■ SIMPLY BALL ■

A silver meteor appeared among the circling squadron of giant dragons. One dragon fell, its tucked wings splayed open, like a parachute. Another dropped like a stone, and the rest scattered in fleeing dives.

Sun glinted on a bright speck, which floated lazily down and paused just above the deck.

"Simply Ball!"

"And just in time, too," came the rejoinder. "I should have known better than to imagine you could stay out of trouble here, Ramsey."

I lowered my gun. "Nice to see you, too," I said.

By William R. Burkett, Jr.

Bloodsport
Blood Lines

Published by HarperPrism

BLOOD LINES

■ ■ ■ ■ ■ ■

WILLIAM R. BURKETT, JR.

HarperPrism

A Division of HarperCollins*Publishers*

🔥 **HarperPrism**
A Division of HarperCollins*Publishers*
10 East 53rd Street, New York, NY 10022-5299

This is a work of fiction. The characters, incidents, and
dialogues are products of the author's imagination and are not to
be construed as real. Any resemblance to actual events or
persons, living or dead, is entirely coincidental.

ISBN 0-06-105823-8

Cover illustration © 1998 by Donato Giancola

First printing: August 1998

Printed in the United States of America

Visit HarperPrism on the World Wide Web at
http://www.harperprism.com

❖ 10 9 8 7 6 5 4 3 2 1

BLOOD LINES

PART ONE

Jo

(Prelude)

High drab overcast.
Another, alien sky.
Fresh blood in water.
In high busy hunting flights,
Dragons dream of human flesh.

The planet Ptolemy, vast and tranquil, filled the transparent dome above the orbital hotel's main lounge. A large irregular splotch of blue and green curved around its rusty dun bulk. The almost-white of cloud cover above the terraformed zone was pleasing to the human eye. Ptolemy's sunlight, and therefore its color spectrum, were not precisely those of Old Earth. But close enough for a human brain to register as homelike and begin to relax after the quantum nightmare of interstellar travel. My brain, anyway. God, I hate space travel!

"Keith Ramsey of Highlands, Acme?"

I brought my eyes down from the view and did a double-take. The speaker was very tall and slender, wearing one of those flamboyant multicolored jumpsuits that seemed to be the local standard. For a heartbeat he resembled Baka Martin—Python—but then the resemblance vanished. Python was dead, sacrificed in a game of interstellar politics several thousand years from here, if you reckoned time in lightspeeds. And Python wouldn't have been caught, even dead, wearing a heavy short sword strapped to his leg. Python hadn't needed any weapon but his body.

"Who's asking?" I said.

"I am Raven of Lao-tzu. Your hunting guide. Welcome to Ptolemy."

I placed my Old Earth bourbon on the bar and accepted the proffered hand. It was slender and long-fingered, and hinted strength. There was a minute flicker of—something else—and then it was gone with the released hand. I could see now he was a good head shorter than Python. Probably not over seven feet tall. Smooth olive complexion, luminous blue eyes, strong but delicate features. His coarse black hair was held off his face Geronimo-style with a wide scarlet headband.

"Lao-tzu is your natal town?" I said.

"Ah! You have studied our customs?"

"I know that much, at least."

A graceful bow. "Ptolemy is honored by your presence."

"How's the gravity up there?" I gestured to the planet above us.

"This hotel is calibrated to local gravity norms. Somewhat light for yourself, a native of Acme." A peaceful smile. "You, Keith Ramsey, will need to govern your strength for the first few days, until you adjust, in order to avoid destruction and slapstick."

"I was kind of hoping Ball would be here to greet me."

"Ah, Ball," Raven said. "A cyborg of many talents. He told me you said that once about him. Or something nearly like that. I have read all your dispatches from Pondoro, in order to familiarize myself with my famous client. Fascinating. You truly believed Ball was no more than an expensive traveling secretary?"

"I thought I paid good coin of the realm for him, too. He kept his affiliation with the Terran Service hidden very well."

"Then you know things seldom are what they seem where Ball is concerned."

It seemed an odd thing to say. But his comment triggered memories of where I had been in my life when Ball came into it: I was a flash-in-the-pan writer with one good book still in circulation and a monumental case of writer's block. I had been doing the occasional stint as an Associated News correspondent, usually in trouble spots, and living the life of a house-trained barbarian among the idle wealthy who considered themselves patrons of the arts. A shooting vacation to Pondoro seemed the chance for a fresh beginning. Ball had been presented to me as the ever-perfect traveling companion every writer should have. A human brain encased in a tough sphere crammed full of life-support and propulsion systems, and supported by all the latest computing equipment. A spherical Friday for a stellar Crusoe, they called him.

But Ball was a covert Terran Services op, with a seamy mission to perform. When the mission required the sacrifice of Martin, his human partner, Ball had rebelled. Part of that rebellion had been to hand me one of the hottest news scoops of my checkered career.

My Pondoro dispatches made me famous
again, and solvent; and generated other writing assignments. I still hadn't written the story
about hunting the Pondoro wolverine I went to
Pondoro to write, and I still was blocked as far
as any other kind of real writing went.

Ball had come straight here from Pondoro,
under Ptolemaic diplomatic immunity, to lecture about the corrupting evils of the Commonwealth and the Terran Service. Rumor said the
Commonwealth Executive had placed a price
on his—well, he didn't have a head. Placed a
price on his carcass. I had received a similar
invite from the government of Ptolemy to be a
guest lecturer, but put them off in favor of those
other writing assignments. It had been almost
four standard years since I laid eyes on his
ornery hide. I was back to using my old Associated News 'corder. Ball's recent voice-post
had reminded me I had a standing invitation to
participate in Ptolemy's annual poetry cycle.
He thought I should use it this year. His message was strongly worded. If I wanted to read
inflection, there was a hint I might find a good
story here. I wondered what he was up to this
time that required my presence.

"How has Ball adjusted to his new career?"
I asked Raven.

"His courses are much sought. Governments from far away send representatives to
his lectures. We are informed the Commonwealth is very unhappy, but unwilling to pro-
voke a diplomatic incident." Raven smiled.
"For two local rotations, I have had the honor to

be one of his teaching assistants at Tezuka University. Ball sends his regrets. His lectures in Tezuka detain him. Since I am a poet, and also hunt, Ball asked me to meet you."

"What kind of sword is that?" I asked. "I hope I'm not breaching local etiquette to take notice of it."

"Sword? I am surprised at you, Keith Ramsey. This is no sword. This is a bowie. One of the most famous hunting and fighting knives of all human history. But forged in the ancient Japanese way. Did you know the original bowie, according to legend, was composed of iron ore from a meteorite? So is this one. I mined the ore from our asteroid belt myself. All kinds of heroic poems have been written about the man who lent his name to this blade."

"Speaking of poetry," I said, "what can you tell me about this local poetry form? The Renga? I have this invitation to participate in one."

"As well as your guide, I have the privilege to be your trainer in the Renga forms for the coming cycle. Time is short, but we will study the ancient forms together."

"You're a poet as well as a hunter and historian?"

"I have the honor to be regarded as a poet on this world of poets, yes."

"There's something else you can help me with, then. As both poet and historian. I need to do research on the history of this Renga form. With special emphasis on off-world poets who died here because their words failed them. I've got an Associated News contract to do a story."

Raven smiled again. "Even on Ptolemy we recognize that Associated News deadlines wait for no one. Then we should go. Our shuttle awaits. Your luggage already is aboard."

My muscles felt compact and powerful in this gravity. I finished my bourbon and stretched luxuriously. I was gradually coming out of the quanta-lag that so unnerves me when star-traveling. I thought my id might catch up to my physical person before too much longer. It always seemed to come unscrewed when a starship left Mr. Einstein's spacetime and began to burrow like a blind mole through quantum probabilities.

But I was here now. The probabilities had aligned properly one more time and deposited those scheduled for Ptolemy—most importantly, me—right where the tickets had promised. I had beaten the odds once more. Ptolemy glowed down with promise. My brains had unscrambled a little on the shuttle ride in from the outskirts of this system. The starship was long since gone. I wished everyone aboard good luck. I know statistics assert that starship travel is safer than automatic aircars on a civilized world, but none of that was any help when a ship vanished into the Lost Dimension, never to return.

I had a lucrative writing assignment in my pocket, and a new world to see. My novels could wait. They'd waited so far. All I had to do was write journalism again, play at this poetry competition, maybe interview for a teaching post, and eventually catch up with Ball to find out just what kind of blockbuster story he was planning to feed me this time. This looked like fun.

I should have known better.

The city of Tezuka spread itself across steep verdant terraced slopes above the wide river. The university grounds occupied the south shore for a spread of kilometers. Its buildings were pastel cubes and pyramids and geodesic domes, scattered like a giant child's toys among a riot of Terrestrial botanical specimens. Broad, carefully tended grass footpaths wound among the trees and shrubs. Tall fountains lifted their misting heads well above the plant life.

Alex Schodt followed his robed guide out onto the wide steps of the interstellar-politics wing and paused. The marble steps descended in a long gentle slope to a river beach. On the beach, an assortment of children of half a dozen species were playing a rapid and complicated game with a large multicolored ball. Their squeals and shouts added a tranquil counterpoint to the lazing silence of the campus.

"It's lovely!" Schodt said.

The shaved head of his host nodded agreeably. "Your first visit to Tezuka University, Alex Schodt?"

"My first visit to Ptolemy at all, Master Inaba."

"Your reputation in your field precedes you. Ptolemy is a world of ideas—and some of your ideas will be welcome here."

Schodt regarded the other narrowly. These Tezuka masters had a wide reputation in semantics. Was there some message in his host's small-talk? Had security been breached enough to permit rumors of the secret purpose of his mission here? Only the emperor and his most closely trusted confidants were supposed to know the truth. Or was the monk simply so astute that the man sensed his public reasons did not square with his actual purpose? Schodt pushed his unruly mop of blond hair back from his forehead with both hands—and cursed inwardly. Would this impassive monk recognize that habitual gesture as nervousness? Of course he would.

"This way," Inaba said mildly.

"Down the steps to the beach?"

"Just so."

"I am on rather a tight time-line . . ." But he followed.

"You have asked for an introduction to the Terran Service cyborg who lectures here, yes?"

"The one named simply Ball. Yes."

They neared the beach. Inaba gestured to the playing children. "Do you know what a beach ball is?"

Schodt frowned. "No."

"A large soft toy ball, filled with air. Played with upon the sands by children since time immemorial. I believe it may have arisen in more than Terrestrial culture alone."

With a whoop of glee, one of the playing youngsters belted the ball with a ropy tentacle. It soared high against the sky, balloonlike, before bouncing across the steps toward Schodt.

"Kick the ball back to the children," Inaba said softly.

"What? All right."

Schodt had played soccer in college. He shifted his weight casually and drove through the ball. Instant pain shot up his leg. It felt as if he had kicked the marble steps. He almost lost his footing. By the time he caught his balance, there was a small tremor of sound in the air. Almost like elves laughing.

"Alex Schodt of Joshua Sayeth, Zion, meet simply Ball." Inaba was almost smiling.

"Of nowhere in particular," said a breezy voice. "And everywhere in general. Stop wincing—there's no permanent damage except to your pride. I let my hide give enough to keep from hurting you."

This close, what had seemed a multicolored children's toy was a dull silver sphere, featureless, and far too substantial to have soared and bounced as it had.

Schodt drew himself up. "There was some reason for this deceit?"

"Sure there was!" The same breezy tone. "You're too damned grim and serious. I'm a joker. Might as well get that settled right off."

The monk bowed, expressionless. "I will leave you." Schodt could have sworn Inaba's eyes were twinkling, but his behavior was flawless. Schodt sketched a return bow and turned to the cyborg.

"You know I tend to seriousness. You obviously know I am proud of my soccer prowess. You consider me important enough to embarrass at first acquaintance." His hands automatically pushed at his hair. "You have studied me."

"Very good!" Ball chose a sincere tone. "I have studied you. You are as intelligent as my studies indicate."

"Then you know why I am here."

"You are a senior project manager for a subsidiary of InterGalactic Cybernetics. You are here to oversee the emperor's project at Ichiro University. You have been informed that in recent months I have become the emperor's confidant. Ready to be admitted to the inner circles. Being the perfect executive, you came here as soon as you arrived. You plan to pick—or at least attempt to pick—my brains."

"How many do you have?" Schodt asked quickly. "And should we be discussing this under the open sky?" He always felt exposed outside the carefully shielded environs of company property.

"How many what?" Ball said. "Brains? One organic—which I choose to style as me—and one artificial one, which I chose to regard as my servant. Plus assorted computing equipment and programming, some of which could be classified loosely as mental quality. You already should be familiar with the specifications. InterGalactic Cybernetics designed my package."

"I know!" Schodt said. "I know some of the engineers who had the honor to work on the design. They had a grand time—designing a cybernetic package for a living human brain. But much of that project was so closely held—each element of the design team hermetically compartmentalized from all the others. I have many questions about how the symbiosis of organic and artificial brain has performed."

"Ask. I don't promise to answer."

"You have never returned to our headquarters for a checkup. Why?"

"Unnecessary. Terran Service medicos and programmers are competent."

"I'm curious about any changes to your limbic system. And your cortex. So much of a human brain's functions are meant to regulate homeostasis of the human body—temperature, blood flow, digestion, breathing. Our brains become physically differentiated in response to different stimuli: the air we breathe, our learning experiences, sex and sexual orientation, even whether we are left-handed or right-eyed."

"I am neither-handed. Nor eyed. As you can see." Ball's tone was dry.

"Just so! Your brain must be evolving in fascinating ways! You are the prototype. No similar platform has ever been produced. You have much to offer the scientific community."

"Well," Ball said, "the scientific community will just have to wait for my memoirs."

Schodt considered that. Then he changed tactics. "There is no indication in corporate records as to why you are the only one of your type. Nor any record of the purpose of your activation. In my present capacity, I have access to every record from every division. I have examined each of the separate elements that went into your composition, except of course the brain-donor file. That is protected by strict confidentiality. But there are no comprehensive records! All the elements were successfully tested. Then they were forwarded—somewhere. There is no record of the team that put you together."

"Did you consider all the king's horses and all the king's men?"

"That's an obscure joke at my expense, isn't it?"

"Yes."

"Have your fun. But it is as if you appeared full-blown! The project, of course, was under the auspices of the Commonwealth of Terra. Your former employer. Perhaps you were assembled by the Terran Service itself. Do you know why they never ordered another package?"

"Maybe they couldn't get another volunteer to surrender his body."

"Volunteer?" Schodt said. And bit his lip. He knew the range of Ball's semantic acuity.

"An interesting implication in your tone," the cyborg said.

"I just meant—"

"Your meaning is clear, if unpleasant. Immaterial. I no longer represent law enforcement for the Commonwealth, so I don't have to report your semantic slip to the Terran Service. If you are kidnapping citizens for some nefarious project, it no longer is my concern. To answer your question, I really don't care why I am the only one of my type. Nor, I would think, do you. Your field is and always has been organic symbiosis."

"True," Schodt said. "More specifically, intelligent symbiosis. Which requires me to study organic memory storage and exchange— the first and most elegant data processing, if you will. I designed the nanodevice that controlled the sybil parasite—which I believe has been referred to as its 'girdle'—to ensure it cannot break stasis and proliferate. A sentient alien virus! I am fascinated by two awarenesses—one alien, one human—sharing the same physical electrochemical storage facility. Your partner, Baka Martin, also of the Terran Service, was one for whom my design was employed. He shared his brain with this Blocked World entity."

"Yes, he did. But he's dead now. And so is the sybil colony that infested him."

"And you have grown a physical clone, at the emperor's request! Here, on Ptolemy!" Schodt's hands shoved at his hair. "My job will be to infect the clone with a new sybil colony, and install the controller." He bit his lip. "Are you sure it is safe to discuss these things here?"

"Perfectly sure. No known eavesdropping device can penetrate the field I have erected. Even a distant observer, skilled in lip-reading, would discover your facial features are blurred."

"You are so well-equipped!"

"Yes. I am."

"In your lectures here, you outline a Commonwealth plan to create a symbiosis between a supreme natural predator on the planet Pondoro and the sybil parasite. A scheme you thwarted. Your partner's role, actually, was that of host to the organism, pending its attempted transfer. But evolution of the sybil is fascinating! I have studied what there is to know. But so little is known. I was permitted just enough knowledge to design my controller. How did the sybil evolve to its present form? Over how many billions of years? How does it manage such seamless integration between such widely disparate beings? Beings from wholly alien ecologies? What effect would it have on a human brain without my safeguards—"

"Sometimes," Ball interrupted, "I miss those hands you mentioned very much."

Schodt blinked and shoved at his hair. "Sorry?"

"I have seen the upheld hand used as a signal to halt the flow of verbiage," Ball said. "You are moving in the direction of a monologue of questions, which is a logical contradiction. What interests you so about this parasite?"

Schodt blinked and shoved his hair. Then he answered a question with a question.

"Why didn't the Commonwealth scientists implant the sybil in you? The sybil nests in the brain of the host. Your brain is supremely protected from outside contamination. Therefore, a breeding colony could not escape you by way of carrion eaters or other means. If they implanted the sybil in a brain of your caliber, within the superb protection of your exoskeleton"—he stooped to rub his aching foot—"they would have had a true superbeing."

Ball used his dry tone again. "I labor under the impression that I already am a superbeing, without any alien goo wedded to my brain cells."

Schodt blinked rapidly several times.

"Don't take offense," Ball said. "It's just my conversational style. I don't know why they didn't select me for the host. But I'm glad they didn't. I'm alive. My partner's not."

"Strictly speaking, that will not be true for long!" Schodt could barely contain himself. "Not when we activate his clone. You—only you— have complete records of his memory and identity over his last days. Only you can help restore him fully, so that I can do my own work."

Ball made a sound like a sigh. "As fully as can be, with modern science. Are you ready to begin?"

We disembarked from the shuttle onto a sun-baked landing field. A hot wind snatched at our clothing. There was a smell like metal burning on the wind. The wide runways were weather-beaten and deserted. A low, featureless building lay at the edge of the rutted paving. Beyond the building, dun-colored earth and patchy gray scrub rolled toward a distant, hazy line of vibrant lime-green.

I paused at the foot of the gangway. Raven turned.

"You seem perplexed, Keith Ramsey."

"I guess I was expecting something a little more inner-planet."

He smiled. "Ah—the frontiersman's view of civilization: wall-to-wall plastic, shoulder-to-shoulder towers, the sky full of commerce and advertising."

"Something like that."

"Ptolemy is old, Keith Ramsey. It was the thirty-ninth inhabitable planet found in the Second Survey. It was well-settled before the Llralan wars. But there still is open space on any planet—even Old Earth. This field lies in the buffer between human Ptolemy and natural Ptolemy. As some areas are reclaimed, others are abandoned, and Ptolemy moves back in."

He started across the scored paving, moving quickly. I noticed that he glanced at the sky several times, with something like apprehension. Even in the lighter gravity, I had to hustle to keep up with him.

We were almost to the building when, from somewhere high overhead, a heart-stopping shriek began, and steadily grew in volume. A shadow bloomed on the paving beside me, and spread. Now it engulfed my own shadow. Something was between me and the sun. Something large.

Raven began to run, hard.

The roof of the building split open and a gun emplacement popped into view.

"Run, Keith Ramsey!"

The honest fright in Raven's voice spurred me after him. The turret gun began to cough. The reports weren't that loud—swallowed in the vast spaces of the abandoned field—but the overhead concussions of high explosive puffed down against me as I ran toward the building. In the light gravity, I was almost flying low.

The falling shriek altered pitch, became erratic. As I gained the doubtful shelter of the building, something came down behind us, hard. The ground shook. I plastered my back to the wall before I risked taking a look.

A smoking nightmare twitched and crawled toward us across the paving. Its lengthy jaws snapped and tore at its shredded body. One of its vast leathery wings was on fire. Raven was in a fighter's crouch, the bowie in his hand. It still looked like a sword to me—if it was an

inch, it was a foot long. Metrics seemed too sis-
sified to describe anything so sleek and deadly.

I heard a low whir overhead. The turret gun
spun its quad-barrels down. A single pop. The
thing's head blew away in a dark mist.

"Status?" Raven called.

"All clear," floated down from the gun turret. "It was just a singleton. No following flocks
on screen."

Raven straightened and sheathed the blade
in a neat motion. I blinked. For a moment he
looked like a different person—shorter in
stature, more finely boned. The moment passed.

"I am sorry, Keith Ramsey. One gets careless within the human zone. Out here, there
always is the chance of an unpleasant surprise."

"What the hell *was* that?"

"A wingfinger. A flying reptile. A native
species. Not unlike the flying dinosaurs of long-
ago Earth. Ptolemy was in its planetary youth
when we discovered it."

My hands were shaking. "Why use old
fashioned high explosive? Why not beamers?"

"Unsporting," said the voice from the gun
turret. I couldn't see who was talking, and I
wasn't about to step away from the wall to correct that deficiency. Jesus!

"This is *sport* here?" I said.

Raven was smiling again. "I knew you
would understand, Keith Ramsey. Your reputation as a hunter precedes you. On our instal-
lations along the buffer zone, there is chance
for some excellent wingshooting depending

upon the season. That one, though"—he nodded toward the smoldering hulk—"was rushing
the season just a bit. I should not have been so
cavalier with you. Your firearms are not even
unpacked yet!"

"You'll get your shots," the unseen gunner
called down. "Won't he, Raven?"

"Indeed!" Raven's eyes shone with some
emotion—relief, excitement?—and he drew
himself up. *"The real work of men was hunting,"* he said, with the cadence of a quote.
*"The invention of agriculture was a giant step
in the wrong direction, leading to serfdom,
cities, empires. From a race of hunters, artists,
warriors, and tamers of horses, we degraded
ourselves . . . to clerks, functionaries, laborers,
entertainers, processors of information"*—this
last with a sarcastic twist of the mobile lips.

"Good stuff," the voice from above approved. "I'm an A.I. tech in Pirsig, myself. But I
like to get afield now and again. Gets the
blood pumping. Was that Keith Ramsey's
work?"

"Not mine," I said.

"No, a late twentieth-century prose poet,"
Raven said. "His name was Abbey. He wrote of
monkey-wrenching society with great glee."

"Monkey-wrenching?" I said.

"As in throwing a monkey-wrench in the
works," Raven said. "Sawdust in the cogs of
progress. Herf-bursts in the computer drive. A
man of delightfully subversive ideas!"

"I think I might like to read some of his
stuff."

"I have the collection of his works aboard my houseboat."

"Your houseboat?"

"Yes, your lodging, as my guest, for the next little while. I am of the river dwellers. Civilization River. Certainly you've heard of it? It is quite famous."

I was beginning to get that feeling you get on a new world: too much information coming in, too fast, from too many directions. The abrupt transition from well-ordered, if chancy, quantum travel to the more familiar terrors of things that want to kill you personally had my adrenaline pumping. It seemed the inner worlds were not quite as settled and boring as I had always been led to believe.

"It appears that you do not know my river, Keith Ramsey." Raven seemed disappointed in me. But he brightened right away. "But how wonderful! That means I have the honor to introduce the famous writer to the famous river!"

Adrienne Taft watched her son ride his new palomino along the beach of the ancient body of water called the Gulf of Mexico. His slender form seemed to meld with the big horse as it swept away down the surf line, sand flying. At age twelve, her son rode effortlessly, as he seemed to do everything. But of course that was the view of a doting mother. She smiled at the thought. That was not precisely her best-known image across the sprawling interstellar Commonwealth under her administration.

Far down the beach her son spun the big horse and came thundering back. The jar of approaching hoofbeats transmitted itself through the sand into her body, where she lay beneath the sunshade. Behind her ear a slight tingle started. The proximity monitor.

"Oh, shit!" She sat up, alarmed. If her son rode headlong into that field . . .

He reined in smartly, bringing the big palomino back on its haunches. Gouts of dry sand cascaded toward her blanket—and winked out of existence. The horse snorted and shook its head. Her son just sat there grinning.

"I thought your son still had unlimited access," he said.

"Oh, honey—you do!"

"But what if I had skinned my knee, Mommy? And was running to you for a hug to make it all better. Wouldn't I have gone poof?"

Her son was the only sentient being who could wring her heart like that. There had been one other—his father—but he was gone. Long gone. Vanished utterly from space and time, so it seemed. When she finally got over the hurt of that last bitter quarrel, she had searched for him—oh, how she had searched. The finest intelligence agents of the Terran Service had been pressed into that task at one time or another, chasing rumors. She did not believe he was dead. She believed she would have known it if that particular life force had winked out—that an unfillable black hole would have opened in her heart. But he was just as gone.

Finally, twelve years ago, as an act of mourning, she had caused the implantation of her lover's semen from the Old Earth banks. She had steadfastly borne his son to term within her own body. Her only natural child in nearly a century of living. Now, she shrugged off those memories. She had no time to drag all that out and agonize over it again. She shoved the memory of his father out of consciousness to concentrate on their son. The coldly rational part of her mind—the part that never blinked regardless the stimulus—knew his reckless display with the palomino was a test. He was teasing her. Being a brat. Being his father's son.

"The horse," she said, refusing to rise to the bait. "The horse could have been a weapon."

"My name-day gift, Mommy? The one you selected yourself?"

Of course she had done no such thing. Her personal staff had found the palomino, which surely amounted to the same thing at her level of responsibility. Her longtime retainers were almost organic extensions of her own brain. They knew her so well, and she trusted them completely. Well—not completely. Never completely. She was, after all, the Commonwealth Executive. Complete trust came at too high a price. Sometimes it seemed everyone in the universe wanted a piece of her, dead or alive.

"Even a personal gift can be corrupted," she said patiently. "Remember who you are. Remember who I am. Remember our place in the scheme of things. Always."

He was bored with the game. "I'm going to cool Caesar off." He reined around. Over his shoulder: "I'll see you our next Qualtime, Mom. Don't work too hard."

Her heart ached. She wanted to call him back for that hug he had joked about. She wanted to cancel her afternoon and linger on the sugar-white Gulf sands of her favorite retreat. But already she felt the tug of duty. She rolled off her beach towel and to her feet, but not with her usual grace. The planet felt heavier today, dragging her down. Mankind's home sun bit her flesh. Her native sun was cooler and more distant from the planet of her birth, and her skin was very fair. She trudged over the barrier dune toward her waiting command car.

Her personal guard arced beyond the car

at a discreet distance, eyes averted from their
leader in the nude. SjillaTen waited for her by
the raised hatch. He examined her dispassion-
ately. Unaccountably, she felt a sensual reaction to the Llralan's gaze.

"You've gained weight."

"You presume too much!" she snapped.

"Your robe."

His practiced gesture did not trigger the
proximity monitor. His blunt four-fingered
hand brushed her slender human one. She had
a brief fierce wish he would snuggle her robe
around her and hold her. Llralans weren't all
that alien. They had raped their share of human
women in that long-ago war. Interspecies relationships were common now. She shrugged
away the inclination impatiently, but she would
have to take some action soon. Some carefully
controlled liaison, real or virtual, or glandular
suppressants again. She shuddered slightly.
None of the alternatives was appealing.

A shadow crossed them; one of the robot
gunships that always flew air cover during her
time on the beach. The armed branch of the
Terran Service left little to chance. Personal
bodyguards, air cover, sea cover, suborbital
fighters in a holding pattern over the horizon—
a full Medfac down the beach, just in case—and
a heavy cruiser in parking orbit straight up. All
because she wanted to spend Qualtime on the
Gulf beaches with her son.

She sighed heavily. Time to go back to
work. Llralans made the best intelligence
agents between the stars, incorruptible and

absolutely loyal to their contracts. SjillaTen
traced his lineage and profession to the time
when the Llralans had controlled their own
considerable sphere of space and viewed
Terrans as just another colonial conquest.
Their mistake.

"You have information for me about this
Ptolemy business?"

"Not out here." SjillaTen frowned at the
sky. "Eavesdroppers."

"If we don't own these skies," she said,
"then there's no hope. Tell me. The synopsis:
what got into those idiots on Ptolemy to offer
political sanctuary to a renegade cyborg?"

"In short, Ball got into them."

"I don't understand."

"Are you briefed on this cyborg? This Ball?
His skills, his performance rating? He was the
best deep-penetration agent we had."

"But he betrayed his oath. Because he was
angry about the necessary death of his partner.
A vengeful *cyborg*, for mercy's sake?"

"Perhaps Ball betrayed his Terran Service
oath. But Ptolemy leadership did not initiate
the immunity proceedings. Ball orchestrated
the whole invitation himself."

"How would he manage that?"

SjillaTen's face twitched in a semblance of a
smile. "When it comes to manipulating information at several removes, to achieve a desired
result, Ball has few peers."

"But I thought this political asylum business
was hatched by the Ptolemy leadership. I
thought they did it as part of some dim-witted

plot to embarrass me—and this administration. Isn't this cyborg lecturing to all comers about Terran Service secrets and procedures?"

"He is."

"Well, then—plainly a traitor. Eliminate him."

The Llralan grimaced. "Traitor? Perhaps. Eliminate him? No. Not while he is on Ptolemy and under their protection. That *would* embarrass your administration. Possibly terminally. But the Terran Service has been looking at Ptolemy for some time. They're up to something there, something deeply hidden. Their security is excellent. We were brainstorming a deep penetration mission before Baka Martin and Ball were diverted to the Pondoro project. Ball seemed the best candidate for the Ptolemy assignment. He does his best work in a civilized setting. He was unhappy about being diverted to Pondoro to baby-sit that news hawk, Ramsey."

"Ah, yes, Mr. Ramsey," Taft said crisply. "Ramsey widened his fame considerably at our expense, didn't he?"

The Llralan studied her. "In certain circles, that bootleg erotic program emulating Ramsey's alleged sexual prowess has widened it even more. My informants tell me InterGalactic Cybernetics designed that under a covert-services contract. The contract came directly from your office. A revenge too subtle for me to grasp."

She smiled grimly. "I know these throwback types like Ramsey. Far from being flattered that women pleasure themselves with his progue, he will feel used and abused." She paused. "Strange you should mention that now. Thanks for reminding me. I have the alpha test model in my office, but I've never run it. It will be just the thing to solve an—itch—I have. I didn't know Llralans pretended to extrasensory gifts."

SjillaTen made the Llralan gesture that equated to a shrug. "Almost four standard years ago Ball used similar erotic programming based on Ramsey's ruttings. He seduced a human female to help extricate him from beneath a rock slide on Pondoro. It appears Ball's thought-processes are similar to yours in some regards."

"What do you know about this cyborg's human brain?"

"The personality shaped by Ball's human donor evidently survived the implantation process," SjillaTen said. "To include emotions like partner-loyalty and whimsy. Perhaps that was intentional. I am not cleared to know the details of that particular experiment."

"Not cleared! You're on my staff!"

"Nevertheless. InterGalactic Cybernetics holds itself aloof from politics in some areas. The Ball project is one. They built him for us, but they hold certain proprietary rights."

"We'll see about that! If we can't eliminate him right now, do you think InterGal might have designed in something we could use to control him? Override chips, something?"

"I'm not sure we want to try to control Ball right now."

"Why?"

"We are developing a Terran Service presence on Ptolemy, slowly but surely. We still don't understand what's happening there. But we know enough to know that Ball soon will know. He is in place. He already is a favorite of the emperor. Ball is working his way into the center of things, as only he can. For whatever reasons, it looks like Ball is still on the job."

"**P**tolemy is a world of ideas, Keith Ramsey," Raven said. "Perhaps the only one. There are worlds of empiric power, worlds of action, worlds of wonder. But here the idea of things is revered almost above the things themselves. Since humanity's traditional communication of ideas has been in words, Ptolemy also is a world of words."

We stood on the spacious flying bridge of Raven's live-aboard vessel, waiting for the longshore 'bots to cast us off. He called it a houseboat. But it was so sleek and streamlined that it seemed underway even at rest. It bore no resemblance to any house or watercraft I had ever seen.

Ptolemy's sun was sinking below the horizon, painting the high cloud cover into a dazzling array of fuchsia colors. What looked like heavy anvil-headed thunderclouds were marching all around the horizon, and the ever-restless wind had turned cooler. The river itself was in deep dusk. In the river port of Champollion, the lights were coming on, rose or pale orange in hue, no whites or yellows anywhere. Other vessels were casting off or docking along the series of wharfs. The quiet hubbub of sounds did not quite mask the gurgle of the river's current against our hull. It was cool and humid on the waterfront. The odors of treated pilings and mud made me nostalgic for the salt bays of northern Acme.

Raven spun the wheel and took us neatly out into the heavy push of the river before he spoke again. I held onto the squall rail and admired his deft handling. I hadn't been in small boats since my teen years on Acme, long ago, breaking skim salt ice out to the *twon* blinds of home. We had heavily sheathed live-aboard garvey boats to break the ice, and to live aboard, while the autumn flights were on.

"You know of the ancient scholar whose name graces this town?" Raven asked.

"No."

"Jean Francois Champollion, nineteenth century. He was the man who deciphered the Rosetta stone and gave us access to Egyptian history. You know of the Rosetta stone?"

"Heard of it anyway. If I remember right, the translated words amounted to a media release describing the reign of Ptolemy the Elder. Your planet's namesake."

"Just so. A report set in stone to record the rule of an enlightened leader. A leader who, from the account on the stone, exemplified the perfect leader, as described by Lao-tzu. You may have noticed most of our towns are named for men of original ideas—Pirsig, Lao-tzu, Pythagoras—but in the world of ideas there also is need to remember the great transla-tors."

We were well out on the river now, and

Champollion was just a smear of light in our wake. The river looked several kilometers wide here. I could make out other scatters of light on both shores, and far upriver the sky-glow of a considerable city. But we were headed downstream, into gathering gloom.

"And where did Civilization River get its name?" I asked.

"Ah! In the vast labors to render this world more hospitable, one approach was to create this entire drainage. They built carefully sculpted watersheds in the mountains, hundreds of kilometers upstream from here. They blasted a channel to the Western Sea. A vast self-replenishing resource for the settlers. The debate to name the river was as spirited as its creation was difficult. Most of our homeworld's great civilizations—and some of its lesser but very lovely cultures—were based on an important river. From the Nile to the Columbia, the Egyptians to the Yakimas. Each great home river had its adherents. In the end, a compromise was effected."

"No one got their way."

"The spirit of the debate was honored." Raven studied his instruments. "We will anchor not too far upstream from the river mouth. Tomorrow we will receive clearance to move out through the buffer zone into the primal tidelands. We will spend tomorrow scouting for locations, and plan to shoot the following dawn. I believe you will find the wingshooting we offer to be quite exciting."

"Given my taste of it this afternoon," I said,

"I have no doubt of that. But for now, I'm interested in how this Renga came to be."

Raven did something to the controls and turned. "I have fresh fruit and cheeses below, and some fine green tea."

"I could eat," I admitted.

"Then we shall. My boat knows the way." He slid down the ladder gracefully. I followed with less grace, still clumsy in the light gravity. The spacious galley's lighting had that rosy glow I'd noticed in Champollion. Raven was placing a loaded tray on the table. For a heartbeat again, his height and shape seemed—odd. The cabin's overhead seemed so low I felt like ducking—but he appeared completely at ease and hadn't banged his head once. I shrugged and took a seat.

"The Renga," Raven said. "An ancient word meaning chain of poems, or more formally, a joint elaboration of linked poems. The first three lines are five, seven, and five syllables, as in haiku. The second two lines are seven and seven. It is believed the form originated in the seventh century A.D., in Japan. Today, the Renga is the official poetic language of Ptolemy."

I sipped some of the bitter tea. "Why?"

Raven shrugged delicately. "Why not? Among the early settlers here were many of Japanese ancestry. They brought the form with them. Settlement life was very rugged in the early terraforming days. The workers were few and their work-stations scattered. Exchange of technical data and crucial information was con-

stant, but someone started a Renga to try to capture the emotion evoked by remodeling an
entire world. Tradition has it that this person
was Kuni Sadamoto, a programmer of earth-
moving equipment at First Landing. Sadamoto
is revered almost as much as Yakamochi."

"This cheese is fine," I said. "Who's Yakamochi?"

"A Japanese princess of the seventh or
eighth century, according to tradition. When an
anonymous Buddhist nun wrote a haiku about
rice harvest, the princess answered in two lines.
A tradition of question and response poetry, the
Renga, developed from there among the
women of the time. Eventually it became a tradition for each tanka, or link, to consist of five
lines by the same poet. Early Rengas often were
marked by covert eroticism."

"Well, covert eroticism sounds promising,"
I said.

"Are you recording all this?"

I gestured to a glowing telltale on my
'corder. "Yes. Wouldn't want to have to go
through this lecture again."

In the rosy light, it seemed he blushed. I
couldn't be sure.

"Forgive me, Keith Ramsey. The Renga is
one of my two major fields of scholarship."

"And the other?"

"Primitive mythology."

"Interesting combination."

"Oh, yes!" He leaned forward excitedly, then
checked himself. "But you do not need that—
lecture—right now. Let us concentrate on the

Renga. As its form developed, some scholars believed it offered the poet a freedom of expression beyond the yoke of family and feudal ties. An opportunity to explore his or her individual genius."

"This is pretty heavy going," I said. "I still don't see where I fit in."

Raven smiled quickly. "You are a spinner of words. The Renga is a new loom for you to master."

I nodded acknowledgment. "Nicely put. Do you really execute poets who fail to perform adequately?"

"Nothing is so simple as it seems."

"Not in this man's galaxy," I said. "But my question was—"

The boat made a subtle change of direction, and the teacups slid. I reacted too fast for Ptolemy gravity and slapped mine across the galley. It burst in a shivering tinkle of sound.

"You did say slapstick," I said.

Raven laughed, a high lilt of sound. "You are every bit as advertised, Keith Ramsey! It is an honor to instruct you. I have more teacups."

Schodt squinted in the bright light of the sterilization chamber. He always fancied he could feel the beams that analyzed him down to the cellular level, but his reason told him this was nonsense. The cool blue illuminated numerals set into the airlock counted down to zero. He waited calmly in the empty white room for the lock to open. He was sure he was uncontaminated. The seconds stretched. He waited what he believed to be a full minute before he spoke to the dimly seen figure in the monitoring station on the other side of the thick glass.

"Well?"

"You have been chipped," the analyst said.

"Chipped? When? How—"

"There is a nanochip lodged in your brainstem, transmitting even now. Of course we have blocked its transmission here. No signal can get out. But it is Terran Service manufacture. It appears they still are trying to penetrate our security."

"But where could I have picked up such a chip? What kind of chip?"

"Evaluating now. Wait one."

He fidgeted now, nervous and impatient.

"How would the Terran Service identify me as a person of interest?"

"Nature of the implant: a simple empath-ometer. Transmission on a very specific band-width. Checking . . ."

Ball's voice cut in over the com unit. "No need to check. I implanted the chip when Schodt tried to use me for a soccer ball. I wanted to test your thoroughness. If you can spot the kind of equipment I implant, you're very thorough. Go ahead and deactivate it."

"Deactivated," the analyst said. "Lock cycling."

The door screwed back out of the way. Schodt found Ball hovering about shoulder height beside the tech, who was bent over his instrument panels.

"In you go," the analyst told the cyborg. "No one and nothing passes this point without full vetting."

"Forget it," Ball said.

"University procedures—"

"Forget it. Unless you want me to scrap this expensive playpen and all its software for you. Nobody runs a diagnostic on me."

"Then you may not proceed past this point."

"What—*you're* going to stop me? You and what robot army?"

The analyst smiled complacently. "We'll see."

"Yes, we will."

Schodt noticed that time seemed to have slowed again. He waited for the analyst to deploy countermeasures. But of course none deployed. He was beginning to understand just how well-equipped the cyborg was. And therefore how dangerous. He saw the analyst realize he was helpless, in seeming slow motion. Across the control room a second door began to screw itself out of the way. The analyst made a gesture as if to lay hands on Ball.

"Don't waste your time," the cyborg said sharply. "Consult your superiors! They wouldn't want to displease the emperor. Lead the way, Schodt. You've been vetted, and I never will be. Not by anything available on this planet! Let's move along."

Past the second door, a bare corridor as white as the sterilization chamber led to a third door, which cycled before they were halfway there. Ball drifted through with centimeters to spare on either side. A single figure awaited them, wearing the rose-hued robes of an Ichiro University lecturer. She was short and curvaceous, and her skin tones bore the dusky hereditary stain of generations beneath a hotter sun than Ptolemy's.

"Elizabeth of Pythagoras." Ball chose a ceremonial voice.

"You know of me then, simply Ball," she answered. "But I was not born in Pythagoras, as you can see."

"The planet Zion," Ball said. "But your loyalties lie now with Ptolemy?"

"Completely. And where do your loyalties lie, Ball?"

"I am my own Ball these days. My loyalty is not to Old Earth, if that is your question. But you already know that, or I wouldn't have been invited here. I have been waiting patiently since I arrived."

She drew in a sharp breath. "You *knew* about this facility? How? Our security—"

"Modulate, dear," Ball said sweetly. "Your ignorance of my abilities is showing."

She stiffened noticeably. Schodt found himself pushing nervously at his hair. The cyborg was unpredictable. "Umm—Elizabeth?" Schodt said.

She exhaled slowly. "Do you antagonize everyone then, Ball?"

The cyborg introduced a happy chuckle. Schodt wondered where it had been recorded. "As many as I can, dear."

"My project superiors are concerned that you would not submit to vetting. The idea of letting a Terran Service operative this near our operation—even a fugitive—has them nervous."

"No wonder. With what I know already, I could buy my way back into the Service's good graces. An antigovernment conspiracy between one of the largest interstellar corporations and the emperor of Ptolemy?"

She blinked. "You will say anything!"

"Get used to it."

"They will have you eliminated!"

"Many have tried. I'm still rolling along. And the emperor would be displeased. Can we just cut through to the purpose of this meeting? This is wasting time. The emperor may be nervous, but I wouldn't be here if he didn't want me here. What do you have to offer in the way of skills to integrate a sybil with the Baka Martin clone? The emperor obviously has great faith in you."

"It is not misplaced. You shall see. But as you know, activating a clone is a complex matter. We have the identical body from the culture tanks on Old Earth. We have all the records of his original nervous-system patterns, brain-wave activity, pulse and respiration from the time he entered the Service until he went on active duty."

"Do you have his earliest memory logs?"

"Yes."

"Memory logs?" Schodt asked.

"Terran Service clone-elects are chipped early," Ball said. "Their thoughts and emotions are transmitted regularly into a master file. Periodic cross-checks are made with vocalization for closer correlation to the concurrent brain-wave, nervous-system, and glandular activity to the closest decimal. It provides a cross-check to the overall life profile. I have the logs dating from our partnership, completely correlated with his every utterance since we partnered."

"Then this will be a particularly excellent copy," Elizabeth said.

"Yes, it will."

"Installing the muscle-memory involved in the Palikar discipline will be—interesting," Schodt offered.

"Simplest of all, actually," Elizabeth said, "The clone begins life with as accurate a compilation of previous motor memory, up to the last memory-log, as we can provide. The clone can then access the memories. Simple physical exercises will return those motor skills and muscle tone to the levels possessed by the original. Integration of his cerebral, or information, memories into his developing awareness is somewhat more complex." To Ball: "Will the clone be given the original's memories of his sybil symbiosis?"

"Of course he will," Ball said. "It was central to his entire adult life. My question for you involves the parasite itself. And of course I can supply a duplicate of the sybil controller that kept his parasite civil. InterGalactic design, of course."

"Of course," Schodt said. "Actually, my design. When I was quite young."

"So my research shows. Your work was quite sound."

"Thank you." Schodt was glad Ball's empath chip had been deactivated. Mention of the control chip had swerved his emotions into very secret waters. The Martin clone would be chipped with an InterGalactic sybil control, all right. But not the ones Ball carried.

Ball had his thoughts on other matters. "You have access to the sybil here? No matter how well we prepare the clone, this whole exercise is meaningless without the sybil."

"Oh, yes," Elizabeth said. "A viable colony of the sybil is under isolation in this laboratory. The emperor has ordered it reserved for this subject."

"How many symbiotic subjects do you have?"

"That is classified," she said crisply. "I have no need to know. Nor do you!"

"You don't have to sound so smug about your ignorance," Ball grumbled. "But the Terran Service would never part with a viable sybil colony. Not even I could figure out a way to get hold of that damned virus, after Pondoro. Which is part of why I'm here on Ptolemy to begin with. I owe Baka Martin a life. Complete with his damned parasite. And the rumors of where to find the sybil all lead here. But I don't believe the Service would authorize access to a viable colony by an unmonitored university project on a world like Ptolemy."

"Well," she said smugly, "we didn't ask their permission, exactly."

"You stole sybil from the Terran Service? I'm impressed in spite of myself."

"Oh, no," Elizabeth said. Before Schodt could intervene, she added: "We stole the virus from one of the Blocked Worlds."

The scaled and fanged form on the laboratory table resembled nothing so much as nightmare gargoyles from Earth's distant superstitious past. Human techs moved about in the subdued lighting beyond the isolation chamber's thick glass. Though determinedly not superstitious, they still were not very comfortable this close to a mythic monster. Ball didn't need empath chips in the brains of the lab crew to tell him that.

"Suspended animation," Elizabeth said softly.

"You have extracted the sybil?"

"No. The subject has been in isolation since capture. We will not extract until the Martin clone is ready."

"You actually visited one of the Blocked Worlds to capture this thing? Avoided the Terran Service blockade?"

"A freelance combat team from Zion made the insertion. Rongor battle robots, controlled from orbit. No chance the sybil could infect a sentient form. The expedition was under the guise of an archaeological mapping expedition. If the expedition had been compromised, the trail would have led back to Zion fundamentalists, seeking new weapons."

"A thin cover," Ball said. "Somebody got bribed big-time."

"I have no need to know."

"Right. You have implanted a monitor chip in this—thing?"

"Yes. The coordinates are there on screen."

"All right. Leave me. Take the lab crew with you."

When they were gone, Ball assimilated the coordinates and probed the still form behind the glass. Here, it seemed, was what all the secrecy was about on Ptolemy. Kidnapped symbiotes from the Blocked Worlds. He would not have considered this planet of idealists capable of such a thing. But here was the visible proof. Had the parasite survived the abduction? For what seemed a long time, his probe revealed no evidence of it.

Then, a formless stirring. Very weak. The nictating eyelids of the thing fluttered but did not open.

There was an awareness of light, bright light, sourceless.

And cold—numbing cold.

The chip was working, transmitting formless awareness through the quiescent host brain from its numbed parasite.

Ball quieted his racing thoughts and listened carefully. *Something* was dreaming in there. But was it the host, or the parasite? He could not distinguish. It was all very sluggish. But he could tell the sleeping beast was supremely healthy, just as Baka Martin always had been. The sybil virus created what had been known for centuries as the interferon effect. It induced its host's cells to produce a specialized substance that made fresh cells immune to any subsequent viral infection. When the parasite set up housekeeping, its first order of business always was to ensure the longevity of its host.

Ball's sense was strong that the symbiotic awareness was lost in a dream. The Blocked World host creatures had a kind of speech. Ball had everything known about those speech patterns on file. But the dreaming upon which he spied was prevocal. Almost like the unformed awareness of an infant. The sensations of brightness and coldness predominated—and lethargy. A deep, deep weariness. And . . . sadness? He paused. Could a thing that nightmarish feel sadness? He suppressed the sheer terrestrialism of that thought, and made a couple of adjustments in his scan.

Lonely. The microscopic goop that infested the monster was lonely. It was aware in some primal way of its physical isolation from its kind. Aware . . .

Ball uttered a small exclamation.

The damn virus knew how far away from home it was!

And at the same instant—was aware that it had never left home.

It was imprisoned here. Yet it was—*not here*. Its loneliness was physical only. His reading was hard to verify through the somnolent state of the host brain. But he did not doubt its accuracy. In some obscure way, the parasite knew its host had been kidnapped, knew it was

in captivity, knew how far away home was—
and, at the same instant, believed in some fundamental way it still *was* home.

That was an awful lot of awareness to be
operating in such an infinitesimal organism
under any circumstances, let alone these.

Ball considered the ancient puzzle: how
large *is* a consciousness anyway? And where in
time and space does it actually reside? For centuries the so-called materialists in brain
research had insisted that all qualities ascribed
to an intelligent mind were merely electrochemical spinoffs of an organic brain. And for
even longer, the dualists, from Anaxagoras to
Descartes, had insisted that the mind existed
apart, somewhere outside Newtonian space
and time. By the time quantum theory came
along, the dualists were ready to conclude the
mind existed in quantum reality. All of that
sound and fury, just over the exact composition
and location of a human mind.

Not one of those theorists ever had to confront the reality of a parasitic microbe with its
own intelligence.

It seemed clear to Ball the sybil had something very like the mind celebrated by the dualists—its potentialities impossible to infer from
its mere physical composition. This was the
property that enabled the virus to blend seamlessly with, and control, the neurons of the host
brain. In this particular specimen, the untouched
native sybil consciousness seemed to be per-
forming in classical quantum-wave-function
fashion. Its consciousness was *here*, and it was

not-here. It was simultaneously aware that it occupied two separate points in space and time, and aware it was indivisible. The quantum-wave-like mental function that originated in this tiny awareness, and its conjugate-wave echo, rippled back and forth across space and time between *here* and the point it knew as *home.* If the host beast had been awake and functional, its parasite gave it the potential to communicate almost instantaneously across the void to its kith and kin. There was no technological communications apparatus that could match its potential for speed and accuracy.

Ball wondered if that explained Inter-Galactic Cybernetics' stake in this little plot. Had their commercial strategists developed plans in which windfall profits would accrue to commercial applications capable of harnessing the sybil awareness? In the modern world, communication was power, and faster communication could come close to absolute power, if used cunningly. InterGal already had a long and enviable reputation for being ahead of every breakthrough technology that might affect its bottom line.

As for Ptolemy, the world in love with ideas, the idea of perfecting such an elegant communications model, based on organic brainpower, would be very beguiling.

Ball mused down upon the sleeping gargoyle. Nothing in his data on the Blocked Worlds provided an evolutionary clue as to why the parasite had developed such a sophisticated communication adaptation.

It must have begun as some kind of herd instinct, race consciousness, to protect the host species—and therefore the sybil—in times of danger, as the sybil's interferon effect protected the individual. But the Blocked World lizards were not star travelers—not even tool users. Which made them all the more mysterious for appearing on several separate worlds in the neighboring solar systems that comprised the infamous Blocked Worlds. Such a distribution stretched the concept of parallel evolution past the breaking point. Some theorists had posited some kind of prehistoric dissemination of the gargoyles by an unknown agency. There were obscure legends of prehistoric star travelers, of course, but none accompanied by anything like hard evidence. Unless this symbiote was that evidence.

The Terran Service was essentially unconcerned about prehistory anomalies. Its purpose was governance, not basic research. Service explorers had found, and been found by, the sybil. The record of that encounter was completely suppressed. And the Blocked Worlds had been ruled off limits for good. The Service was determined that the unregulated sybil should never be permitted to break free into humanized space. At least that was the official position. Use of carefully controlled parasites in agents of Terra argued another purpose. Sybil symbiotes could help the Service maintain superiority for Old Earth among the competitive governments of the sprawling Commonwealth.

From that view, Ptolemy's experimentation could be perceived as a threat to Commonwealth security. No wonder the emperor's people were nervous about his presence.

This was Ball's first opportunity to examine an untrammeled example of the virus. The cerebration he witnessed in the brain of the sleeping gargoyle made him a little uneasy. The virus clearly had the native potential to give its host near-instantaneous communication outside Einsteinian spacetime. Any star-traveling aggressor bonded to the sybil could run rings around Terran technology. No wonder the Service was so nervous about this thing.

Was Ptolemy the only world that had dared to infiltrate the Blocked World blockades? Just how many of these damned things were loose among the stars?

Ball continued to ruminate, analyzing parallel streams of data from his artificial brain at high speed. It was definitely time to activate the Python clone. Baka Martin always had exhibited near-telepathic gifts of acuity. It was why the Service had chosen him as a sybil host in the first place. Ball was counting on that ability to manifest itself in the cloned brain as well. He supposed that allied him, to a degree, with the so-called materialists. With something like the old Python alive again, functioning smoothly in tandem with his regulated sybil, it shouldn't take long to discover the extent of Ptolemain—and InterGalactic—plans for the sybil.

If Ball could have smiled, he would have. The emperor remained convinced it was his own idea to have Ichiro U. bid on the Baka Martin activation. The conspirators now viewed the Martin clone as central to their schemes. Getting them to arrive at that conclusion without wondering why had been a clever piece of work. They now viewed Python as an experimental subject for their project. *Another* experimental subject.

Schodt's semantic slip on first meeting had been suggestive: they already had other experimental subjects—probably unwitting ones—under study. Perhaps already wedded to the virus. Based on his longtime successful symbiosis, Martin would be the control against whom to test the others.

"I'm done here," Ball said.

Elizabeth of Pythagoras came back into to the lab. "The sybil, in your opinion, is suitable for a brain of Martin's power?"

"Yes."

"You can supply us the final records of Martin, before his death?"

"That, and a sybil-control chip. Python wouldn't want to miss this dance for the world."

When the silent vibration from the houseboat's engines altered rhythm, slowing almost to a stop and then powering up again, the change penetrated my sleep and brought me half awake in the aft cabin. After a full day aboard, my subconscious seemed to be attuning itself to waterborne life again.

The cabin was dark, but weak light leaked around the porthole curtains. The bulkhead clock said it was nearing dawn in this hemisphere. The engines slowed again, and the boat almost stopped. A queasy tidal swell lifted the stern in a slow corkscrewing motion. On terrestrial planets, water is water, right: H_2O? But under the lighter gravity of Ptolemy, influenced by the tug of Ptolemy's single, manufactured moon, the wave actions felt—odd. My stomach shifted in sympathy. The engines altered revolutions again, picking up speed. I crawled out of the bunk and pushed back the curtain.

Something was moving on the stern deck. In the washed-out pinkish light it was hard to distinguish details. A formless blob humped out of a low turret back there and heaved itself overboard. A heavy splash, a brief show of spray above the deck. Raven was setting out decoys. A second blob began to tug itself free of the turret. I could see a little better now. Raven had called them jelly-slugs—a much preferred food group of the flying dinosaurs we would be hunting.

The thing swelled and undulated as it extruded from the turret orifice. It hesitated, broke free, and rolled over the rail. In the boiling wake, the two blobs bobbed and wallowed like live things on the surface.

I stepped into the fresher for a quick wake-up before I pulled on the Ptolemy coverall Raven had supplied me. Its climate controls were deactivated here; the cabin was cool and dry. But Raven said I would welcome the coverall's protection while waiting for the flights out on the flats of the Western Sea. The hunt had been laid on for me by Ball, as a kind of welcoming gift. I found myself intrigued at the prospect of the shooting—and strangely reluctant. I had been changed more than I realized by my hunting of the Pondoro wolverine. I didn't see how any hunting on any world would ever match the greer. But it seemed I was committed. I found Raven in the main cabin with a bulky rifle in his lap.

"Ah, the decoy placement must have awakened you," he said.

"What have you got there?"

He offered it to me butt first. "A dragon-slayer. A sporting arm based on ancient designs."

I hefted the weapon. It was heavy, but well-balanced. "A double-barreled bolt-action rifle?" I said. "I've never seen anything quite like it."

"Two completely separate firing systems," Raven said. "If one firing pin breaks, you have another. If one primer fails, or the cartridge jams, you have a separate barrel. Two independent firing systems for dangerous game is a concept as old as smokeless powder."

"I understand that. But those ancient elephant guns back then were strictly two-shooters. This thing has box magazines for each barrel!"

"A late twentieth-century design," he said. "It came too late in that century—and was too costly to produce—to ever gain wide usage then. The design was resurrected by Ptolemy craftsmen during settlement days. With modern tooling, these were simpler and cheaper than beam weaponry. They became standard issue for hundreds of isolated terraforming settlers who were endangered by Ptolemy's fauna on a daily basis."

"You mean like the thing that tried to eat us at the landing field?"

"Just so. Call them dragons or call them wingfingers, they were a planetwide menace in those days. Today, the settled areas are protected by sonic barriers they can't penetrate. We try to leave the rest of the world pretty much as it was."

"Wingfingers?"

"That's the literal translation of the ancient term 'pterodactylus.' Flying dinosaurs. The term comes from the finger-joint of the upper appendages, which evolved and adapted to support the beast's flight wings. The local versions are a striking example of parallel evolution. Many people here still call them dragons—the Japanese influence again."

I worked the bolt of the bulky rifle. It was slick and glassy, and had the solid camming action of a quality design. I closed the action and handed it back. "Nice weapon. How many decoys will you use?"

"A couple of hundred—all activated, to resemble a feeding school. The churning of the water can be seen from quite far away. Our Ptolemy wingfingers have very well-developed bulbous optic hemispheres and large keen eyes. These shallow seas teem with jelly-worms. The predatory species of our wingfingers fly enormous distances from their roosts when the jelly-worms are schooling. My decoys swim and dive just like the real thing. You'll see."

"We're to shoot this morning, then?"

"If the flights cooperate. I have been tracking the early flights on screen. So far they are working almost a hundred kilometers from here. But that can change rapidly."

He had several slender rifle cartridges from my shooting kit secured to a compact analyzer unit. They were dwarfed by the thumb-sized rounds for his dragon-slayer. But to my eye they were sleek and efficient. I had used them with success on a wide variety of game, from Old Earth leopard to Pondoro wolverine. I hefted one of them.

"What do you think? My rifle is a seven millimeter, built on Acme. The ammunition is

Acme design as well. Will my primers detonate adequately on this world? Will my gunpowder give me a useful power curve?"

Raven shrugged delicately. "You will get a good flash—and reasonable burning. Your rounds will not generate the energy you are accustomed to in this atmosphere, but there should be no dangerous power excursion or pressure build-up. And the lighter gravity will offset some of the debilitating effect on the burn rate. All our shooting will be at effectively point-blank range. Under three hundred meters as a rule. But this caliber is very light for a wingfinger. I would use the pencil-bombs to ensure a clean kill, not the game loads. In the meantime I will have the analyzer extrude a few cartridges and develop a suitable powder and projectile which will duplicate your native ballistics."

"Until then, you can back me up with that dragon-slayer, right?"

"If you wish. But I have a battery of these heavy rifles which you are welcome to use."

I shook my head. "I don't think so. I'll start with the pencil-bombs. High explosive seemed to work on that thing at the landing field. And I've used that same rifle all my life. One firing system, one barrel, one magazine. Even against the Pondoro wolverine."

"It is always best of course to use the weapon you know." He rose gracefully, perfectly balanced against the rolling jolt of the vessel's motions, and plugged the analyzer unit into its somewhat larger manufacturing component, built into an overhead cupboard. "We should have some breakfast and move into position among the decoys not too long after sunup. I'm sure we will get some small flights by mid-morning. But we need to be in place well before then."

The morning sky was occluded by a high thin overcast. Ptolemy's sun seemed in no hurry to rise out of the sea, but it was gilding the underbelly of the overcast with deep pink highlights. The headlands around the mouth of Civilization River were a dim smudge off our starboard. The short slow bathtub waves rolled under our keel without moving us. We were tucked in among crustacean-covered rocks still wet from the falling tide. Raven had let down hydraulic stabilizers from his hull to embed in the shoal and provide for steady gun-handling. All around us his flock of ersatz jelly-worms humped and rolled and cavorted.

Far off across the pallid water, a dark line of aerial shapes plowed along with a steady wing-beat. At this distance they were no bigger than mosquitoes.

"They may turn," Raven said softly.

He was fiddling with a portable console that controlled his boat's color scheme. The vessel's brightwork was dulled down to the color of thinned blood, to match the encrusted rock. Its heretofore glossy hull was as mottled as a Zion siege tank. We were seated on the bridge, beneath the dusky arc of an interruption field. We could see out, but even the sharp vision of a Ptolemy dragon would not be able to penetrate the exterior diffusion.

"For a sporting vessel, you've got some awfully sophisticated stuff," I said. "I've been on worlds where the local military would kill for stuff this good."

The line of dots merged with the sea and was lost to view. I adjusted my coverall's thermostat. It was terribly muggy out here on the flats. Raven studied his monitor screen. I noticed the water around us seemed to be deepening to a dark rose hue.

"Is something bleeding down there?"

Raven smiled widely. "Red shrimp! A good sign."

"Red shrimp?"

"Shrimplike, anyway. Close enough. They feed on algae in these shallow bays. That's where they get their coloration." He was watching his monitor again. "Excellent!"

"What?"

He pointed aloft. "Use your field glasses."

An echelon of fliers was high above us. Their lighter underbodies flashed in the sun like the bellies of mallards. But these were no ducks. Almost as soon as they were in focus, the leader executed a wing-over and dove. The rest followed with the precision of a battle squadron of Zion suborb jet fighters. The slanting morning sun seemed to strike crimson from their wings. The wind-shriek of their combined dive wasn't quite as piercing as that of the thing that dove on us at the landing field, but it was loud enough.

They hit the water, one after the other, in a series of tall columns of spray. The closest splash couldn't have been a hundred meters away. I realized my hands were cramped around my rifle and glanced at Raven.

"Bristle-tooths," he said dismissively. "They feed on the shrimp. That's where they get that bright pigmentation in their wings and backs. Notice how from above they blend in with the red bloom in the water from the shrimp school? Excellent camouflage from the more predatory dactyls. They remind me of a tanka."

"A tanka?"

"One of the links of a Renga I forged in a regional competition. Listen:

Wake to blue-sky days.
Crimson birds pop here and there.
White-patterned snow.
Cardinals of the sun, they
slake a thirst from melting tears."

"Have you ever seen a Terran blue sky?"

"Not relevant," he said. "But I have seen much crimson. And many tears."

The bristle-tooths were foraging among the ersatz jelly-worms, ignoring them.

"Try a tanka, Keith Ramsey. Look at the day spread before you, and compose."

"A tanka? Now?"

"While we wait for larger game." He made a neat, economic movement and seated the shockingly big-bored double rifle against his shoulder. He fired the instant the gun was

against his shoulder. One of the bristle-tooths
convulsed and went over on its back in a blather
of spray. Its wide wings beat a diminishing tattoo, their almost-white undersides semaphor-
ing vividly against the heaving red water.

I noticed there wasn't much recoil, and no
report. His dragon-slayers were heavily com-
pensated, and he was using safari-grade hush-
ers.

"Good eating?" I said.

"Not bad, actually. But he's not for us. He's
bait." He was studying his screen again. "There
are interesting flights on screen. Spin us a
tanka, Keith Ramsey. The competition begins
in one standard week."

"Five syllables, seven, five—and then seven-
seven?"

"Just so."

I counted syllables on my fingers while he
studied the screen. I was torn between feeling
silly and imagining the feature story I could get
out of this: shooting flying dinosaurs and
inventing ancient poetry.

"Okay," I said. "How's this?

"High drab overcast.
Another alien sky.
Fresh blood in water.
In high busy hunting flights,
dragons dream of human flesh."

Raven looked up from his screen. "I am
moved, Keith Ramsey. You will be welcome in
the Renga. Your words of blood and death will

be strong magic. And now, we have game worth shooting—"

This time the shriek was exactly the same pitch as I'd heard at the landing field, multiplied. They came from far up against the overcast, almost invisible at first, dropping like a pair of stones.

"You shoot, Keith Ramsey. The one on the right is a prime hunting male."

I tried to catch the falling shape in the crosshairs. Failed. Tried again. There was a heavy double whump and splash, and the newcomers were all over the floating bristle-tooth, their beaked mouths tearing ravenously. The rest of the red-backed fliers had not flinched when Raven shot their squadron-mate, but now they struggled aloft and away.

My crosshairs centered on a huge glittering eye, above a beak full of steaming flesh. The seven gun seemed to nudge my shoulder the same instant the pencil-bomb blew that long crested head apart. The explosion of the round was not hushed. The concussion rolled off across the water. The second beast was too busy ripping chunks of the bristle-tooth's flesh to notice. Without even thinking about it, I killed that one, too.

"Well-fired, Keith Ramsey! A double! And with your first two shots on Ptolemy. Your hunter's reputation is justified."

I put down my rifle. I felt vaguely ill. It was the adrenaline rush of a kill that had come too easily. Something every hunter knows. But there was something else, too. This was the first shooting I had done since Pondoro. There, I had labored under the extrasensory terror the Pondoro wolverine used to harass its quarry. You didn't sit around and invent pretty words when a greer was hunting you. Men who hunted beneath that fear were changed for all time, so the legend went. For some the terror became like a drug, always drawing them back. For others, it broke their spirit for good. I hadn't really thought through how hunting and being hunted by the greer might affect any other shooting I might do. Now, I just felt sick.

The tangled bodies of the three wingfingers heaved and rolled, awash in the ground swell. The stench of burned flesh came strongly. I thought I might throw up.

"Something is wrong, Keith Ramsey?"

I was groping through my memory for a phrase to capture how I was feeling. Some ancient phrase I had heard somewhere. Finally it came to me.

"Fish in a barrel," I said.

"I don't understand your meaning, Keith Ramsey." Raven looked concerned. "Are you all right?"

"Like shooting fish in a barrel," I said. "Too easy. Not very sporting."

He didn't have time to be disappointed in me again. On the heels of my words, that diving shriek began again. Directly above us. We both glanced up at the same time. A Ptolemy predator twice as big as the ones I had shot was diving right at us.

Ichiro University was an eagle's aerie, perched on man-built crags that formed the upper watershed of Civilization River. From the ceremony room at the top of the Ichiro Tower, the river itself was a bright thread that glittered oddly beneath the morning sun and the rose-hued sickle of the early moon. The emperor of Ptolemy stood at the room's best vantage, hands folded behind his back, absorbed in the view.

Ball cleared the entranceway's ceremonial doors with plenty of room to spare and coasted dead-silent above the opulent carpeting. The emperor would have passed unremarked in a crowd of his fellows—tall, spare, draped in a simple and colorful jumpsuit. His iron-gray hair was caught back in a simple ponytail. His expression—like most of his fellows, most of the time—seemed contemplative and tranquil.

"Your presence graces our world, simply Ball," he said without turning. "Your teaching serves better government far and wide by casting a bright light on the perfidies of the Commonwealth administration."

"Your own reign exemplifies the wisdom of Lao-tzu." Ball used his ceremonial tone. "Your modesty and good works would make Ptolemy the Elder smile."

The emperor smiled. "Your diplomatic skills are well-honed. Where does Ball, the well-programmed machine, end, and Ball, the human intelligence, begin? An interesting question! You know that our main industry here is robotics and artificial intelligence. Since first settlement, human and machine effort have blended here to build this pleasant land."

He unclasped his hands and made a wide exuberant gesture to encompass the view. "Human plus machine can build mountains such as these! My ancestors and their machines did. They shaped a raw world into harmony and pleasant living. Created a well of knowledge and hope for all mankind. Are you familiar with the ancient expression, 'He hung the moon'? No? It was a term of romance, implying a lover's power. Well, *we* hung Arsinoe, our moon! With a carefully calculated mass and orbit to generate life-blessing tides and seasons on this planet. To govern such as my people is a privilege and an honor. It is easy to be modest among my people!"

"A world of ideas," Ball said softly.

"Just so!"

"Ideas fashioned into hardware and software for galactic commerce. Your people can afford to study their navels as long as their designs are considered superior in the marketplace, and marketed aggressively by Inter-Galactic Cybernetics."

The emperor continued to smile. "Ball the

cynical observer. Do you know there are those
among your admirers who consider you the
very epitome of the ancient Japanese concept
of the Zen robot? The sacred tool of civilization.
The samurai's blade, the poet's quill. Of course
you are much more. You are a sentient being—
a consciousness. We modestly aspire here to
one day raise our machines to that estate. In
the endeavor, we adhere to Hasegawa's seven
rules of robotics, more complex and comprehensive than Asimov's three."

"You caused the reprogramming of Rongor
battle robots for a raid on the Blocked Worlds.
I'm sure my erstwhile employer, the Commonwealth Executive, would consider that a more
profane than sacred use of tools."

"One uses the tool at hand in support of an
overarching idea!"

"This new idea of yours is . . . encompass-
ing."

"Ideas must be communicable to have
strength!"

"You plan a demonstration, then."

The emperor rounded on Ball. "But our
demonstration is no threat to Commonwealth
security! Quite to the contrary. I believe our
demonstration will show the essential harmony
of things. Of course my esteemed colleague, the
Commonwealth Executive, is suspicious of our
design. But then, it is her role to be suspicious,
isn't it? As shepherd to all civilization?"

"It is my impression she would appreciate
that description."

"I believe she would. Tell me, simply Ball—

how much personal knowledge do you have of Adrienne Taft of Yok, Belkin's World?"

"No personal knowledge," Ball said. And paused, surprised by a stray wisp of—something. Memory? He reached for the wisp and found nothing. "No personal knowledge," he repeated. "If I ever was in her presence, I do not remember."

"Yet you were one of her most trusted agents! Some of your exploits are legend within the secret world of intelligence and counterintelligence. Worthy of a Renga all their own."

"I had some success in my endeavors," Ball said.

"Modesty," the emperor said, "is not a trait of yours I have heretofore been privileged to observe."

"I failed to protect my field man in my last assignment. I was required to take . . . unorthodox measures to ensure his sacrifice was not in vain. I see little reason for preening."

"Spoken like a principled entity. Then you will take deep pleasure in resurrecting your friend. As nearly resurrection as we yet can accomplish. Will you furnish him with memories of his death?"

"He died twice on Pondoro. Memory of his second death will not serve him well. No. He will remember only his first reawakening there. And perhaps keep his idealism intact. You have others like Martin in place? On other worlds? Awaiting his resurrection?"

"Right to the point! I like that."

"How many?"

The emperor gestured vaguely. "Irrelevant at this juncture. Enough. Enough for an adequate demonstration."

"And you have enough sybil for them all? You have spread undiluted sybil throughout civilized worlds? What are your safeguards?"

"Adequate—as you saw here. The host creature is in suspended animation. Fully isolated. The transfer will not be effected until we have fully integrated Martin. The procedure has proved efficient. Do you know who named the sybil, by the way?"

"A Terran Service Scout," Ball said. "The only one who survived the first Blocked World expedition. A man with a sense of humor, evidently. He named it for a woman he said had infected his heart as surely as the sybil infected his mind. Why do you ask?"

"It's not important. There was an ancient, almost-prehistoric oracle of that name. I believe the spelling was different. But that can change over scores of centuries. How marvelous to learn of a romantic in the Terran Service! Isn't life marvelous in all its aspects?"

"The only omen the sybil represents is potential danger to humankind," Ball said. "What powers of mind do your other candidates have in common with Baka Martin?"

"Must they have something in common besides a brain receptive to symbiosis?"

Ball introduced his patient sigh. "Aside from the fact that the sybil considers *any* brain receptive, harmony is a tenet of your faith.

Beauty all around you. An amalgam of Zen and Navajo precepts. You would not miss the chance to introduce a harmonious element into the selection of candidates for such a demonstration as this."

The emperor inclined his head. "Well said. They are not clones of Terran Service agents killed in action, if that is what you are asking. They all are idealists of a sort, but they also share another point of commonality. As well as being your field man, Martin was essentially a storyteller, yes? A wandering teller of tales?"

"Poets," Ball said. "All your host candidates are poets. You used past Renga competitions to select them."

"You are astute. The administration of InterGalactic would be terrified to know I had shared that information with you. The Terran Service lost one of its best and brightest in you. But you will be the bridge that brings our achievement into harmony with the government, in the end."

"I'm glad you think so. And your demonstration?"

"Ask yourself: what are words to ideas?" The emperor's eyes glowed with excitement. "Why, words are like quantum wave functions for the ideas they represent! Do you see? A word is merely a potential until it is received and comprehended. Which collapses the wave into a perceived reality. What is a communication between sentient beings but an exchange of quantum wave and echo wave? You see it? A reflection of the very manner in which the sybil communicates outside normal time and space."

"So you have chosen poets for the experiment."

"The poet does not create his work," the emperor said. "Are you familiar with that idea? Nietzsche it was, I believe, who said that. An ancient philosopher. The poet's intellect is merely the field of conflict and of reconciliation to the impersonal and masked forces that inhabit us. Masked forces! What better poetic description of quantum phenomena?"

Ball made a slight sound. The emperor's brows creased. Ball made the sound again.

"Are you laughing at me?"

"Maybe a little. By the standards of the Commonwealth, you are quite mad."

"Ah!" His brow smoothed. "Of course I am! By those standards. I am not injured by your assessment. I am unimportant in the grand scheme of things, don't you see? Such things as ego are not an infirmity. They are an illusion. We all are part of the great circle of things. The great unity. As our project will demonstrate with great elegance!"

"And when do you plan this demonstration to occur?"

"I should have thought it would be obvious to one of your gifts!"

Ball was silent for a space. Then, "During this year's Renga," he said.

The emperor clapped his hands. "I knew you'd see it!"

"Yes, I see it." Ball paused again. Twin

incoming data streams diverted his attention: his Keith Ramsey empathometer was spewing with more force than it had since the crisis on Pondoro. And Raven's was nearly as busy.

Something was trying to eat them.

"Excuse me, Excellency," Ball said calmly. He activated the mechanism on the ceremony room's balcony doors. "I have friends urgently in need of my presence."

The emperor's attention was diverted by the sliding doors. "What?" he said. "Ball—"

Air collapsed with a loud whoop into the pocket of space Ball had occupied. The emperor's garment flattened against him in a rush of air.

Ball was gone.

The interruption field held under the impact of the huge predator. It hovered there, trying to grasp the slippery field with its cruel talons. I didn't trust the field to hold. I was trying to climb under my seat. Raven calmly tipped up the double muzzles of his dragon-slayer and shot the beast through its gaping maw.

It spasmed overboard, spraying bright blue blood and bits of flesh across the shimmer of the force field. I had time to register the color of its blood—its physiology was based on copper, not iron.

"Unusual method of attack—" Raven started to say.

And that shriek of air across cocked wings came again.

Another of the huge ones slanted in, as if trying to come under the edge of the field. That seemed wrong, but I didn't have time to ponder it. My first pencil-bomb exploded on its shoulder and knocked it into the water. My second one tore its head off.

Wind-shriek again. Another one was coming down on us.

Then the interruption field shut off.

Raven muttered some word I didn't recognize. It sounded like profanity. He fired upward quickly, twice. Then rolled fluidly to one side. I went the other way, clumsy but fast in the still-unaccustomed gravity. Something huge and foul-smelling hit the bridge a hell of a whack. The boat jounced on its stabilizers.

One of Raven's big slugs sizzled a hot tunnel through the air too close to my ear. It hit like a meat cleaver. Blue blood and raw tissue sprayed again. A convulsing wing swept me off the bridge. In seeming slow motion, I tumbled onto the aft decking. I didn't weigh as much as I was accustomed to weighing, but the impact still hurt.

I came to my knees fumbling in my ammo belt. This work was too close for the PBs. I needed solids.

The wing of the thing hung above me, twitching like some gigantic hell-born kite. There was a single spurlike projection at the wing joint. It glinted red. Raven crawled from beneath the wing. His colorful coverall was sodden with reeking, purpled blood. Copper-blue and iron-red mingled. He was moving as if dazed. Again, just for an instant, he seemed smaller and frailer than he should have. His arm rose and fell. The bowie flashed in the weak light. There was a dull *whunk* of sound. The wing bone parted at the joint and dangled free. He made a graceful slashing gesture. The wing membrane parted like paper, and the severed half went over the side.

I had no more time to admire the knife-work. Another of the big ones came in at a shallow slant, right at me. I had a solid chambered in the seven gun, and another in the magazine. All my attention focused on the crosshairs. I fired twice in quick succession, and ducked.

Massive claws rattled across the boat. Raven screamed, a high-pitched sound. Then his body thudded into me, knocking me down again. His heavy rifle banged across my shins with eye-watering force. But he still was conscious, squirming off me, reaching for his rifle. I noticed he had somehow resheathed his blade. Marvelous self-control.

The dragon I had shot heaved up into view. Its jaws fastened on the transom. Its wing arched over us like a leather tent, its spike searching for us. It was trying to lever itself aboard. I single-loaded a solid and fired into the dactyl's jaw hinge. It sagged back out of sight.

"All systems are out!" Raven said hoarsely. "I don't know where this flight came from! Something is very wrong—"

My pulse was pumping now, all right. I was scared enough, but at my core I was calm, steady. For all their horrific zeal in trying to eat us, these things still were just primitive organisms. They couldn't freeze my bowels with terror as the Pondoro wolverine had. This was shooting! The greer would be proud of me. I almost laughed out loud.

"More of them coming!" Raven said. "Circling." He crawled toward the cabin door. "Need more ammunition—"

I rolled flat on my back. There must have

been another half dozen in a tight orbit up there against the overcast. Almost as soon as I saw them, one broke formation and stooped. I jammed my eye to the seven gun's scope and tried to lead it.

But its plummet was interrupted dramatically before I could fire.

It slammed to a stop. Right in midair. Its tucked wings splayed open like a parachute. It fell away like a brain-shot *twon*, coasting on fully extended wings.

A silver meteor blazed away from it, glinting in the weak sunlight.

The sphere described a wicked turn and towered into a high climb. In a heartbeat it was in among the circling squadron of giant dactyls. It was like seeing a hawk explode among pigeons. One fell immediately, like a stone. Then another spun down. The rest scattered in fleeing dives to all points of the compass. Sun glinted again on that bright speck way up there against the cloud cover. It hovered up there for what seemed a long time. Then it floated lazily downward, swelling into a familiar shape and size, and paused just above us.

"Simply Ball!" Raven said.

"And just in time, too," Ball said. "I guess I should have known better than to imagine you could stay out of trouble here, Ramsey."

I propped my back against the cabin wall and listened to my heart pound for a long minute.

"Nice to see you, too," I said.

The emergency-response forces
of Ptolemy were a model of efficiency. Within
half an hour of Ball's arrival they dropped a sonic
barrier two kilometers wide around Raven's vessel to fend off further feeding flights of wingfingers. An ambulance with full Medfac dropped in
beside us and took Raven aboard. The crew
insisted on examining me. The ambulance
stayed alongside. Word came shortly that Raven
would be fine and could rejoin us before the day
was out. By then Ball was supervising a forensics
team that was probing Raven's on-board software.
Robots wearing the emblem of the emperor's
personal household cleared away the dragon
carcasses, consigning them to the sea.

"Sabotage," Ball told me.

We were on the flying bridge, watching the
Ptolemy crews work. "Sabotage?"

"No question. Raven's on-board systems
were tampered with from a distance. Herf-
bursts, precisely targeted. You didn't see any
other vessels out here this morning?"

"No. Nothing."

"Doesn't matter. They would have been
well-camouflaged. The early scan of satellite
images in this sector show nothing strange,
either. But someone was out here."

"What the *hell* is going on?"

"My hypothesis is that somebody wanted you to be eaten. Raven was just in the way. You probably have been under close observation since you arrived. There's something else. The forensics 'bots are scoping these beasts. This last flight represents the largest predator here—average wingspan of sixty meters. Every one of them was chipped—programmed for anomalous dive patterns. They couldn't have broken that orbit above you if they starved to death circling. The forensics 'bots are trying to plot a backtrack to their roost, but my bet is they won't be able to. This was carefully arranged."

"That's an awful lot of trouble to go to, just for me. "

"You tend to make powerful enemies."

"You mean the Commonwealth Executive?"

"So the emperor believes. He already is directing a formal protest through open diplomatic channels."

"Open?"

"Publicly monitored ones. To ensure Associated News is aware one of its own has been put at risk. You're famous again."

"And I don't get the byline on the story? Shit."

"You've already got a contract for your work here. Don't be so greedy."

"Do you think Taft arranged this?"

"No. This doesn't square with her style. She'd want to be able to claim credit, at least covertly. But even the attempted execution of a famous journalist, here as a guest of Ptolemy, will cause her nothing but grief. This is a setup."

"If not her, then who?"

"That is the question. I must say you handled yourself calmly under pressure here. The greer would be proud of you."

A weird little chill got loose along my spine. "You *can* read my damn mind, can't you? I was thinking that very thing during the attack!"

He ignored the remark. "I also must point out that you are a little hard on the women I entrust to your care."

"Women? What are you talking about now?"

"You got Kathryn's neck broken for her in that aircar fall on Pondoro. Now you almost got Raven killed before I could get here."

"Raven?"

He introduced one of his nastiest chuckles. "She was much taken with the idea of meeting the great Keith Ramsey in the—well, flesh. I suspect she has one of those Keith Ramsey erotic progues aboard this vessel, in her stateroom. But she was afraid you would balk at a female hunting guide, since you are such a primitive."

"Raven is no woman!"

"Sure she is. I just tinkered with your chip a little, so your reticular activating system got its references a little scrambled."

"I thought that damned chip was just an empathometer!"

"Relax. It was a harmless stunt. It tickled my fancy to do it for her. Her other field of study, and her chosen name, just made it seem so fitting as an introduction to Ptolemy."

"I'm getting lost here, Ball."

He produced a patient sighing sound. "Raven was the ancient shape-changer and trickster for Indian tribes in the American Pacific Northwest on Old Earth. One of the legends says Raven stole a ball of fire from the gods to give to humanity—a kind of Salish Prometheus. Get it? Ball of fire? That was how the greer on Pondoro thought of me, remember?"

"So Python said. What's that got to do with Raven?"

"Primitive mythology is her second field. Our Raven liked the idea of seeming to be . . . anybody—a lot. Exploring alternate identities, male or female. She had her name officially changed to Raven a long time ago. And she asked me to help her with you in this latest personification. Male bonding on the hunt. A new role, you see."

"Goddammit, Ball—"

"Relax, I said. I've corrected it now. No time for any more fun and games. Not when somebody decides to kill a news hawk."

"Sabotage doesn't make any sense! Who am I a threat to here?"

"I don't know that yet. You're just a broken-down news hawk who's going to try to fake his way through a poetry competition. Other than harm you might perpetrate on our shared language, I don't see a threat, either."

"What in hell is going on here, Ball?"

"Well, for one thing, a local university is under contract to activate a Baka Martin clone."

That stopped me for a minute. "Under contract to whom? The Terran Service?"

"Not so's you'd notice. Somehow Inter-Galactic Cybernetics got the rights."

"Them again. That company is getting too big for its britches."

"You have the most delightfully archaic way of saying things, do you know that? I'm sure Raven will be—has already been—utterly charmed."

Images of Raven from our first meeting replayed themselves behind my eyes. If Ball wanted to confuse me thoroughly, he had done a masterful job. Raven gravely shaking hands in the orbital hotel. Raven running for cover on the shuttle field. Raven reacting calmly and with courage under this morning's attack. Only once or twice had something seemed—odd. My muscle memory replayed the feel of Raven's body as he fell across me in the last heated moments of that skirmish. And told me my brain had failed to register a certain softness and roundness—had repressed them—during the skirmish. Registering those sensations now, I felt a carnal stirring. Tried to suppress it.

Impossible, of course, with Ball and his infernal empathometer.

He chuckled. "Try to be flexible in your thinking," he said. "She really is a woman. That seems to matter a great deal to one of your frontier upbringing."

"What the hell do I do now?"

"You should definitely leave these flats and get back inside the main terraformed zone. The plan was for you to do some sightseeing up the river while you train for the competition. I see no reason for that to change. The emperor is very disturbed that a distinguished visitor—a journalist, at that—has come under attack. Since he suspects the Commonwealth in this, his pride is on the line. Local security forces are quite good, and they will be babysitting you from now on."

"There must be a story here. One hell of a story."

"Perhaps there is," Ball said. "You may even live to write it."

PART TWO

Hen

(Start)

Everybody
Cries here. Tears burn memories,
Scattering damp ash.
Lovers cry because nothing
revealed is forgotten.

The Ptolemy headquarters of InterGalactic Cybernetics occupied a vast and remote compound in a foothill valley a little over fifty kilometers downstream from the city of Tezuka, and forty kilometers inland from Civilization River. An anonymous plas-teel wall marked its boundaries and kept ground traffic away. The surface film of the wall was programmed to blend so well that nature-walkers had been known to blunder into it full force. It had just enough pliancy under such impacts to minimize personal-injury lawsuits.

Alex Schodt's aircar paused halfway to the walls from the river, at the required interval for clearance, then swooped neatly above the wall. A shimmering interruption field domed the complex, and Schodt involuntarily closed his eyes, as he always did. The field dilated to admit them, and closed seamlessly behind them. The surface structures of the complex were featureless amber cubes one story high, lined with military precision along lush lawn-like thoroughfares. The car drifted to a stop in front of the administration building, and the hatch sighed open. Schodt got out and stretched luxuriously. He always felt safest within the protection of the company's elaborate security precautions. The clear rose-hued sky of Ptolemy was undistorted by the interruption field. It was a cloudless, lovely day.

He waited out the white-room scanning patiently, and knew a sense of relief when he was pronounced clean. He didn't trust that damned Ball one bit. His executive assistant was waiting on the other side.

"Your quarters are ready for you," she said.

"Let's have a look."

The first sound he heard as the door opened was the fluid mating song of a male canary. His face relaxed into a happy smile. "He's singing!"

"Yes." His assistant smiled back at him. "Isn't it lovely?"

He barely heard her, walking toward the small bundle of avian life perched on a truncated branch that seemed to grow out of the wall. The suite was decorated in Schodt's favorite deep green, with substantial furniture of real wood and pale green leather. The canary stopped singing and cocked an eye at him, rocking slightly on the branch.

"How has he adjusted to the local gravity?" Schodt asked.

"He hasn't had to. We set his cage area for Earth-normal."

"Ah! Excellent." He brushed his fingers against the slight friction of the cage-field in something like a caress. "Sing for us, Tony!"

But Tony kept his beak closed.

"Would you like lunch now?" his assistant asked.

"No. Just give me a few minutes and then I will be going below. Time for a report to the home office."

When she was gone, he sprawled in a leather recliner and whistled a few tentative notes. Tony ruffled his feathers and looked unimpressed.

"So I'm not very good at carrying a tune," Schodt said tenderly. "You're a lucky bird, you know that? To be alive now, and with me? You could have been a miner's canary, you know. Dragged into the bowels of some dank pit to test the air by dying for them so they could live. But you're an executive sort of bird." He laughed out loud.

Tony was Schodt's one executive affectation, traveling with him on his business jaunts for InterGalactic Cybernetics. Every executive needed something to set him apart in this vast corporate bureaucracy, and Tony was Schodt's trademark. Schodt enjoyed the joke of it, for Tony also was an icon of his field of knowledge—a knowledge shared only by a select few inside the giant company, and not including even the board of directors. InterGal thrived on internal secrets and rivalries. Schodt had lied to Ball about his total access to all records. The key data involving the cyborg's activation was so closely held Schodt didn't even know where to look. He suspected direct intervention in the project by one of the outside directors.

Schodt brushed his hair back from his forehead. Male canaries sing a new mating song
each season. It was ancient knowledge that the
portion of a canary's brain that learned the
song grew to double its size for the annual ritual. And then shrank back to its normal dimen-
sions after the mating rituals were done, the
song entirely forgotten. When the season came
around again, that portion of the bird's brain
began to swell again, and it regained the ability
to invent, and remember, and sing, a whole
new song. But past songs were gone beyond
recall.

"You showed us the way, Tony," Schodt told
the bird. "Well, not you, but your kind. Humanity
still has much to learn from its fellow beings,
you know."

Tony launched himself from his branch,
flew several meters along the wall. He banked
gracefully just before he would have encountered the cage perimeter and flew back, circling the invisible boundaries.

"Getting restless, huh? Not to worry, you'll
have a more appreciative audience soon. I'll
have my assistant release Mary into your space
tomorrow." Schodt climbed to his feet. "I wonder if you remember your past loves, Tony?
How can you, if you don't remember the songs
you sang to them?"

Tony regained his branch and studied his
master, evidently listening to the familiar
voice.

"No matter," Schodt decided. "Different
mores for canaries, right, Tony? Enjoy yourself,

sing a little. I'll remember, even if you don't.
But now I've got to go sing to the boss."

He rejoined his assistant in the reception
area and they took the elevator twenty stories
deep into the bedrock of Ptolemy. Another
white room. Schodt endured it patiently. His
assistant tapped her manicured fingernails
against her wrist computer and released a
long-suffering sigh. She hadn't been outside
the complex since they arrived, but procedure
was procedure.

The room at the end of the corridor was in
semi-twilight. A soft spray of light illuminated
the transparent case in which a woman lay,
writhing slowly, her face loose and disorganized by passion. Perspiration shone on her
nude body, which was too angular and bony for
Schodt's personal taste.

"She's cybering again," his assistant said
with prim distaste.

"Shhh," Schodt said. "Let her finish." He sat
at a console near the head of the creche.

His assistant joined him, and crossed her
legs tightly. Her body was much more pleasing
to Schodt, though he would never for a moment
let her know that. To reveal personal need was
a weakness. It could be turned against you. Her
filmy jumpsuit material outlined her shapely
thighs. A slight pulse beat in her throat. Schodt
suppressed a smile as she struggled against
her voyeuristic impulse. Her own personal discipline still was lacking somewhat. He didn't
yet have to worry about her as a threat to his
position in the corporate hierarchy.

He keyed the console.

"Yes, Mr. Schodt?" The voice hung in the air.

"Remaining duration of this episode?"

"It should conclude in five minutes. Unless you wish me to interrupt?"

"No. Leave her to it. But stimulate the sybil to suppress the hypocamus and begin opening the usual neuronal linkages."

"Initiating."

The woman in the case was panting hoarsely now, her hips lifting in a steady rhythm. Her hands roved restlessly in thin air, as if caressing a lover. Schodt's assistant crossed her arms tightly across her breasts and stayed that way, unmoving. There was a slight sheen of perspiration on her brow. Schodt leaned back, closed his eyes and tried to remember the exact notes of Tony's new song. The woman in the creche was crying out now.

"Mute the audio," Schodt said without opening his eyes. "Give her that much privacy."

In the silence, he heard a silken rustle of clothing beside him, and an audible gulp. His assistant's breathing was quiet, but uneven. He smiled, and tried to remember Tony's last mating song. He couldn't, but he had it recorded. He might play it back later.

"Episode concluded," the attendant said. "She is resting now. The virus has initiated traumatic automatism. She is ready for communications mode."

Schodt straightened and opened his eyes. "Activate audio again. Miriam?"

The woman's eyelids fluttered, but did not part. "Who is it?" Her voice was soft and gentle.

"Alex, Miriam. Can you reach Arthur for me?"

"Arthur's right here. He's always right here when somebody asks me. Wherever *here* is. I don't know where he is when nobody asks. Isn't that strange? This is what he is saying to me right now—

"Like open secrets
Wings take flight from mountaintop
peaks to oceans deep.
Lodged in the deeps, they wait to
reveal their secrets to none."

Schodt heard his assistant's sharp intake of breath. "Easy," he muttered to her. "Arthur doesn't really remember anything."

But he did wonder, briefly. The orders to organize the wingfinger attack on Keith Ramsey and his companion had come from the home office. Schodt thought it was an overreaction for a corporation of InterGalactic's size to fear a run-of-the-mill news hawk just because the cyborg, Ball, had invited him to this planet at this precise juncture. As to suspecting Ball's teaching assistant of being a Terran Service spy, that seemed ludicrous. But Schodt had not risen to his elevated position by questioning orders unnecessarily.

"Very poetic," Schodt told the recumbent woman. "What are you saying back to Arthur?"

Miriam said:

"Rain draws its curtain,
across all sense of distance
Blurring time and space
Is that your breath on my neck?
Oh! That rain could make this be."

"It's not raining today, Miriam. The weather is fine."

"It's always raining somewhere, Alex," she said softly. "Always in my heart. Why am I always your prisoner, Alex?"

"Oh, sweet Miriam—not my prisoner! My honored guest! The best-known erotic poet ever to come from Chisholm. One of the few off-worlders ever invited to participate in a Renga here on Ptolemy. Remember? Of course you do. You felt you were at the end of your string that year. You signed away your life. You wanted to die here, in the poetry competition. Go out in glory. And you did. Your lines from that competition are famous."

"But I didn't die. Unless the ancients were right and this is Limbo."

Schodt sighed. "How can it be Limbo, with Arthur to console you? And with your poetry reborn? I know you believed your art had deserted you, but you still spin words like threads of precious metal."

"I don't remember any poetry I've created since I came to Limbo!"

"Ah. But the universe will! Your words will survive us all. I promise you that."

"I have forgotten so much, it seems." She

stirred restlessly. "Would that I could drink from the lake named Lethe, and forget this Limbo, and be born again."

"A fine classical reference," Schodt said. "Why don't you fashion a poem about that lake?"

"Have we had this conversation before, Alex?"

Schodt pushed back his hair. "Many times, Miriam. Your short-term memory is gone, dear. If I left this room for five minutes and came back, you would not remember this conversation. And we would probably have it again!"

"Oh!" she exclaimed. "Listen!"

"What?"

"Arthur already has answered me:

"Everybody
cries here. Tears burn memories,
scattering damp ash.
Lovers cry because nothing
revealed is forgotten."

"That's beautiful!" Schodt said. "Arthur is showing off again." In an aside to his assistant, he said, "Have all Arthur's tankas scanned for semantics. He's being a little too cute with all those memory references." Then back to the woman in the case: "Miriam, love, would you ask Arthur if JonHoward is standing by?"

"Isn't JonHoward always standing by when you are here with me?"

"You remember that?"

"I seem to. I don't know. Is he?"

"You're right, of course—from your perspective. Please let JonHoward know I am ready to report."

It was ceremony day at the Commonwealth Executive's summer palace. Adrienne Taft had selected a severe charcoal business suit, set off by a blazing yellow kerchief, to preside over the festivities. She loved this part of the job: meeting and greeting, conferring honors, bestowing medals. Personifying the majesty of Old Earth and the Commonwealth, all in one. She was not above inserting a few deft political comments into the extensive news coverage of the event, because this kind of feel-good stuff played very well in outlying precincts of the Commonwealth, and was less critically edited before it got to the public.

The ceremony stage in front of the palace rose behind the broad esplanade far above the St. Lawrence River. Bleachers had been erected on the lawn all around it in homage to the fine weather. Clusters of giggling schoolchildren, who had received firsts in everything from genetics to rhetoric, were shepherded to her podium for the benefit of their home-planet news cameras. She hugged the small ones and gravely shook hands with the older ones. Her body language and gestures, when the recipient was nonhuman, were flattering and fluid imitations of the recipient's native greeting rituals.

Among the youth was a procession of Terran Service veterans or, in more than one instance, their survivors. They were all here to receive their Commonwealth Palm, for extraordinary peacekeeping efforts among the stars. For each of these, she extemporized appropriate remarks from the data-feed com tucked into her left ear. The media veterans who covered her activities knew she was milking each medal for all it was worth. They didn't care. There was nothing hotter in sight, and they had to fill air time. They could always spice it with rebuttals from the contending factions that drew her barbs.

The summer palace of the Commonwealth Executive was picturesque and widely recognizable. To billions, it represented the central role that humankind's home world played in modern politics. The palace grounds commanded the St. Lawrence River. The imposing gray-stone edifice itself was designed to emulate the vanished Quebec chateaux that had once crowned these heights.

Down on the river, the strong current was alive with pleasure craft. Air traffic was brisk along the far shore. Air space was of course severely restricted above the former site of the ancient Quebec City, but on ceremony day Terran Service security managed to be inconspicuous. To all outward appearances, the executive stood alone and undefended to greet Commonwealth subjects, as befitted the most far-flung human government yet devised. The wind off the river popped the flags of over a thousand planetary governments that lined the esplanade. The official Terran Service band played light and cheerful airs in the garden behind the stage.

Taft was in the middle of her remarks to a group of teenage nanotechs from WhitePeyton when a large crimson-and-silver aircar broke from the restricted paths along the far shore. It cruised toward flat ground beneath the palace bluff. It didn't hurry, it didn't pause at the mid-river force field, and it didn't evaporate in spinning atoms because Terran Service weaponry resented the intrusion. Only those who knew Taft very well indeed would have realized that the sight of the vehicle had distracted her. She hugged several winners, kissed the cheek of a twelve-year-old prodigy, shook hands with the older youths, and offered commentary as if nothing had happened.

In a very few minutes she noticed SjillaTen step off the lift in the wings of the stage. He was the only one who looked directly at her. The bodyguards were of course watching the crowd for trouble, and her advisers were watching for portents about how she was selling her programs today. She finished her praise of the young geniuses despite a subtle, hardly seen gesture from her intelligence chief. He needed to talk, and right now. As if it had been planned all along, she graciously handed off the remainder of this ceremony to dour Hennesy, her first deputy, after telling the assemblage he himself was a native of WhitePeyton. She stepped discreetly back, listened with all appearances of attentiveness, then drifted offstage, out of view of the crowd.

The Llralan's features twitched in his version of a smile. "Deft extrication in plain sight," he said.

"What's so urgent?" she asked, controlling her impatience.

"JonHoward Tomas awaits your presence below. The urgency is his."

"Well, wonders will never cease!" she said. "The mountain has come to Mohammed."

"An obscure reference," the Llralan said.

"Never mind. And why does the chief executive of InterGalactic Cybernetics presume, with no notice, to interrupt the affairs of the Commonwealth Executive?"

"There is news from Ptolemy he would share with you. InterGal's intelligence is quite as good as our own."

"Ptolemy again! This Ball?"

"Not this time. Not precisely. Shall we go down?"

JonHoward Tomas was waiting at the lift door, alone. His cyborg bodyguard stood well across the reception area, blocking the entranceway. No one else was in evidence.

"You presume, sir," Taft said, "to dismiss Commonwealth staff and meet me with an armed . . . thug at your back?"

Tomas was a mountain of a man, almost seven feet tall. Big head, hands, body. The expense and severity of his business attire, per-

fectly tailored to his bulk, was at least the equal
to Taft's. The accent color was a silver and crimson logo over his right breast—InterGalalactic's
familiar colors. He beamed fondly down at Taft.

"Wonderful to see you, too, Adrienne."

She cocked her head up at him. "So we're
back to first names? Then you must want something."

His laugh boomed out. His ample girth
shook gently. "In that, my dear Adrienne, I am
very like one of the most famous and enigmatic
warriors in all history. Though I personally
couldn't fight my way out of packing plastic."

She glanced at the Llralan. "Which famous
warrior?"

"General Robert E. Lee," Tomas said. "A
man honored even by his foes. A man with
everything his world could offer, or so history
seems to relate. Yet the quote most attributed to
him is 'I am always wanting something.' So am I.
Today, I have something to offer in return."

"I'm rather pressed here, JonHoward, for
history lessons. Perhaps you could be a little
less oblique?"

"As you wish, my dear. The emperor of
Ptolemy is lodging a formal diplomatic protest
against your administration through open
channels. Which means the media will know it
as soon as he releases it. I thought you might
appreciate knowing it first."

"Ptolemy," she said. "What in blazes does
that land of lotus-eaters think I have done to
them?"

"Well—they think you commissioned an

assassination attempt against an honored guest on their world. One that very nearly succeeded."

She glanced at SjillaTen again. "Do we know anything about this?"

"No."

"Tell me who," Taft said, turning back. "Who did we supposedly attempt to terminate? This cyborg, Ball?"

Tomas's booming laugh came again. "Not even the Commonwealth Executive would violate diplomatic immunity. Well, at least in no detectable way! In point of fact, Ball broke up the assassination attempt against an old friend of his, just arrived there."

"Ramsey," SjillaTen said.

Tomas shot him an appraising glance. "Just so. The news hawk, Ramsey. Who of late has been a bit of a thorn to the Terran Service."

"How do you know this before we do?" Taft asked him. "And why tell me? InterGal has a very profitable relationship with the government of Ptolemy, doesn't it? Still? Their factories produce a number of InterGal products under license. They are a growing force in the market. Why offend a business partner by alerting me?"

"The emperor will take no offense. He doesn't mind your being alerted ahead of time. But he remains determined to make a public issue of this aborted assassination. Ramsey's status with Associated News will guarantee this gets a lot of publicity."

"And what do you want from me in return?"

"I love your directness, Adrienne. When your term is done—or when somebody finally gathers enough Assembly votes to kick you out of office—please remember me. You would be an excellent addition to InterGalactic."

"Is that some kind of a bribe?" There was a dangerous edge in her voice.

"Of course not—a simple observation. This is a private conversation. You have the best witness you could have, in your Llralan there." Tomas shrugged. "I have no protection here. Charge me with bribery if you like."

"What do you want?" she repeated. "Your time is almost up."

"All right. There is talk backstairs in Assembly about some new antimonopolistic legislation. So far, just talk. While I do not believe we are the primary target, some of the language under review could cause us severe difficulty. I urge you to throw your considerable prestige behind free-market concepts, if it comes to that."

"That's all? I tend to support an unregulated marketplace anyway."

"Just so! See how easy I can be to get along with?"

"When do we expect this formal protest from Ptolemy to materialize?"

Tomas gave a shrug almost too delicate for his massive frame. "It has materialized. It is traveling the com-links as we speak from Ptolemy, ringing alarm bells in every Associated News bureau along the line. Before the day is out, I would say."

"Thank you, JonHoward. I won't forget."

"You are most welcome, dear Adrienne. I am counting on it." Tomas sketched a half-bow, and gestured to his cyborg.

The bodyguard was as tall as the executive, and nearly as massive—but his mass was the coiled energy of a lethal machine, guided by a sapient mind. The bodyguard activated the seals on the outer door. Slanting sunlight poured in. The cyborg went out first, shielding his master.

"Damn!" Taft said. "Somebody really tried to murder Ramsey?"

"So it would appear," SjillaTen said.

"I can see a jealous lover murdering him. For spreading himself around through that damned erotic progue. But is he really important enough for a political assassination?"

SjillaTen's face had twitched at mention of the erotic program. "To be seen."

"How the hell does JonHoward *do* it," she wondered. "How does he get information like this before we do?"

"A corporation that size must have adequate intelligence to survive in that oh-so-free marketplace upon which he dotes."

"Adequate! It's better than *ours*, for pity's sake."

"No," SjillaTen said. "Just several magnitudes faster."

She regarded him narrowly. "Am I missing something?"

"We all are," he said patiently. "We have the best communications equipment known, and so does InterGalactic, of course. But they have something else they keep closely held. Something that denies known communications logic. InterGalactic remains effectively a law unto itself."

"Find out what it is. I want some!"

"We have been trying," the Llralan said. "Our luck has been limited. The corporation's internal compartmentalization makes our own bureaucracy almost transparent by comparison. But we have a very tentative lead. Ptolemy's name has come up."

"Ptolemy again! You've been concerned for some time that something top-secret is going on there."

"Yes. That was the mission Ball wanted before he was diverted to Pondoro."

"Don't remind me!" She mused a moment. "There actually is some talk backstairs in the Assembly about that new legislation Jon-Howard spoke of. His intelligence must be very solid, or he wouldn't risk mentioning what he wanted me to do in the same conversation. He's convinced he has a marker to call in now."

SjillaTen said nothing. Legislative politics bored him.

"I need to go back up to the stage," she said. Above their heads, Hennesy was being uncharacteristically flowery. Taft was listening on her ear-com. "The home folks really bring Hennesy to life, don't they?"

The Llralan gave his version of a shrug. "You seem quite lively today yourself. Top form. I know it isn't these ceremonies. Given your reference to a believable motive to murder Keith Ramsey, I hypothesize you found that erotic program you commissioned . . . diverting?"

She stiffened. "One of these days you're going to go too far with your impertinence."

SjillaTen was unmoved. "It is time for you to go back up to the stage."

*Death, terrible and utterly si-
lent, came and fastened white-hot claws in his
flesh. Python's warm shocked life poured
thickly, horrifyingly, almost eagerly out. A single heartbeat to control the outflow of his life
before it all was pumped away. Then he must
dodge again, all that was left of his life force
unequally divided between fending off inrush-
ing death and stanching the outpour of blood
that welled into the back of his throat, to stran-
gle him . . .*

The violent memory faded like a falling
star. This new world to which his spirit woke
was without strife. There was gentle dusk
always, like the dusk that always quivered
between the end of the day and the onset of
evening in the troubled vale he left behind, and
had always been his best-loved time there.
Peace held him motionless, utterly content.
Motion is strife. The only motion his newly liberated spirit would forgive was that of the tiny
silent firefly that periodically shared his dusk
with him. Coming into his awareness without a
sound, it would pause and study him, then
move about its business in a steady rhythm. He
sensed in some way that the firefly was
charged with his well-being, and at least

shared in the responsibility for this blessed immobile quietude.

There followed a blank time, and then drowsy awareness again of the gentle dusk, patrolled by the solicitous firefly. It occurred to him to wonder if all the ancient monotheistic religions had been near the mark after all, and if this tiny bright sentinel was their God. He would be quite content to offer what remained of his weary soul if that were so. His soul had stains on it . . .

The processional began again in memory, as it always did: the arena, the final bout. Through the funnel focus of his sybil-awareness, Baka Martin saw Iron Fennec clap his hands and start to twirl. Martin clapped his hands, and the arena began to revolve.

He was peripherally conscious of the announcer, far above: "The ninety-fifth playing of the Twelve-System Games has been one for the histories in Palikar, a discipline old before the Terran Service. Baka Martin, parentage unregistered, was accepted by schools of Old Earth before his first birthday. A foundling, nothing is known of who brought him to the first home of mankind . . .

"Look: Martin has stopped!

—I must not fight this man. He wants his medal, too hard . . . there is death in me, his death. How do I know? How does the crowd?

For the crowd was growling steadily now, low and harsh, and it sounded . . . hungry. The unaltered part of him warred against the purring strength of the sybil parasite, and lost.

Fennec charged. Martin moved, in a leaping step that flexed his wiry body like a whip. Flex, reflex. Fennec coming with force and fury. The computer alarms shrilling, extrapolating too late what the crowd had known by instinct. Baka Martin's foot took Fennec in the chin and nearly tore his head off . . .

The dusk endured. The firefly came and went upon its rounds, and his reborn spirit doted on its travels. *Forgive me, Father, for I have sinned . . .* But the unvarying routine of the firefly began to worry his groggy brain. Would God never vary His habits? The question supplanted his nightmare memory of the Games.

Python slept dreamlessly until the firefly came and went again. When it left this time, the dusk was not as complete as it had been, and now more nearly resembled false dawn. The change was subtle but undeniable. His spirit yearned with all its strength for the former condition. Baka Martin thought that if he were a baby being born for the first time, this was when he would begin to cry. Hours bled past.

A kind of crisis occurred later, when his brain served up a new rhythm of faraway alien brain-wave activity. The alien brains were hardly distinguishable, at this distance, from human brains. Distinguishable only because they were so hard to read. He nearly yelped aloud when they rendered up vivid and familiar images: Pondoro's queer ruins, queerly seen. Mountains exploding in titanic fury, a mush-

room cloud towering into the skies. A flashing, twirling ball of fire and an odd, elongated stick figure that stomped and capered in a fool's jerky parody of the dance of the Palikar.

As others see us! *flashed like heat lightning in his mind.* As others see us! *Ball . . . and stick man. Over and over now, Ball and stick man. And the mushroom cloud of doom . . .*

He tried to awaken fully with his new-won knowledge—but a dark flood of sedation eclipsed his churning awareness. He went deep into alpha sleep again. He woke once more when the firefly came back, its holy glow diminished in the dawn of his rebirth. God spoke for the first time, but not to him.

"Activation sequence complete. Mr. Martin will awaken soon."

That emotionless voice had absolutely no reason to exist in his fading dusky paradise. He recognized it without understanding how he did. It was the voice of a hospital creche.

"You are identical to the Central Receiving creche on Pondoro?" A different voice, accustomed to command.

"Not identical," the creche said. "No more than he is identical to the original Baka Martin—"

"Hush!" The word was a whiplash. "He can hear you now. The sybil is active. Monitoring his environment."

Python groaned and shifted. There was something—wrong—about the conversation. There had been a conversation when he was brought back from the dead on Pondoro, yes. A medical consultation. He reached for the memory, but it eluded him. He had been too eager then to be off and racing back to the continent of the greer. . . .

"I'm no longer on Pondoro?" he asked the dusk.

"No," a third voice answered. An entirely too-familiar voice. "You are on Ptolemy."

"Ball?" Martin said. "Ball?"

"Yes. Relax. A change of assignment, that's all. You remember we had Ptolemy on the charts even then?"

"I remember." Martin stirred. "But the greer—"

"Dealt with," Ball said crisply. "Your work was exemplary. As usual. Satisfactory conclusion." Python registered an atypical emotional charge lacing the cyborg's words. Did cyborgs cry? Why was his enigmatic partner so sad?

"There is no record this specific entity ever was on Pondoro," the creche said.

"Shut that creche voice off," Ball said, "or I will scrap it for you. And leave us!"

"Yes, yes—it's done. Sorry." The command voice was apologetic. Somebody Schodt? Martin felt a smile stretch his face. It was almost painful—as if his face had never smiled before. Big shots often found themselves reduced to that humble state around Ball. Memories of a thousand shared adventures roiled in his awakened brain.

Despite the oddity of the conversation, Martin felt the compulsion to report. "The

greer, Ball. They are—they must be—paranor-
mals. They know us! Know us for what we are!
Ball and stick man, hunting their secrets. They
still remember us, Ball—even now—"

"Wait!" Ball interrupted. "You made contact
with the greer here? Now? From Ptolemy?"

"If that is where I am. Yes, moments ago!"

"Were any of them infected with the sybil?"
Sharply.

"What? Oh, no. No! What would make you
ask such a thing?"

"Never mind. Interesting that the greer still
remember us. I guess they always will. I must
say your sybil exhibits new range. Pondoro is a
thousand lights from here. Let it go. Your contact with the greer is done. Over. Case closed.
New planet, new problems. Same old Commonwealth."

"I was killed! The greer came and tore me
in the dark! Oh, pain . . ."

The Ptolmey creche, though rendered
mute, was alarmed by the unquiet mental state
of its patient. It attempted to short-circuit the
flaring, clashing memories that caused his distress. Like the Pondoro hospital creche before
it, those efforts were shunted aside brutally
by . . . *something* . . . hidden in the reborn
brain. The creche analyzed the malfunction in
order to prescribe adequate sedation. But this
creche was programmed somewhat more com-
prehensively.

"Permission to make status report?" the
creche asked.

"Yes," Ball said.

"The sybil will no longer permit sedation. But the patient needs his rest."

"The patient's own resident demon, in this case, will decide that."

The patient's accelerated brain activity continued to register a wholly indecipherable pattern that deeply troubled the creche. Whatever the patient was now doing, he was certainly not resting.

"Abnormal, atypical brain activity," the creche reported.

"I don't need your help to know that," Ball said.

The creche adjusted demand and fed the organism what it needed to stay alive under this extraordinary demand. Minutes ticked past.

The interior passage of impulses through the vast labyrinth of the brain was creating incalculably swift new connections, weighing, assessing. The cloned body appeared to be little more than a conduit for the energy to drive the cloned brain and its new parasite. Much of the activity was the processing of taped memories, integrating them into the new brain. Python developed an awareness of his identity. Accepted that he no longer need concern himself about the Pondoro wolverine.

But it was obvious to Martin that his new sybil was goading him toward some goal of its own devising. The sybil was active, fiercely active, invading neuronal processes and altering synaptic sequences. He knew the creche could not clearly identify the trigger for each synaptic burst as wholly human, or wholly viral. Nor could he. Integration was complete, and functioning. His awareness turned outward.

"There's someone here," Martin murmured.

"Just you, me, and the machinery," Ball said. "Don't give me carnival crap that belongs in a séance."

"I don't mean *here*." Martin was annoyed. "I mean *here*, in my mind. A mind-contact. From somewhere on this world. Another sybil symbiote."

"Ah! I thought that's what you meant. Explain. Is this *other* nearby? Down the hall? On the other side of the world? Where?"

"Here," Martin said simply. "*Here*. And— somewhere else. Oh . . ."

"What do you mean?"

"It is her sybil! It is not controlled as it should be! It is—there's no governor control! Wait. Yes, there is—but it is different from mine." His voice trailed off. He had recognized a new truth. The distant sybil was *not* different from his.

"What?" Ball said. "Something alarmed you then." Martin had forgotten Ball's empathometer.

"Her controller permits her sybil liberties that mine never had," he said carefully. For some reason, he wanted to conceal the new strength of his own parasite. That had to be the parasite's doing, of course—a survival stratagem. He knew, without knowing how he knew, that the sybil feared Ball.

"Where is this other sybil?" the cyborg asked.

"It resides in a human woman! Very old— she is very old. But she is not aware of her age. The sybil helps her mind be *here*—and else-where—all at once. At the same moment . . ."

His voice trailed off. If he said more, he would reveal his own altered state. Ball might take remedial action. Might extinguish him again. And he had the simple drive of every organism since the beginning of life—to live at all costs. In one beleaguered corner of his con-fused mind he wondered who would authorize infection of a human with a sybil of such power. And why? Didn't they realize the deadly dan-ger? A lifetime's Terran Service conditioning was not so easily suppressed, even by his new parasite.

"The patient is growing agitated again," the creche said.

"No lie." Ball chose his dry tone. "Relax," he said to Martin. "Relax. You need to rest. Is this other symbiote here, on this world?"

"Yes." That was safe enough. "But also . . ." The sybil held his tongue.

"Yes, I know," Ball said. "Also far away at the same time, insofar as we understand time and space. And you're right, it must be her sybil which creates that *here-not here* effect. Amazing your own parasite could find her and share that information with you before you were even fully alive. Is there a malfunction in your controller? Don't try to answer that—no way you could know."

Python said nothing—but his sybil cringed with fear.

"Relax," Ball said soothingly, misinterpreting the sybil's fear for Martin's. "I am a little surprised there is another symbiote actually on this planet. Friend Schodt is being cagier than I realized. I hadn't expected that. Not yet anyway. Does this symbiotic woman know that you have found her?"

"Her sybil knows!" Martin managed to say.

"I understand that. Does *she* know?"

"No, the host is unaware. The host is—not all there."

"What the hell does *that* mean?"

"Not all *there*," Martin said impatiently. The sybil evidently saw no danger in his words. "Not all there mentally. She seems to be focused only on—poetry?—and sex. A kind of sex. There is specialized damage to the host brain. I— That's all I can see. But her sybil knows me!"

"Not all there," Ball said. "Slang from the creche. It appears you are back to something close to normal. As normal as you ever were. I'll give the creche something to put you to sleep. If your sybil will let you. This is too much activity for your first day among the living."

"Don't you mean *back* among the living?"

"Good question. You're coming along fine," Ball pronounced. "Rest now. You will need your strength before too long."

The two of us sat in the darkened lounge of Raven's houseboat, watching a three-dimensional action flick. Sometimes we seemed to hang suspended above the rolling sea, witnessing the attack of the gargantuan wingfingers. Other times the view was from various vantage points on the houseboat.

Raven was a feminine silhouette across the cabin, sitting perfectly still as the drama played out. My brain felt as if it were overheating in its struggle to reconcile cortical memory with the images unwinding before it. I had set off on a shooting junket with a male far taller than me. My memory was adamant on that point. But Raven was sitting right there, and she was actually just about my height. Every sense in my body, from visual to olfactory, was busily advising my confused brain of her complete femaleness.

The figures before us tumbled together on the deck of the vessel as the Ptolemy dragons swooped and clawed. Raven was as agile as I remembered, but the unwinking cameras showed her active form to be voluptuous and disturbing. My motor-memory was gaining the upper hand now, as the battle drew to its close. It asserted tactile sensations of softness and roundness that my reticular activating system had screened out, thanks to Ball's meddling. Meanwhile, somewhere in all those madly firing synapses, was a nagging suspicion that Ball could just as easily have reversed the process: turned my erstwhile hunting guide into a desirable woman through the agency of his empathochip in my skull. And somehow edited the video to match whichever reality he chose for me.

If he had done that, I decided, I would probably have to find a way to kill him.

With all due respect to individual sexual preference, I am hetero born and bred. I knew there was no way I was going to leave this boat before I knew Raven in the carnal sense. She of course had known that long before I did. Women always do, it seems. But I knew it now, all right. Watching us roll and tumble and fight for our lives side by side was an added aphrodisiac. Her coverall was ripped to the waist—a detail that had been irrelevant to me during the attack. But the cameras had faithfully recorded the peekaboo appearance and disappearance of her breasts, heaving with exertion.

The tape went black just before Ball put in his appearance. Raven left the cabin lights down. The silence between us stretched.

I cleared my throat. "You edited the tape already? Those transitions were too smooth for raw footage."

"You like it?" Her voice was a soft contralto. It did things to my insides. How in *hell* could I not have heard that on first meeting?

"Very skilled," I said. "It flows. How many cameras did you have in place? And why?"

She laughed softly. "Disposable miniatures. Several trailing the boat on microdrones, the others sprayed here and there all over the boat. Two dozen, I think, all coordinated by a stand-alone computer in Champollion. Most of the cameras were cooked when my on-board defenses were, but not the off-site computer. As for why—to record for posterity the Ptolemy hunt of the famous Keith Ramsey. "

"You're doing freelance journalism?"

"No!" She sounded vaguely offended. "I am a loyal fan." Then she laughed again, an intimate kind of laugh that made me want to wag the tail I didn't have "A *very* loyal fan."

The fever in my brain seemed to have worked itself to my skin. I could feel heat on my neck and in my groin at the same time. I was breaking a light sweat.

"Hot in here," I said. "I need some fresh air."

"The lights of Pirsig are quite lovely," she said. "I'll join you on the stern in a few minutes."

There was an overcast obscuring the stars, and a gentle, cooling breeze off the land, carrying smells of dirt and flowers and cut grass. We were anchored out from shore in a cliff-lined cove.

The river's course had been sawn through solid rock here, and most of the city was well above the water line. The soft lights of the sprawling city undulated over unseen hills and cast a reflected glow against the low-hanging overcast. The effect was of some aloof and mystical fairy kingdom. There were only a few dim lights along the shore of the river to mark the city's limited docking facilities. We were ruled off the docks—Pirsig did not permit off-worlders to wander its streets.

The hatch opened and closed behind me. I caught a vagrant whiff of the subtle perfume I had noticed since Ball unblocked my noticing ability.

Her body seemed to radiate heat to mine through the cool air. My eyes were adjusting to the dark. As she came and stood beside me, I could see she had changed into another jumpsuit—this one the sheerest gossamer, with a small pin above her left breast. I had one of those vague thoughts you sometimes have—wondering how many centuries women had been slipping into something more comfortable as an aid to seduction. My mouth was dry. And my brain still was at war with my senses.

"Shape-changer," I said.

"Oh, yes! I wanted to experience—so many things! And I did. I have a marvelous prosthesis—a Ptolemy design—of the male sexual organ. Programmed to supply all the sensations through my nervous system to my brain. It is extraordinary!"

"Saints preserve us," I said weakly.

"How can I make love like a real woman if I don't know how a real man feels?" she said. "Does this disturb you? That I have assumed roles? Does it disgust you? Perhaps—in some dark way—excite you? I have studied the mores of your home world, Acme. But your culture appears prudishly silent of the hedonistic pleasures of the flesh. Even your own writing draws a curtain over the flesh details."

"Shape-changer," I said again. "I've done a little research of my own. One story says Raven stole a 'bright ball' from the Sky Chief and gave it to humanity. Mr. Poe's bird was actually a kind of Salish Prometheus, according to Ball. I can see why Ball liked you, with delivery of a flaming ball to humanity as part of your persona."

She was gazing up at the overcast. "The big white trail is obscured tonight."

"The big white trail?"

"What some tribes called the Milky Way. Coyote—another trickster—shot an arrow into the sky, shot another to stick into the first arrow, and so on, and built a ladder up there to arrange the stars just so."

"Him and William Tell," I said.

She laughed again. "Careless research, Keith Ramsey. William Tell shot apples off the heads of children. Robin Hood shot arrows into other arrows. Isn't it a lovely night?"

"Yes," I said. "To all appearances."

She glanced at me. "You are worried about the assassination attempt. There is no need. The emperor's forces are all around us. You should be considering words, Keith Ramsey. The Renga is close upon us."

"What words come to mind?"

"Well," she said softly. "There are these . . .

"Words upon the air
freighted with feeling and thought
Fan sparks of wanting.
Sparks assemble themselves, breathe
this sad heart alive again."

I could feel my own heart thudding under my ribs. She was watching me with shadowed eyes. I said:

"Words, hung like city
Lights. Bright Japanese lanterns
Afloat in the night.
Burning, they expel a smoke.
The breath of our heated thoughts."

"Are your thoughts heated, Keith Ramsey?" I could barely hear her. "Despite your upbringing?"

I cleared my throat. "Yes. But I am distracted by fear."

"The emperor's forces shield us. Even from your inquiring colleagues who want quotes from you about the wingfinger attack. How long the emperor can manage to protect us from the media is an open question. But they will and can slay monsters."

"Monsters?"

"Another Amerind legend, the slaying of monsters, the evil-chasing way. Strong magic against the stalking evil. I know all the rituals."

I shivered slightly. "You think there is an evil stalking me?"

"Perhaps. But not tonight, unless you view me as evil. Tonight, I am stalking you."

My face felt heavy and awkward. "You are? Then it's going to be an easy hunt. Because I'm right here."

"Yes," she said serenely. "You are." She pressed the pin at her breast. Pin and jumpsuit melted away like the illusions they had been. My breath caught. "Fish in a barrel," she smiled.

And then her fevered body was in my arms.

As the Commonwealth Executive's intelligence chief, SjillaTen commanded a far-flung network of operatives and analysts, completely independent of the Terran Service chain of command, and a fair-sized bureaucracy of his own to support the field operation. He also enjoyed the privilege of locating his headquarters where he chose. Here he had succumbed to whimsy. His administrative and support-staff functions were housed in decommissioned subterranean planetary-defense sites on the high plains where what once had been Kansas blended into what once had been Colorado. These deep-buried and hardened facilities had been part of a planetwide defense system, mothballed since the Earth-Llralan wars.

No Llralan bomb ever had touched them. But Llralans had walked here once, thinking themselves conquerors of all they surveyed. Among them had been his namesake ancestor, whose name eight generations before SjillaTen had borne with gloomy pride. The original Sjilla had been chief intelligence officer for the Llralan battle fleet which almost turned that long-ago war in favor of Llrala. SjillaOne's detective work in an attempt to save Code-name *Sleeper* from falling apart had been exemplary, but too little, too late. The rest was history.

SjillaTen rocked back in his office chair and rested his eyes on a bank of monitors that for the moment were not transmitting data or talking heads. The audio on these picked up the prowling wind in the tall prairie grass and the grumbling thunder of a buffalo herd on the move. He watched the shaggy beasts flow over the open prairie they had reclaimed long ago from dry-land farmers and dusty crossroads towns. Earth was turning into a theme park of its own colorful past. Even some of these old planetary defense systems were tourist attractions now.

The Llralan briefly envied the life of those primitive native nomads whose whole lives had cycled around the beasts stampeding high above his head. He fancied he felt a tremor through the room. That was imagination, of course. Direct hits of significant megatonnage would not stir the dust here. His own home-world had its history of nomad cultures just as colorful as Earth's, before the empire organized them all into garrisons to feed interstellar ambition.

All history now; hostilities long forgotten. A Llralan commanded the innermost intelligence-gathering apparatus of the Commonwealth Executive. Other Llralans held similar positions of trust on scores of worlds. Their private joke was that in the end they had inherited just what their vanished empire sought: the headaches of trying to administer a sprawling stellar civilization. He rubbed his eyes and went back to work. This was work he loved: detective work, not unlike that his namesake ancestor had pursued on this world in the long-ago. Putting together bits and pieces and looking at them in new ways.

First, the Ptolemy question.

The Terran Service had harvested innumerable rumors about some major secret project on Ptolemy. Since Ptolemy excelled in production of specialized robots, cyborgs, and some of the most sophisticated programming between the stars, it was distinctly possible the secret work had strategic value. But Ptolemy was a tough nut to crack. Terran Service penetration missions had been largely fruitless. And Ball and Baka Martin had been diverted to that harebrained scheme on Pondoro just when the Service really could have used them.

But Ball was on Ptolemy now. For whatever motives, he unquestionably had managed his own insertion, and curried his way into favor with the emperor in a very short time. Indications from embassy sources on the planet were that Ball had somehow worked himself into the heart of whatever deeply secret project was afoot there. And now he was activating a Martin clone.

SjillaTen called up and reread summaries of intelligence from his own picked spies within the corporate structure of InterGalactic Cybernetics concerning the clone contract. Someone had carefully orchestrated the decision to create a clone, and weighted the bid process to ensure Ptolemy academia would be selected for the project. It was clear in retrospect that there had been a guiding force—but no trace whatsoever of the nature of that force. Which amounted to Ball's personal signature on an operation. Ball clearly had some kind of clout within the sprawling InterGalactic Cybernetics organization that even its CEO couldn't figure out.

So Ball wanted Martin's clone to come to life on Ptolemy.

Inference: he needed his Palikar-trained field man.

SjillaTen considered that briefly. What else was Baka Martin? He was a sybil symbiote with latent extrasensory potential that seemed to have bloomed on Pondoro.

Was Ptolemy tinkering with the Blocked World parasite?

SjillaTen felt an almost superstitious fear shiver along his nervous system. The Blocked Worlds had that effect on every one of his race familiar with ancient Llralan history. Llrala had twice attained space travel before contact with terrestrials, though that was little known these days. The first venture into space brought them afoul of an immeasurably older race of beings which had almost contemptuously brushed them back into a near stone age, and went away. From those ruins rose the grandly named Empire of Four Thousand Suns.

We called them the Workargi. We never knew what they called themselves. But we hurt them before they fled. And then went on to be just like them—until Terrans came along.

The Blocked Worlds included what was left of the Workargi home system. No in-depth exploration ever had been done to determine where they went—not with the sybil as watchdog. The Terran Service had ruled all but the most cursory probes out of bounds.

He issued a few terse commands, then leaned back and looked at the prairie monitors again while he waited. This time he saw butterflies, not bison. And a cruising red-tail hawk.

His subordinates found what he needed to know before the hawk found lunch. He smiled faintly at the speed of execution. The information received was less pleasing: though all known sybil within Terran Service control were accounted for, there had been breaches to the Service blockade over the decades. Not all had been cleared. Sybil could in fact be loose outside the Blocked Worlds without Service knowledge. He directed exhaustive further evaluation. Adrienne Taft was not going to be pleased that some of the incursions had occurred during her tenure. And that would translate into considerable pain down through the naval chain of command. But SjillaTen was on a different scent now: Inter-Galactic Cybernetics.

Aside from its vast power and near total dominion in its field, what was unusual about InterGalactic?

In recent years that answer was simple: their near-instantaneous access to information across thousands of light-years. Information was the coin of the galactic realm. It was one commodity that could exist in more than one place at a time simultaneously, and have far different effects depending upon its location. What was of no value on one planet might be of incalculable worth a few hundred light-years away. The entity that could defend its information best—and move it most swiftly and accurately—always possessed the upper hand.

InterGalactic had leveraged its information-gathering speed into attractive contracts on literally hundreds of worlds, causing the competition to scream foul and demand investigation. And to begin to lobby the Assembly for antitrust measures. InterGalactic was feeling the pressure, or JonHoward Tomas would not have been so direct in his request to Taft for help. And certainly would not offer as trade goods some advance information that relied upon that very communications speed so galling to opponents.

Something was missing, some vital link just beyond grasping.

Was InterGalactic's communications secret part of some undisclosed Ptolemy design? Was that where Ball was going in all this?

If so, the cyborg was playing a deadly lone game, far beyond the support of the Terran Service. If the mandarins of InterGalactic Cybernetics so much as suspected such a thing, they would eliminate him. Would they somehow place the blame on the Service, since Ball was there under diplomatic immunity? SjillaTen nodded to himself. Of course they would. Perhaps that also explained the near-fatal hunting accident for Keith Ramsey. They were turning up the heat on Taft already.

By casting Ptolemy, widely known as a land of eccentrics and lotus-eaters, in the role of injured party, InterGalactic could give Adrienne Taft too much to think about to worry about their possible bid-rigging. Implicit in Tomas's visit had been an offer to act as intermediary with the outraged emperor. If Taft accepted his help, she would then be bound by the strange code of politics to protect the corporation's privileged position. Politics, for all their murkiness, followed simple rules, after all.

But Ball was a pretty tough customer. Elimination might prove more trouble than JonHoward Tomas would expect.

Tomas was no fool. Even though he could not find Ball's specifications within his own corporate hierarchy, he would have to know Ball was formidable. He would have alternate options available to deal with the cyborg if he saw Ball as a threat. Ball had been activated by a special task force of experts, each working in self-contained cells. One of SjillaTen's best double agents in the company had worked on Ball's gravitation drive, and had over the years met others who had worked on life-support and communications. None knew where their work product had been assembled; there was no known record of control-chip insertion. Aside from a direct hit with sufficient energy, which he was superbly equipped to avoid, where was Ball vulnerable?

SjillaTen called up another file. The Executive's legal department hadn't had much luck penetrating the privacy laws of Belkin's World, ostensible home of the adult male who had voluntarily donated his brain to the Ball project. There was no case law to support such an intrusion. But there was a legal footnote of interest: the donor's body had been preserved intact on life-support, rather than parcelled out to the organ banks.

There was an escape clause in the Terran Service contract that had created Ball. If the cyborg ever wanted to renounce his contract, he could do so. And be returned to his original body at Commonwealth expense. The date the contract had been witnessed and filed in court on Belkin's kept nagging at the Llralan's awareness; something significant about that date, and that world. Some other investigation? He queried a subordinate and kept reading.

It hadn't taken his operatives, with the authority of the Executive behind them, very long to narrow the choice of places to search for Ball's dormant bipedal body. The first and easiest guess had been correct: it was secreted on Belkin's itself, in private storage, waiting. InterGalactic owned the storage facility. Perhaps Tomas wasn't worried so much about trying to eliminate Ball directly. Perhaps he planned to hold the cyborg's original body hostage if things began to fall apart.

Would such a threat stymie Ball?

Hard to know. SjillaTen felt a clench of unease worm though his intestines. This business of leaving your real body to go adventuring in what amounted to a hardened satellite shell evoked superstitious chills. Llralan culture never had liked the idea of spirits liberated from their physical bodies. SjillaTen was a product of his upbringing.

His subordinate responded quickly. SjillaTen forgot his superstitions in a surge of even greater unease: the date he had been worried about was the last of record in which a particular individual had sent a personal communication to Adrienne Taft. A farewell letter. And then essentially vanished from the cosmos. The vanished one was her erstwhile confidant and lover. As vast as the galaxy was, that was just too much coincidence.

SjillaTen had dispatched agents far and wide during his years of service to Taft, hiding the expense in his discretionary fund, each time a rumor of this man's presence had touched his network. Alone among her household staff, SjillaTen knew the whole story of the genesis of Taft's rambunctious offspring.

Adrienne Taft was a native of Belkin's World. Had grown to maturity and entered politics there. From early on her every successful foray had always been in company of this other native, her principal adviser, mentor, and, it was widely believed, lover. But pragmatic decisions she made in her rise to power had spawned disagreements, separation, estrange-

ment. From quietly blocking some of her blood-
ier decisions, he moved to campaigning openly
against her as she fought for the Executive's
position. He had openly attacked some of her
initiatives in the early days of her administration. And then vanished, without a trace.

Or perhaps with at least one trace. This privacy document.

SjillaTen reflected briefly, then asked for a
summary of all Ball's assignments over the
years. He already knew Ball's last assignment
had openly stymied Taft's designs, and embar-
rassed her enough that she had wanted Ball
eliminated. Now he was looking for any evidence the cyborg had shaded the outcome of
other assignments more cleverly—arranging
for some of Taft's more cold-blooded flights of
fancy to fail aborning. As SjillaTen himself had
done, come to that.

Once he knew what he was looking for, the
record of Ball's exploits became undeniable.

All Ball's assignments but Pondoro had
been concluded successfully. But in every
one, the butcher bill had been lower than
expected—or even explicitly commanded.
Where death would serve a mission purpose,
death had been swiftly delivered; but where it
would have served a Taft purpose in securing
her political future, it had almost always been
avoided. No one but Taft, of course—or the tiny
core group of advisers as close to her as
SjillaTen—would have been able to see such a
pattern. Indeed, SjillaTen never would have
looked for the pattern absent the events on

Ptolemy. The whole chain of command had been pleased with Ball's work. Taft would have perforce remained silent. Her erstwhile lover had, to all intents and purposes, devised an exquisite continuation of their life-long debate by other means.

SjillaTen began to develop an authentic headache. There was no way to predict his volatile leader's reaction to such speculation. But he knew it would be extreme.

Something woke me toward morning. The gentle tugging of the houseboat at anchor had worked its way into my dreams. I dreamed I was a young man again, back home on Acme, asleep in my bunk on my father's gunning garvey out on the big salt bays. I even dreamed I heard *twon* calling down the wind beneath the twin moons of winter.

The houseboat had shifted slightly, dipping to one side, and there had been a whisper of sound. A light thud against the hull, almost imaginary.

For an indeterminate moment the dipping motion melted into my dream. The light thud was my father stepping aboard from a launch after his morning farm chores, to wake my brother and me in time for the morning flight. I always woke up when the launch touched the hull and he transferred his considerable bulk to the side deck. The garvey always dipped gently sideways in response to his weight. Then an alien, fetid odor penetrated my dream.

I opened my eyes to unrelieved darkness, and the slumbering warmth of Raven's back. She was curled spoon-fashion against my chest and thighs. We were in her stateroom bunk, forward of the houseboat's main cabin. My body still was utterly lax, sated by a long, erotic night of lovemaking. My mind, until moments ago, had been the same way, finally and blissfully free of any persistent edginess about her shape-changing exploits.

But now my brain was abruptly wide-awake, buzzing with primitive fear.

There was something in here with us. It smelled like death.

My rifle was in the main cabin's gun rack, along with Raven's dragon-slayers. It might as well have been on Pondoro, or home on Acme for that matter.

A faint dry slither came to my straining ears from the deck near our bunk. My primitive brain said *reptile*. Adrenaline surged.

Without even thinking, my hand went out to the bunk's headboard. Found the haft of Raven's businesslike bowie where it swung from its leg harness. Thumbed the scabbard release. It made a tiny click as I drew the blade. I turned my wrist to lay the blade along my inner forearm, edge outward. Something I remembered from an interview with a Zion commando. Raven stirred and murmured—

A band of steel snapped around my wrist with shocking speed. And recoiled in the same instant.

Hot wetness sprayed over my forearm. Whatever had grabbed me had grabbed cold steel, too.

I heard Raven's muffled exclamation as the goop hit her naked body. I almost dropped the

knife from nerveless fingers. Lunged and got it
with my left. I felt her trying to turn out from
under my sudden weight. A ropy tentacle,
thick as a hawser, lashed across our lower bodies. There was a sibilant hiss that froze my
blood. Raven cried out.

The tentacle wrapped my ankles together
and dragged me irresistibly across her struggling body.

I slashed, backhanded and blind. Then I was
on the floor, pressed down by an obscene weight
that slimed my naked chest. Another tentacle
wormed roughly under my body and closed
around my trunk. I kept stabbing blindly.
Scalding spatters of something flew in my face.
The stench was indescribable.

The hawser around my trunk tightened
inexorably.

Blobs of colored light danced in my vision. I
couldn't breathe. A third appendage wrapped
my knife arm before I could resume my defensive grip. My hand went numb on the haft. I
punched with my right, with all the strength of
muscles that had matured in heavier gravity
than here. It was like punching an age-rotted
tree trunk. My fist sank deep through collaps-
ing fibrous stuff. But this fiber was hot and
pulsed with furious life.

The stateroom lights flamed to life somewhere up above me. The thing that had me
pinned was a bulbous gray-green glistening
obscenity. My vision was fading fast. I was
thinking what a silly way to die, out of all the
chances I had over the years.

There was a singing metallic hum, and a human grunt of extreme effort.

The coils around me tightened convulsively. I almost went completely under. The metal sang again. The coils released their killing pressure. I choked down great gulps of air. My sight cleared momentarily. I saw a dark-haired naked angel. Her unbound hair swirled like smoke around her shoulders. She wheeled a shimmering arc of light above her head and down. My guts sucked up in anticipation of the blow—

The bowie cleaved the monstrosity neatly as a melon.

But the blade came to rest precisely against my chest. For an instant the nerves in my skin registered the almost-bite of that razor edge. Then the halves of the thing peeled apart messily. I felt a horrid hot oily spill engulf my midsection. I promptly threw up. Violently.

When I looked again, Raven was gone. I shoved the wrecked thing off me and tried to scramble to my feet, still gagging. Footing on the deck was slippery. I went down twice more before I made it to the still-dark main cabin. Raven was at the helm. The engines purred to life. Outside in the gray wet river dawn a vast dark shape settled beside us. I started for the weapons rack.

"Don't," she said shortly. "That slime on you will ruin the finish on my guns! The crisis is past. Those are the emperor's bodyguards arriving. We are safe."

"You said that before," I said. But I didn't touch the rifles.

"There was no real danger from that—" She made a guttural sound. Her voice held a fine contempt.

"I don't know that word," I said.

"Literally, it means bottom-feeder. A scavenger. It shouldn't be this far upriver."

The cooling matter on me seemed to be etching itself into my hide. I rubbed at it absently. "Maybe I should wash this crud off?"

"Right away," she said. "I've dialed medicinals into the fresher to handle any infection. The more you rub it in, the more skin you lose. It was predigesting you."

She activated the boat's automatic pilot and swept her hair back out of her eyes with her gore-spattered knife hand. The bowie blade had lost its sheen. In the binnacle light her eyes still blazed with combat. Even in my sorry state I couldn't help but notice the dramatic erection of her nipples. I wondered whether that was in reaction to fear, excitement, or residual passion. Even adjusting her vessel, muttering a few quick words into the com, and looking everywhere at once, still ready for battle, she noticed me notice. The fire of battle muted to a softer glow.

"Frightened half to death, covered with corrosive slime and your own bile, still you ogle me, Keith Ramsey. I like that in a man. It will make strong poetry when you write it."

I started to say something. I have no idea what.

But she used her besmeared bowie in the ancient finger-to-lips gesture to be quiet. Her other hand took mine. She led me to the fresher. She turned into my arms as I stepped into the stall behind her. Her arms went around my neck. I would have sworn her nipples branded my chest more permanently than the poisonous slime.

I was confused about what the hell had tried to get me this time, and afraid there was more where it had come from. But her body in my arms stirred raw, simple, celebratory lust. Human had survived sabertooth again. And our floating cave had a foaming, healing shower in which to celebrate.

Raven's kiss left no doubt she was completely into celebratory mode. Well, she knew this godforsaken world better than I ever would. To hell with it, we all die sometime. If I was going to die, in her arms would be a fine place. But I did hope she was being careful with that damned knife. The medicated, cleansing spray came down to steam us clean.

■ ■ ■ ■ ■ ■ ■ **19**

The woman in the creche pursed her lips. "I'm not sure," she said, "a second assassination attempt on Keith Ramsey was wise at this point."

Miriam's voice. But Schodt could hear the flat tones of JonHoward Tomas's disapproving voice as clearly as if the Chief Executive Officer of InterGalactic were in the room with him. Schodt cast a warning glance at his assistant. She silently got up and left. He knew she would block all audial access to the room as soon as she was clear, to protect her boss from rumors of a reprimand from Old Earth headquarters. It was good to have loyal staff.

"I'm not sure I understand your meaning, JonHoward," he said carefully.

"You know I appreciate and reward initiative, Alex. But your authorizing another attempt of Keith Ramsey's life without my approval is pushing it. Even more, waiting so long to tell me. It will be very difficult to arrange timely notification for Adrienne Taft at this late hour. I assume another protest is planned by the emperor?"

"The emperor's protest already has been transmitted from here," Schodt said weakly. "I just learned of it. Within the hour, local time. I did not authorize this attempt. I knew nothing of it until our agents notified me. And Ptolemy security forces completely blanketed Civilization River after the attempt. They were furious their protection of their guest had been compromised."

Tomas did not reply for so long Schodt wondered if Miriam and Arthur had somehow lost their rapport; it happened occasionally, when their sybil parasites seemed to tire of the exchange and just shut down. Schodt felt himself blinking and couldn't stop. He pushed at his hair nervously. He could not escape the uncanny notion that Miriam was reading his terrified thoughts and sharing them with Arthur. If that were true, Arthur would be sure to convey them to his ultimate boss. Arthur didn't like him. Never had.

It shouldn't matter, Schodt thought. Like the male canary and his mating song, Arthur should forget these communications as soon as they were over. Arthur's creche on Old Earth would activate the nanodispensary in Arthur's sybil-infested brain. The electrochemical compound of Schodt's own devising would goad the resident sybil into sealing forevermore the neuronal pathways it had activated for the communication session. Those specific pathways should be as incapable of remembering the words transmitted as the canary's brain was of remembering its erstwhile mating song. There should be no memory bleed-over. Arthur shouldn't remember how much he hated him.

In the test phase of sybil linkage, Arthur's

first poetry to Miriam had been about being buried alive with a predatory canary that drank his brain. Schodt shivered. But Miriam soon had him drooling with virtual lust, addicted to her eroticism. Again it had been Schodt's genius to use the sexual centers of the brains of the sybil hosts to bond them to one another outside time and space. The rest was simple engineering.

But still he wondered what information Arthur was conveying to the CEO, and felt sweat trickle from his armpits. JonHoward had never been this furious with him.

"I am forced to accept your word," Tomas finally said, speaking through Miriam. "For now. For once in your scheming career, Alex, your word had better be good."

"But this latest incident may work to our advantage after all," Schodt said eagerly. "The emperor was having second thoughts about his initial protest. Taft's diplomatic response to his first protest scorched him. I think he's actually afraid of her."

"The emperor is not a fool," Miriam said crisply. "Taft is not to be trifled with."

Schodt pushed at his hair again in his uncontrollable tic. Berated himself silently. Did it again. Miriam's eyes were closed. Did she know he was doing it anyway?

"Ramsey survived this second attempt?" Miriam asked.

"Yes. This Raven destroyed the centopod with all the dispatch of a trained warrior."

"Well, that seems to square with my suspicion that Raven is Terran Service." Miriam's words conveyed a self-satisfied Tomas tone that Schodt had often heard in person. Too often, it sometimes seemed.

"This attack made the emperor furious again," he said, almost pleadingly. "He is absolutely convinced now that Taft is playing him for a fool."

Miriam frowned in mimicry of the emotions pouring into her brain through her link with Arthur.

The silence stretched again.

Surprisingly, Miriam gave a small laugh. "This attempt occurred right under the noses of the emperor's household security forces?"

"So our agents say. Ramsey has been under their protection since the incident with the dragons. They were enraged at the audacity."

"I bet they were! And of course the very fact this attack went right through their best defense *does* cast more suspicion on the oh-so-clever Terran Service. There is nothing to trace this creature that was used back to us?"

"There is nothing to trace, JonHoward." He hated the supplicating note in his voice. "It is a native scavenger to the shallow bays where the first attack took place. Probably drawn to that houseboat by all the dead dragons in the water. Sucker scars on the boat hull supposedly show that it attached itself there, and clung. Eventually the fresh Terranized water of the river drove it onboard. Then it smelled flesh. It must have been very hungry by then, to attempt living prey."

"You're trying to convince me this was a natural event? A coincidence?"

"Not natural. Just not instigated by us. They found angstrom-sized traces of a chip that had been keyed to self-destruct upon the creature's death. Obviously to avoid investigation. The traces showed a chip with Terran Service registration code. One of the very most up-to-date ones."

"You think the Service actually *wants* to kill this news hawk?"

"Well, who besides the Service has access to such chips?"

"The manufacturer, of course. This chip was not one of our designs, surely?"

"Actually . . ." Schodt cleared his throat heavily. "Yes. One of ours."

Miriam actually laughed out loud this time. Schodt heard Tomas's hard bray in her tones. A trick of the mind surely. He just didn't know *whose* mind.

"You *are* clever, Alex. I never said you weren't. It *would* be suspicious if the Service didn't use the best nanochip technology available. And that, of course, is ours! Perhaps even such short notice will work to our advantage. I apologize for sounding so grumpy. Do you have any idea where the clock is here at headquarters?"

"I'm sorry. No, I don't."

Though of course he always did, within the standard Terran minute. He had scheduled his notification for JonHoward's sleep period, in hopes of escaping the CEO's wrath in the confusion of the moment.

A lesson learned: he wouldn't try that trick again.

Meanwhile he was struggling to decide whether to try to claim credit for the attack, now that Tomas's mood had shifted so dramatically. No. He had seen the CEO trap more than one unwary executive with that particular ploy. And dammit, he had *not* laid this attack on. For the first time he felt a pang of doubt: had one of his own subordinates taken a flier on his or her own? Perhaps intending to garner individual glory, move closer to a challenge to his own status?

"I must compliment you, Alex," Miriam said softly. "This second attempt will intensify media attention on Ptolemy very nicely. Raise dozens of queries as to why Taft insists on picking on the lotus-eaters. The media will be on the prowl for anything resembling a scoop. And we are ready to give them one. They will have to draw the obvious conclusions. Well done. But . . ."

She paused. Schodt pushed at his hair repeatedly.

"Don't do it again, Alex," she said. "The stage is set. Let this play out now. No more initiative on this assignment unless you clear it with me personally. Clear?"

He released pent-up breath. "Very clear, sir."

"Don't 'sir' me, tough guy." The woman's lips curved into a sweet smile. "Just follow orders. Got that?"

"Yes, JonHoward."

"That's better," Miriam said. "Anything else to report, Alex?"

"No, JonHoward."

"Then let's leave our randy poets here to relax and have some fun. You know how emotionally stirred up they get from all this deep collaboration. You should see the physical state poor Arthur's in, here!"

Miriam smiled beatifically. Schodt wondered if those were JonHoward's words or her own. He was beginning to be confused by his own emotional engineering. His usually precise mind didn't seem to be functioning as well as usual. Surely Arthur and Miriam and the rest of the captive poets were no threat to his well-being. He became aware Miriam was speaking again.

"Keep an eye on things, Alex," she said. "I need to wake up Adrienne Taft. She's not going to like it any better than I did!"

"**Y**ou're schtupping her, aren't you?"

Tanner's moody features, framed by his trademark prophet's beard and tangle of iron-colored hair, were larger than life-size on Raven's main communications screen. His sunken eyes were looking somewhere over my shoulder. I didn't have to turn to follow his gaze to know he was eyeing Raven's shapely bottom as she went out on the stern deck to give us privacy.

"What does schtupping mean?" I said.

There was the usual pause as my question flashed to Associated News Central desk on Sirius III. Finally his eyes swiveled back to me and he adjusted his little black skull cap—icon of some ancient religion whose name I didn't recall right then.

"Get the meaning from context, Ramsey. I have to retrain you?"

"Is your first question on the record, then?" I said.

After the time-lag, he made some kind of mouth noise. I had learned over the years it meant resignation. "It was never like this when I was out in the field chasing news. Have times changed? Or was it always just me?"

"You're burning up a lot of expensive transmission time for personal nostalgia," I pointed
out. "Though I admit it's kind of a pleasure to
be close enough to you for once to see your ugly
mug. And where the time-lag's not too awful.
This is more like a real conversation. And you
damn well know your exploits are legendary to
the youngsters. How did you get through the
local communications blackout, by the way?
The emperor's secretary of state assured me it
was total."

He swallowed a grin. He liked flattery as
well as anyone.

"Even the emperor understands you never
say no when A.N. Central calls. Guess I'm
known more for my temper than my schtupping skills. Such is life."

"So you're going to interview me?

"Hell, no! I've got more important things to
do. I'm relationship-building, is what I'm up to.
With a hot news source. That would be you, my
lad. When are you going to give the local boys
and girls of the media out there a break and
feed them something? This is a good story,
Ramsey—a scrap between Ptolemy and Her
Nibs. With a journalist in the middle of it! The
emperor's people are running interference for
you, keeping us away. Don't you like being
famous anymore?"

"I just wanted some time to myself."

"Yeah. You know how you'd get if it was you
on this end. With somebody trying to hide from
you. Give me something! For instance, I hear
there's some sexy tape somewhere that shows

you and that babe battling the local wildlife. Blood and exposed flesh, the whole thing. Tasty."

"Now where would you get a rumor like that?"

When the lag let his expression change, it had become a sour smirk. "You know how many thousands of rumors Associated News gets an hour? Even on an off day? Of course you do. At least you should. It's my job in this pest-hole to rank them from implausible to impossible, and allocate news crews. You going to try to hold on to this for your own byline? Is that it? Ain't you rich enough off that Pondoro business?"

"If you want that hunting tape, do a contract with Raven. It's hers. As for any high-level name-calling between the emperor and the Commonwealth Executive, I don't know a damn thing more than you do. I'm just here for the poetry competition. You know that. You authorized the feature contract."

"What makes you so damn special that the Executive risks diplomatic troubles just to wipe you? Any ideas?"

"Don't put words in my mouth, dammit."

His grin turned sly. "'Ramsey said he had no idea why he was important enough for the Executive to take extraordinary steps to have him assassinated'? Like that?"

"Just like that."

Pause. "You still going through with that poetry business?"

"That's the general idea," I said.

"Yeah? Well, how come Ptolemy's name keeps popping up in all the rumor mills all of a sudden? And I do mean all of them. This business about the emperor's formal protest is just the tip of things."

"Give me a for-instance," I said.

"For instance, keep your ears open for anything about Arthur Galatis, will you? You know the name?"

"One of the poets who died here in the Renga. Years ago."

"Yeah. We've got a rumor that some of his unpublished work is about to be released there to kick off this year's festivities."

"Well, that's why I'm here, to cover a poetry contest."

"Yeah, right. You and that renegade cyborg are getting ready to stick it to Adrienne Taft again, aren't you?" He gave me an awful leer. "Figuratively, I mean. Have you ever wondered how verbs for sexual intercourse often interchange with verbs for being had? See what I mean?"

"I'm not out to get Taft!"

"Then why did she go to all that trouble to have a bootleg erotic progue, featuring you, spread all over everywhere?"

"That's speculation," I said.

"No," he said, "it isn't. InterGalactic Cybernetics got the contract. Want to know where the only outside copy of the alpha test model went? Right to Adrienne Taft's office, eyes only for the Executive. Wonder how she liked it?"

I could feel my ears burning. "You can't be

serious. You're not going to put something about that damned progue on the news."

"Not yet, anyway. If you manage to get killed out there, we just might. At least when you die, you'll know your software doppleganger is looking after all those lonely ladies you never got to schtup in person. Come to think of it, maybe that was Taft's idea for a fitting revenge. For you to die knowing that. She must know you pretty well to know how that would grate on you. How it would burn you to know that your essential—um, *functions*—had been taped for posterity. That you—you personally—wouldn't be *all that* missed. Not in the flesh. So to speak."

"Are you going to patch me through to a reporter, or just sit there spending the A.N. budget to give me crap?"

"Keep your pants on." He leered again. "Oh. Guess I'm too late with my advice, huh? Learning exotic verse forms, slaying local wildlife, schtupping that delicious bit of fluff. You live some life, you know that? One last question, though. Humor me."

"Yeah?"

"Adrienne Taft took a heavy cruiser and two frigates from her personal armada and left Old Earth within standard hours of the second protest from Ptolemy. Sealed orders. Security of the Commonwealth, that line of guff. So far, we haven't been able to turn a trace of her." He fairly bristled with that eternal satisfaction a newsie gets when he's in on breaking news. "Hennesy is running things in her absence, and keeping his mouth *shut.* What do you make of all that? Think it's connected to Ptolemy?"

"How the devil would I know?"

I thought he would leave the screen, but he had one final dig.

"Be sure to tell my reporter all about that shape-changing business that your newest conquest is so good at." His bristling whiskers gave him a predatory air. "Is this the famous hairy-chested heterosexual's first drift toward normal ambiguity? Inquiring minds want to know! It will make some spicy gossip for the lifestyle 'casts."

The last thing I saw of him was his grin, like that mythological cat.

PART THREE

Dai

(Theme)

Blood the argument.
Indignities untold stain
All the bloody years.
Stars collide, explode, expire.
Blood drums hot until it cools.

Lifeguard and Shipping Lanes Station Huitseptdix had a storied history of rescuing disabled craft falling outbound past the fringes of the Belkin's World home system. Watch Officer Mondesi had congratulated himself on drawing Huitseptdix of all the similar stations posted in a loose sphere around the system beyond its final asteroid belt. For the first months of his tour he'd been bright-eyed and alert, ready for a deep-space-bound disabled pleasure craft, or a runaway asteroid.

But he was a veteran now. The more prosaic task of monitoring system tugs out to pick up barges sling-shot from nearby systems had dulled his excitement. Those cargoes didn't warrant starship handling, but were nonetheless of high value: burial urns scheduled for interment in home soil, containers full of foodstuffs, and manufactured goods in exchange for products of Belkin's going the other way. A five- to ten-year lag in the produce and products getting to nearby markets made for interesting commodities trading in the sector, but Mondesi didn't care about stuff like that.

He knew his work was valuable. But it was dull. Even organizing shuttle service for the once-thrilling arrival of scheduled starships had paled. Now a solo shift on the control bridge was just a job of work, an interruption to his hobbies and to participation in intrastation romantic intrigue.

So when an unscheduled starship probe popped into normal space a million kilometers out-station, his reflexes were slowed just the slightest bit. He took time to goggle at his instruments. Seconds, really, but that was enough.

A second probe materialized.

"Holy shit!" He sounded general quarters then.

Before the first raucous caw alerted the station, a third probe arrived. The three formed a tight wedge, pointed straight at Huitseptdix.

Three ships! Three unscheduled starships, arriving that close together, defied logic, defied economics, defied probability. But the instruments didn't lie. The probes were there. They were operational, sweeping space for any obstructions, feeding the data back into the nothingness from which they had emerged, vaporizing any questionable matter that tried to occupy space selected for the arriving vessels.

"This is the station commander, Mon. What have we got?"

"Three ships, skipper! Starships. Their probes are hot and cooking."

"*Three*? I'm on my way!"

Mondesi still was alone on the bridge when the first ship came through. His screens came to sparkling, murmuring life. Seconds later it identified itself on local frequency.

"Terran Service frigate *Standfast*. Do you read, Belkin's?"

A warship! "Aye," Mondesi said. "Station commander on the way to the bridge."

"Acknowledged. Frigate *Stout Heart* and cruiser *Forthright* due momentarily—"

More screens blazed. Data feeds scrolled. The other ships were there. Mondesi was reading the ships' pedigrees off the main console when his commander arrived, her brush-cut hair still damp from a shower.

"Terran Service, Skipper," Mondesi said. "Household fleet of the Commonwealth Executive!"

"Get me the president, now," she gritted.

"Terran Service cruiser *Forthright*," came a second hail from the warships.

"Belkin's World, Huitseptdix, state your purpose," the commander said crisply.

"Launching landing craft in under five minutes," *Forthright* said.

"Landing craft! What's the meaning of this?"

"Direct orders of the Commonwealth Executive. This does not concern the government of Belkin's World."

"I think my president will be the judge of that—"

"Stand by for the Commonwealth Executive on visual," said *Forthright*.

"She's *with* you?"

The central display console flickered. Adrienne Taft's well-known features swam into view. She was on the cruiser's command deck, framed by uniformed Service personnel. In contrast, she was in a simple black jumpsuit with a white scarf at her throat.

"It's Mary Rinearson, right?" she said.

Mondesi heard his skipper's intake of breath. "You know me?"

The famous smile flashed. "I make it my business to know the important people on my home world, dear. Please relax now. Your government is not a suspect in any crimes against the Commonwealth. This is a straight law-enforcement exercise."

"Against whom?"

"Sorry, dear—that would impede the investigation. Please connect me with President Somenon as soon as possible—I'd like to reassure him personally of my best wishes."

"We are hailing him now, Excellency."

"Please! Call me Adrienne. Alert your defense forces to our landing craft, please. I don't want any unfortunate incidents. You may know I use Llralan shock troops for my household guard. They tend to resent unwarranted interference."

Mondesi kept his eyes glued to the data flowing in. Other bridge personnel dropped into their places around the bridge. But he had the central con and wasn't surrendering it, short of a direct order.

"Small boats away," he mumbled to his skipper.

"You've launched already?" she asked Taft. "I cannot authorize—"

The famous smile went away. "Your authorization is not needed. Nor your president's. I am acting on a Commonwealth Court warrant. A certified copy is transmitting now."

Mondesi watched *Forthright*'s brood of landing craft accelerate in-system. He shivered. Llralan shock troops in-bound for the planet of his birth. The thought was almost too much. Somebody down there was about to get an ugly surprise.

"The president is standing by," someone said across the bridge.

"Excellent!" Taft replied. Her smile was back. "Furnish my bridge with coordinates, and he and I will go to secure talk. Thank you for your time, Mary."

Mondesi's skipper opened her mouth—but the screen was blank.

The manager of Sweet Repose Body Storage had made it his business to study the history of body management. He liked to shock his guests with the irony that ancient graveyards once had similar names. But his luncheon guest seemed unimpressed. He decided he would have to try harder, for he really wanted to impress her. Well, he wanted to *start* by impressing her, and see where it might lead. She wore the latest spray apparel boldly, with no little shimmers to shield her most intimate treasures. And the body that glistened in the fashionable rust and earth tones was worthy of such flaunting. He found it hard to concentrate on her eyes or her words.

"You're new to the board of the organ bank,

aren't you?" he said. "I haven't seen you in any of the previous meetings. I would have remembered."

"Would you?" Her eyes seemed to be laughing at him.

They were in a window-bubble in the rooftop restaurant atop two-hundred-story Taft Tower, the centerpiece of Belkin City. The tower, too, had been named for the scout who found Belkin's World. Then one of their own became Commonwealth Executive. The view of the city and the rugged, snowcapped hills beyond was splendid. He could see the installation where he'd worked for forty years. But he was leaving now, moving up the corporate ladder.

"You had questions about the bodies in our care," he said. "I had thought we explained all that satisfactorily. Most of our clients are well-advanced in years, and were simply bored. They wanted to skip a century or two, see what might happen in the future. Our earliest were taken on before the restoratives became fully effective, but their estates do not spin off enough income to awaken and restore them. Where survivors have inherited power of attorney, we have obtained the necessary permissions of organ donorship. That accounts for just short of eighty percent of our capacity. The rest your board will have to pursue through legal avenues—or continue to maintain. It's all in the contract."

"You bought off the survivors with cash settlements from the estate trust funds?"

He grimaced. "You make it sound so harsh."

The dining bubble began to vibrate gently. Water danced in crystal.

"Earthquake," he said. "Make that Belkin-quake." He smiled at his own wit. "Don't worry." He reached for her hand, though she didn't look worried. "These towers can withstand—"

A thunderclap pealed across the city. Even muted by the building, it was loud.

He jerked in spite of himself.

"Ahhh," the woman said. "They're coming in hot."

Her words were drowned in a rolling roar, punctuated by several more booms. She was gazing out the window in rapt attention. He followed her look.

Lazy coils of smoke lifted from Sweet Repose. A rain of blue haloes was floating in above the smoke. As they watched, lightning bolts flashed and struck out of clear skies.

His ear-com chimed. He listened in disbelief. "We're under assault!" he said. "Those are paratroops!" He keyed his throat mike. "Yes, yes!" he said. "Activate the Rongor—"

Something closed his throat. His vision darkened for a moment. When it cleared, she was leaning across the table toward him, her arm extended, smiling.

He quite clearly saw the muscles ripple in her slender arm, and his vision darkened again.

"No," he heard her murmur. "Cancel the

order to activate the Rongor battle robots. It is quite illegal to have Rongors on a civilized world in the first place. You're in enough trouble. Use of illegal weaponry will compound it, and be useless. Those are Llralans out there!"

He gagged, and her grip on his throat lessened slightly. "Llralans? My God, but why—"

"Countermand the order," she rapped out.

"Cancel the Rongors," he cried. His blood was pounding in his ears.

"Tell them to stand down and surrender," she said. "We are executing a Commonwealth Court search warrant."

"But—"

"Tell them!"

He told them. She released her grip and patted him kindly on the shoulder. He shuddered. "You've destroyed some of those bodies!" he said.

"No. We destroyed your defenses. Very precisely. And the troops took out the guards trying to fight back. That's all. It's a clean mission. It could have gotten messy if you activated that squad of Rongors, but it wouldn't have changed the outcome. The Exec's troops are the best there are at this kind of thing."

"The Exec! But why?"

"You had somebody in there she needed. That's all I know. And all you need to know. All you need to do now is show up for the magistrate. I'm going to assume you intend to do that, right? So I don't have to embarrass you further?"

He swallowed. "No, you don't have to. My

God, are you Palikar? You must be, if you're Terran Service."

She smiled at him. "You may as well relax. It's over. They're mopping up now. Mission accomplished."

"What mission?"

"Need to know, buddy-boy. And you don't need to know." She leaned back in her chair with lazy grace. "Now, you were about to begin your seduction by showing off your knowledge of local cuisine. And you are kind of cute, at that. Don't let this distraction ruin a beautiful lunch."

In his dream, Python performed his Palikar ritual in the ruins beside the river on the continent of the Pondoro wolverine. In the pale dawn, he fought with phantoms. Lavender mists rose off the slow sliding of the broad water. Off where the world was piled up in jagged battlements against the sky, black crags were touched with soft deep orchid tints from the autumn sun.

"Come—out!"

His body blurred into a shadow that repacked into solidity three long strides away, behind a flashing foot that struck at nothing and recoiled, in venomous imitation of the name its owner carried.

"Come—out!"

Another blurring, interlocking series of moves, murderous fist and leg strikes at nothing. Flood-deposited rubble grated beneath his moccasins.

"Wherever you are!"

Spin me a story, storyteller, and I just might!

There was only the slightest hitch in his fluid movements. But on the next pass he interrupted his routine with an abrupt, broad-legged stance of total immobility. He could feel sweat running freely over his naked body.

Where had his utilitarian coverall gone? He blinked. The river, and the crags, and the sky, seemed to lose their sharp focus. Was his vision going as well?

Oooh! I love a man who keeps his physical body in such tone! May I watch you sweat? How—basic!

It was Miriam, of course, speaking in his mind through the agency of their joined sybil-awareness.

He blinked again. Never had his sybil opened communication with another of its kind in all his long years as a Palikar contestant, though he knew full well there were others similarly infected. But his sybil had been a genetically reengineered descendant of native rootstock, carefully monitored and controlled by Terran Service technology.

The sybil infecting him now was far stronger. And he had no sense that it was subject to any control but its own whim. This had troubled him when he first realized it. So much of his Terran Service conditioning had been dedicated to protection of humanity. And the untrammeled sybil was a threat. An incalculable threat. But he had forgotten his concern swiftly, as the new sybil integrated smoothly into his brain. He wondered if a clone brain was not perfect clay for the parasite. He still tried to think about things like that.

The emotion behind Miriam's perceived words was so freighted with bold carnality that he couldn't concentrate.

"I don't understand how this works," he said.

Does it matter? What matters is that is does—and we've found each other.

He had no memory of ever having been the object of so much candid lust. His blood already was stirred from his exertion. He was distressed to feel his internal rhythms alter from the joy of simple exercise to something just as primal. He sensed, but could not hear, her merry laughter. He closed his eyes. Pondoro was illusion, after all. He was somewhere else.

From some nearby point in that somewhere else, Ball spoke to him.

"You're in an exercise sphere, regaining your form. Your short-term memory still is shaky. The sphere is controlled by a reanimation creche located within Ichiro University, planet Ptolemy. You've already known all this. You don't remember?"

"Exercise phase coming to conclusion," said another voice.

Python's memory flickered and delivered a tidbit of information. This voice belonged to the Ichiro University creche.

"Muscle memory improved by another 12.393 percent," the voice went on. "The clone is nearing optimum physical efficiency. The atypical brain activity still is troubling. Short-term postactivation memory function still is erratic."

"He's dreaming," Ball said. "Let him alone."

"Clone?" Python said.

He heard—*heard?*—Ball make his long-suffering sighing sound.

"Yeah. Clone. You might as well know. There wasn't much of you left after Pondoro. But you're back now. Healthy and hearty."

And better than ever, she whispered in his mind, *unless the original was amazing!*

He shivered. His physical reaction to her was as unambiguous as a pubescent teen's, and deeply disturbing. Meanwhile, Ball and the creche went on discussing him as if he were merely an interesting experiment they were conducting, one who had no awareness of their words.

"He is doing far more than dreaming," the creche said. "His sybil is activating extraordinarily high combinations of synaptic sequences. Focusing on those centers where the clone brain tests high on paranormal function."

"Of course the sybil is doing that," Ball said. "That's why he was selected as a symbiote in the first place. The sybil is trying to train him to use his brain like its native host species does. "

"The parasite is succeeding. His brain's conversation centers show that he is bonding with another of his species via the sybil's unique communications mode."

Are we? she whispered in his mind. *Bonding, I mean? I know I'd like to bond with you—in every possible way.*

Python moved again, into a slow whirling spin, arms out and drooping like the weary rotors of ancient hovercraft. His head was back, eyes still closed. The sweat cooled on his skin, and the sound of his breathing was heavy in his ears. As he whirled, long-ago images of his training years played across his memory, refreshed by the input from his purring musculature. He felt powerful, fit. He knew, with years of knowledge, that he could perform well enough right now to earn a place in the next Twelve-System Games. But he was a clone. His memories were synthetic. His confidence was based on flesh and blood gone back to dust on Pondoro's bloody soil. Was his confidence as synthetic as his memory?

Would you wear my kerchief—like the ancient knights of Manhome?

Just like that, his doubt was gone. As Palikar, Python was the closest thing modern times had to a true knight errant. His deepest, earliest beliefs centered in those ancient dreams of selfless dedication to his fellows. He felt a stunning surge of immense devotion to this feminine presence in his mind. She knew him as had no other—ever.

His breathing and pulse steadied, but other chemical changes flushed through his system. Her words—and the emotional and erotic force behind them—were stirring him in unremembered ways. No thought remained of himself as a flawed and altered being. His was a unified awareness, questing for full rapport with Miriam.

Not just the kerchief, love. Wear some clothes, too. If all those men and women see you in that state, I'll have too much competition!

Python felt his ears burn.

"Sweet spirit of space, preserve us all." It was Ball's disgusted tones. "Initiate a glandular suppressant."

"Initiating," the creche said.

Python's sense of union, of singleness with his sybil, was essentially complete. Now, sensing an unwanted intrusion to his lusty coma, he shrugged off the creche's attempt at inoculation. He would not *permit* unwanted outside intrusion. His immune system instantly attacked and neutralized the suppressant.

"Initiation unsuccessful," the creche said calmly. "Suppressant neutralized."

"By the sybil?" he heard Ball ask.

"By the patient. The symbiosis is complete. Host and parasite act as one entity now."

"Damn!" Ball said. "Martin?"

"Yes?"

Miriam still was there, whispering encouragement. *That will show them!*

"Is it this Miriam you told me about that you are in communication with?"

"Yes." He was once more lost in an erotic daydream, lost in her words, lost in her presence in his mind.

"You remember where you are now?"

"Ptolemy. The new assignment. Oh!" He sighed deeply.

"What?"

"Sweet Miriam. She is quoting poetry to me."

"Poetry?" He heard utter disbelief in the cyborg's voice.

He dropped into a position called lotus long ago, until preempted by the Palikar discipline, meditating to the cadence of her words. He didn't want to talk to Ball anymore. Perhaps that was unfair to his old partner. But her words were so moving! He tried to explain.

"Yes, poetry. The local form, she tells me—the Renga? Her words dance like a Palikar *kata*—so disciplined, so interconnected. Would you like to hear?"

"Spare me." The cyborg's voice was wintry. "I think I get the general sense of things from your reactions. You are literally spewing pheromones. Yet you said, when you first became aware of this other symbiote, that the woman is ancient. And 'not all there,' I believe you said."

Python felt a surge of sad empathy. Poor Ball! Trapped in his genderless sphere, isolated from anything that gave sentience true meaning.

"Age is an illusion," he said. "Time is an illusion, after all. And what is sanity?"

"Sometimes I am grateful for no digestive tract," Ball said. "Otherwise, I might just throw up."

Python felt himself frown. "You mean I implied her mind was damaged in some way? I don't remember saying that. How could I? You don't know anything about her. She is so wonderful!"

"So it would seem." Ball was not impressed.

"As to whether I know her, you have clearly forgotten my resources. *Miriam* and *old* were all the clues I needed. Miriam Trane, a female poet of Chisolm. Her vitals show her to be a wiry dark-skinned woman half your height with a frizz of yellow hair and large dark eyes. Her appearance is almost simian. Her poetry had a vogue among sybarites when she was in her seventies. Then she stopped writing for publication. She died at age 157. Here, on this world. While participating in one of these Renga cycles. She signed away her life, willing to die if her verses should fail the local standard. A fairly extreme attempt to conquer writer's block. I consider it barbaric to murder visiting poets, no matter how banal their words. But who am I to judge local customs? In any event, you're lusting for a ghost. Go shower and cool off!"

Miriam withdrew, stung. Python opened his eyes in alarm.

He was in a bare exercise dojo very like those of his childhood Old Earth school. Pondoro was just another memory—or a dream—or an illusion. He had been Python on Pondoro, itinerant yarn-spinner. Before, he had been Baka Martin, athlete and covert op for the Commonwealth of Terra. Who was he now, in this incarnation? He felt fresh and new, and weary of his old memories.

"Where did you go?" he asked the blank walls softly.

If I'm such an ugly wizened little old ghost, what do you care?

"Oh, Miriam, I am so sorry."

She wasn't laughing anymore. She was hurt. Her pain stabbed at him. For the first time in his questionable memory, Baka Martin considered ways he might visit similar pain on his cynical partner. There was no easy way. Ball had struck right to the heart of Miriam's self-esteem. Oral abuse was one of the cyborg's principal weapons in civilized environs. As for shaping words to hurt Ball as he had hurt Miriam, the damned cyborg's self-esteem was as well-armored as his hide. It would be a great challenge.

Miriam was up to it. *Your wonderful partner is an—*

No comprehensible word followed. But the image that boiled out of her mind was fetid and caustic. Python hoped Ball's empathometer recorded its full intensity.

"Yes!" he said with vindictive glee. "He is exactly that!" Then, worriedly: "You aren't really a ghost, are you? Will I ever see you?"

Oh, sweet man! You will do far, far more than see me! Poor Arthur. He would never understand these feelings I have for you. . . .

"Arthur?" He felt something like a physical shock. Had he awakened after all to a myth-world? Only moments ago, she had touched on ancient knights and kerchiefs and tournaments.

Do as the nasty cyborg says, sweet man. Go take your shower. Mmm. I'll be right there with you, dear. You won't believe how fully I will be with you. You'll like that. Trust me.

He heard Ball's voice as from a great distance. "Where do you think you're going?"

"To shower," he said, with great dignity. "May I have some privacy? Please?"

"I may throw up anyway," Ball said.

Ball's spherical hull rocked gently back and forth in a curved couch meant for three humanoid passengers. His transportation was a luxury vehicle from the emperor's own garage. He was being royally summoned. A spare synapse or two fired off a small curiosity as to whether his rocking motion was some limbic shadow from the time he had been a biped. He ignored the question. Irrelevant. There were far more urgent ones to consider.

Ball was unhappy. Of all things he detested, none ranked higher than being outmaneuvered. He was beginning to suspect it had happened again.

Yes, the Pondoro wolverine had fooled him and trapped him. Buried him ignominiously under an avalanche. A primitive culture without fire, without tool, without any advantage other than that eerily alien intelligence of theirs.

That didn't count. He had never been meant to operate in a frontier setting.

But this was different. Ptolemy was his natural element. Interstellar politics, and their seamier underside, were precisely his domain. Despite the reverse on Pondoro, it had not crossed his mind to doubt his ability to perform here. And perform he had, ingratiating himself with the simpleminded monarch, bullying and insulting and charming his way into the inner circle of those at work on the secret communications project.

He had needed a safe haven from the wrath of the Terran Service after Pondoro. And he had a history with Ptolemy. At least there was a good deal of information about the world in his personal archives. Probably from the full mission briefing he had received before being diverted to Pondoro.

Managing to obtain diplomatic immunity had been simplicity itself.

Arranging for Ptolemy to bid on the project to clone his erstwhile field man, Baka Martin, had been equally as simple. Ichiro University had wide renown in clone research. An opportunity to work on so celebrated a case as the former Twelve Systems Palikar champion was one they could not pass up. Ball felt a moral obligation to make the attempt. He'd let Martin down on Pondoro. Also, he was sure reanimating Martin as a free agent would infuriate the Commonwealth Executive.

He wasn't really sure which motivation was stronger.

It was almost fortuitous that Ptolemy's secret project involved the Blocked World parasite. Almost. Martin's symbiosis with the sybil had been one of the reasons they initially were tapped for this assignment. There had been suspicions even then.

His vehicle was programmed to find the peripatetic ruler wherever on his world he happened to be. The emperor did not sit in one place awaiting a command appearance. The automatic pilot lifted the craft over a low range of forested foothills whose streams all fed back into Civilization River. On the far side of the crest the flora changed and spaced itself out in economic dryland fashion. A few kilometers farther out, the drab colors of unclaimed Ptolemy stretched to the foreshortened horizon.

He had been so clever, bringing a clone of his field man into play. A Terran Service symbiote to penetrate the ultimate secrets of the Ptolemy experiment with symbiosis. But Schodt had somehow palmed Ball's sybil-control chip and inserted another, with different programming. Martin's new sybil had not been reengineered to drain away some of its unguessed potentials. The linkage of Martin's still-not-fully-integrated awareness with a sybil of that power made Ball very nervous.

Python's mellow baritone spoke in one of Ball's com channels, in a peculiar cadence:

"I have known horror,
Done horror, all innocent.
My soul, dark-stained, seeks
Sweet surrender in your arms.
Cleanse me between your warm thighs."

Python still was back in his Ichiro U. creche, resting. The tremendous torque placed on human flesh and bone and gristle by full

Palikar routines had taken its toll of the cloned body. Though the sybil could just as easily have mobilized Martin's own resources for the rebuilding, it permitted the creche to work uninterrupted. The parasite was busily siphoning large amounts of glucose to Martin's brain to facilitate his continued neuronal linkage with Miriam Trane. Martin's brain had learned the almost-telepathic trick in the Pondoro creche, as he reached for rapport with the minds of the greer. Ball had left the sequences in the reanimation tapes to strengthen Martin's effectiveness. Maybe not the best decision he had ever made, he reflected.

Martin recited another few lines of blank verse.

Ball keyed a speaker in the creche. "That's pathetic."

"Go away." Martin's voice was dreamy and soft. "I have nothing to report to you anymore. No reason to report. We no longer are Terran Service. This particular me never was of the Service to begin with. You forgot to mention that when I was resuscitated. Well . . . reanimated. But I don't mind. I am free at last. Free of my oath. So are you. Free to be ourselves! Perhaps even to find love—"

"Love?" Ball gave it a bitter twist. "You are engaging in what amounts to a pornographic séance with a 157-year-old monkey-faced bitch. Who is supposed to be dead. Whose poetry was so bad she chose death rather than go home in disgrace from a poetry exhibition. If she likes the drivel you spout, no wonder!"

"I have explained to Miriam about your odd personality and how it came to be," Martin said. "She has overcome her hurt at your crude remarks. She now finds you cute. Can you imagine that?"

He still sounded dreamy, and callow as an adolescent, to Ball's jaundiced hearing. Well, this clone was only standard days old. Perhaps it was just a phase. But Ball didn't think so. Miriam's intervention was too well-timed. Martin's sybil was leading him too smoothly astray. None of this should have happened. Martin had been taken out of action before the game truly began.

Ball really *hated* being outmaneuvered.

Up ahead, a rambling splash of blue-green, not quite terrestrial blue-green, bloomed in the sere landscape. The emperor's aircar made straight for it. The structures and plant life were so cunningly fashioned that it seemed he approached some uninhabited Garden of Eden.

"You're reciting this drivel to Miriam, aren't you?" Ball said.

"I don't have to recite aloud, you know. She hears me fine without that. And since it seems to disturb you so, I won't. I'm not being manipulated, Ball. Maybe for the first time in my life I'm not. Miriam wouldn't do such a thing. She's nothing like you."

"What are you talking about now?"

"You manipulate people, Ball. It's one of your best things. You manipulated that poor woman on Pondoro to help you escape that rockslide. You used her emotions to bond her to you. And then you abandoned her."

Ball experienced some trace of emotion. Trace of memory. Something deeper than his memory of the abbreviated interaction with Kathryn Kinsella on Pondoro. That memory itself was clear and bittersweet. This was something else.

Engram? The word popped into his awareness. An ancient word for a memory-trace left on the brain. Did emotions leave traces? Of course they did. They often supplied the acid to etch the engram deep. Of what corrosive stuff, then, was this deeper, aching trace composed? Was his brain trying to remember *guilt* about something? Some ancient leave-taking? Perhaps from before he assumed his present form? He considered it, rejected it. No way to know.

But Martin's words woke other questions. "That rockslide on Pondoro happened after you were dead permanently. Well, in a manner of speaking. Therefore it is not part of your memory. The memories I supplied your present incarnation stop after you awakened in the creche after that greer savaged you."

"Miriam told me about it," Martin said.

"She supposedly has been out of circulation a lot longer than you. How would she monitor obscure news squirts from frontier worlds like Pondoro? And why would she have bothered?"

"She knew about it. She told me about it. That's good enough for me."

Ball uttered several oaths. "Don't you see there's a lot more going on here than just your simple—or even complex—lust? Who turned her loose on you? Who took you out of circulation this way? Who controls her? Report, dammit!"

"I have already told you: I have no obligation to report to you anymore. Or to anyone. That part of my life—the body that lived that part of my life—is gone. I am new. All new. And free. Freer than I ever could have imagined . . ."

The garden below Ball's vehicle was not uninhabited, nor, he knew, was it a garden. It was Ptolemy's version of a major industry. This one was used to design and assemble machines out of the stretched parts of molecules, or in some cases, specific atoms. The assemblers then built smaller machines into chips for a variety of applications. Tolerances were measured in angstroms, down on that almost mystic level where distinctions between any kind of actual existence and probability blurred. Exacting work. There was abundant room left over in the complex for meditation chapels, game courts, spacious dojos, and even lawn bowling. Ptolemy's version of the frantic corporate life.

Ball was in no mood to appreciate the beauty. "Orbit the perimeter and ask for landing instructions," he told the car.

"Why do you want to know where Miriam is, Ball?" Martin asked.

"I need to know who's controlling her. Her sybil girdle is flawed, dammit. And so is yours. They have too much autonomy. Somebody is being incredibly stupid. We need to get those damn parasites trimmed back before something awful happens."

Martin's empathometer wavered drunkenly. The sybil was reacting to Martin's perception of Ball's words. The parasite already had attempted to mobilize Martin's immune system against the empath chip, and failed. Now its reaction to Ball's words was powerful. It recognized a threat. It feared—*feared?*—that Ball could somehow curtail its freedom. The sybil didn't want its freedom curtailed.

"It has to be Schodt, of course," Ball said. "He's got more courage than I imagined."

"I'm not going to listen to you anymore right now," Martin said.

"You're useless anyway. Enjoy yourself while you can."

Ball *hated* being outmaneuvered. He had badly underestimated Schodt ever since the other had arrived. Or, more likely, had underestimated the cultural paranoia rampant within Schodt's corporation. Someone high up the chain of command had decreed that no anomaly should be viewed as harmless. No matter how artful his penetration, his arrival had been treated as a threat from the beginning. He had focused on earning the trust of the quirky emperor and his inner circle. But the emperor wasn't running things here. Inter-Galactic was.

"**P**ermission to land has been obtained," the car said.

"Then do it," Ball said.

They came down in a swale ablaze with mutant wildflowers. The emperor of Ptolemy, in a many-hued jumpsuit, appeared with a sorcerer's flourish out of the blooms. "Simply Ball! Thank you for coming so promptly. Let's go below. I can speak with you before my tour guests arrive."

"I could have made it under my own power," Ball grumbled. "You didn't need to waste a vehicle."

"Let's go below."

Floating behind the emperor, Ball took note of heavily armed troops dispersed across the surface of the establishment. They were carefully tucked out of sight, but easily discernible to him. He thought maybe he was supposed to notice them. There were cyborg gunmen—a Ptolemaic specialty design often favored as VIP bodyguards—and a squad of refurbished Rongor battle robots. He wondered if the Rongors had been part of the Blocked World insertion force, or if Ptolemy was going into production of the old, outlawed design.

The deployment of forces could be defensive—or imprisoning. Either way, some kind of showdown seemed in the offing. The subtle show of force made Ball even more irritable.

Well beneath the surface, the lift door opened to a spacious, blue-lit chamber.

Humans and machines moved with quiet purpose between random work stations. In one corner, a woman with straw-colored hair was plucking softly on a stringed instrument. No evidence of heightened security here. Only a pair of the emperor's personal bodyguards, humans nearly as tall as Baka Martin, weaponry concealed beneath loose coveralls in the imperial colors.

Ball registered a variety of soft scents drifting through the work space.

"Frantic pace," he said to the emperor's back.

"Well, we need to put on a little show of industrious enterprise, you know," the emperor said. "Some important InterGalactic clients are coming. "

They passed into a smaller, brighter room. Alex Schodt popped out of his chair, smiling and pushing at his hair. He looked very pleased with himself. The emperor returned Schodt's bow and settled into a broad, approximately human chair, spreading out his long legs.

"You are aware your former employer is in space?" he asked Ball. "With three ships from her personal fleet? That observers report unexpected Terran Service naval movements in many quadrants?"

"I usually am aware of current events. So?"

"My fleet is on standby alert. We will not be cowed. But surely she would not take armed action against us?"

Ball made his laughing sound. "Do you have any idea how many conflicts and conspiracies she deals with hourly? Let alone natural disasters, to include most of the Assemblymen. I thought you said ego was an illusion. If you're right, then you're delusional."

"Harsh language, simply Ball."

"Um," Schodt said, "how many of her hourly decisions have to do with the sybil?"

"You're paranoid," Ball told him. "Terran Service naval movements are always unexpected. Except by their admirals."

The emperor nodded. "Perhaps you're right. Ptolemy is too populous and important for protectorate proceedings. My protests were within acceptable diplomatic norms. But if we must cross swords with the Executive, then we must. She had no right to attack a guest of this world."

"You have no proof she did. She may have proof she didn't. If so"—Ball introduced his official tones—"she might well use your protests to convince the executive council you aren't fit to rule such a technology-intensive planet. The council might go along with protectorate status just long enough for your removal and replacement."

"You can't be serious!" Schodt exclaimed. His hair was getting quite a workout.

"Stick to symbiosis," Ball told him. "Stay out of interstellar politics."

"She wanted to silence Ramsey! In an obvious hunting accident! To avoid any media attention. He was the only media rep even remotely interested in this year's Renga."

"Somebody," Ball said, "wanted media attention focused here. So they chose an attack on an accredited news rep. Adrienne Taft could care less if the media does or doesn't take notice of this land of navel-gazers. With all due respect, Excellency. Try again, Schodt."

"There were two attacks," Schodt said weakly. He no longer looked pleased with himself.

"There won't be more," Ball said confidently. "The media is here in full force. Mission accomplished. Haven't you ever heard of a conventional media release?"

The emperor cut his eyes at Schodt. "What is he talking about?"

"This is the year you have planned your elegant little interstellar communications demonstration," Ball said, "to coincide with the Renga. To establish how innocuous it all is."

Schodt looked vaguely ill. "You *told* him that?"

"Excellency," Ball reminded gently.

"What?"

"You sound as if you are reprimanding the ruler of a full member of the Commonwealth. You, a corporate underling."

The emperor straightened in his chair. "We are a very relaxed society, simply Ball. Still"— he turned a sorrowful look on Schodt—"you *did* sound recriminatory, Alex Schodt."

Schodt was blinking rapidly. "Forgive me, er—Excellency. No affront intended. I, ah—assure you, InterGalactic holds nothing but the highest regard for you. JonHoward mentions you frequently and with great friendliness."

"*Does* he? I find that pleasant to know." The emperor settled back with a smile. "You are very adept at fomenting trouble, simply Ball."

"So is InterGalactic. They've already spread hundreds of rumors about a scientific breakthrough here. Deftly handled, I am forced to admit, so that any attempt to eliminate the visiting celebrity journalist would trigger a feeding frenzy. Just in time for your Renga. And your demonstration of speeded-up data transmission. With the added bonus that the Commonwealth seems afraid of this new breakthrough. Perhaps likely to take drastic steps to curtail it. Every government will want some. And many major enterprises. InterGal should be able to name its price on a thousand worlds."

The emperor's eyes narrowed. "Your implication is unseemly, simply Ball. Ptolemy would not be party to such a subterfuge."

"And you weren't. You were a puppet."

The emperor reacted as if slapped. "Your bluntness ill becomes your legendary diplomatic skills, simply Ball. You are an honored guest here, but guests have duties to their hospitality."

Schodt cleared his throat forcefully. "Um—it is the best of our belief, Excellency, that simply Ball is here under false pretense. That he in fact managed his own diplomatic immunity from afar, through surrogates."

"Well, of course he did," the emperor said. "I was his main surrogate. And the university monks, of course."

Schodt shoved his hair viciously. "You were? I don't understand. Your agreement with InterGal—"

"Our experiment will benefit all sentient life," the emperor cut in. "Enhance communications by almost incalculable magnitudes. But not if the Commonwealth opposes us. Ball is our bridge to them, don't you see?"

"He's the damn puppet here! He's still Terran Service to the core!"

"Well, I certainly should hope so." The emperor smiled. "I am counting on it. He will report how fairly we have selected and treated all our experimental subjects. The Commonwealth will have no cause for action against us. You see?" He turned back to Ball. "Now do you understand why I am concerned about these naval movements? Not because I fear strife, but because I fear the Commonwealth has misunderstood."

"I can't believe you informed Ball without JonHoward's approval!" Schodt said.

The emperor frowned. "You forget yourself again, Alex Schodt. JonHoward is not the emperor of Ptolemy. I am."

"Are you *crazy?* Taft will seize all our sybil subjects, all our equipment! Declare eminent domain or something like it. Plead Commonwealth security. Of course the navy is on the move! Ball already has briefed them."

The emperor stood. "I believe this audience is at an end. Control yourself, Alex Schodt."

"Not quite at an end." Schodt's voice cracked with tension, but he somehow mastered his nervous tic and held his hands rigidly at his sides.

The emperor went quite still. "You overstep, Alex Schodt."

"Um—please hear me out, Excellency." Schodt was blinking rapidly now, but his voice firmed up as the words spilled out. "The—um—Rongors and so forth on the surface up there? They're programmed to let no one in or out. Except me, of course. For your own protection. Ah, that is, JonHoward has information of some kind of coup attempt. You are the target. Probably supported by the Commonwealth."

"That's asinine," Ball said.

"It's absurd!" the emperor said. "I'm returning to my palace, right now."

"Um—that wouldn't be wise. There is some kind of explosive device believed to be hidden in this facility, keyed to your nervous system. If you set foot on the surface, um—then this place will—ah, vaporize."

"Then come take the ride to the surface with me, Alex Schodt." The emperor started toward Schodt, who shrank back in alarm.

"Colonel!" he croaked.

One of the emperor's bodyguards stepped into the room. He pointed a blunt, bell-mouthed handgun at the emperor. "Stand still," he said tensely.

"Mathis of Decartes," the emperor said. "I knew your father! What have you done to us?"

"It's not Mathis," Ball said.

The bodyguard touched something at his waist. The gaudy colors of his coverall faded to the mottled tones of desert camouflage. He shrank, and as he did, his facial features changed. He was less than six feet tall, squat, muscular, with leathery skin and cold eyes.

"A Zionist?" the emperor said.

"A hired gun," Ball said.

"Don't mouth off," the gunman said.

"I don't *have* a mouth," Ball said. "Good night."

The gunman wilted on the spot. His military blaster made a heavy thud on the thick carpeting. The emperor made a graceful swoop and came up with it. Schodt's eyes seemed to start from his head.

"Now you stand still!" Ball snapped. "Don't make me narco you, too."

"I should save you the trouble." The emperor gestured with his captured weapon.

"No. This is complicated. We need Schodt alive. He has the code to those robots. I don't think your one remaining bodyguard could take on a Rongor squad. Assuming this mercenary left him alive in the first place."

"You knew this"—the emperor indicated the fallen man—"was not Mathis."

"Of course I did. But I had to play this out to see whose side you came down on." To Schodt: "What were your orders?"

"To—um . . . that is none of your business!"

"Don't be terminally stupid, Schodt. Don't you want to live to see how this turns out? *What were your orders?*"

Schodt was visibly trembling. "To, um—that is, to return to local headquarters and wait further instructions. I can't order the Rongors away! Nor the cyborgs. Our planning took into account that I was—um, vulnerable."

"A pawn," Ball said.

"Well, I ah . . . How about a rook?"

Ball made his laughing sound. "You surprise me more and more, Schodt. A sense of humor under pressure? Maybe InterGal does know how to pick executives."

"A pawn—a rook?" The emperor shook his head. "Is this some vast board game, then, and all of us merely pieces?"

Ball ignored it. "Your orders, Schodt! For the emperor. And myself. You wouldn't like the ways I'd use to force it out of you."

"Um—well, that is . . ." He swallowed and started over. "You're just to stay here until we have the news of our breakthrough properly managed and released. Both of you. We're doing that now, out in the orbital hotels. It's for your own safety, Excellency." He edged almost imperceptibly toward the door.

"Anxious to leave?" Ball said.

Schodt froze. "I—"

"Want to call your Rongors down here to bail you out?"

"I—um, no, of course not! We know your capabilities. We built you!"

"So what's to keep me from going up there and weeding the emperor's garden for him? This infernal device set to go off if I go upstairs, too?"

Schodt pushed furiously at his hair. "We weren't sure you'd come here. But two things should, um—deter you. First, um—Rongors are not toys. They can fire and maneuver better than anything else ever built. Out in the open, against a squad, one of them would acquire you before you could disable them all. You, um—are of course familiar with their firepower."

"That's only one thing," Ball said grimly. "Suppose I feel lucky?"

Schodt eyed the emperor's weapon. "Um— do you remember when you volunteered your brain for the Ball experiment?"

Ball experienced a momentary blankness, as if his brain had shut down. He said nothing.

"Well, *do* you?" Schodt's back straightened. He seemed to sense Ball's confusion. "Would you like to see the contract you signed then, refresh your memory?"

"*You* have a copy of my contract?" He couldn't seem to think clearly.

"Of course we do. We built your package, remember? Would you like to see your escape clause?"

"What escape clause?"

"You weren't sure you'd like being a ball," Schodt said. "InterGal agreed to preserve your human body indefinitely. And to reintegrate your brain with it, upon demand."

Ball's mind reeled with the implications. "You know who I was?"

"Of course we do! And *that's* the second thing that will keep you here." Schodt no longer sounded hesitant. His mood seemed to have elevated to vengeful glee.

"What? That you know who I was?"

"That we have your body. If you don't stay here until we release you, we sell your human body to an organ bank on Belkin's World."

"Belkin's World?" Ball felt his memory jink dizzily at the name, but nothing would form.

"Your home planet, of course."

"You could be lying."

"They'll dispose of your body anyway," the emperor said sadly. "These are not ethical creatures, simply Ball. I know JonHoward Tomas. Better, perhaps, than I would wish to. He will dispose of your body for spite. I know you will ensure he lives to regret it. Let's just kill this worm now. If we all go into the great otherness together, so be it."

Schodt looked as if his legs would buckle. Ball didn't need an empathometer to know Schodt had never expected this much spirit from the emperor of lotus-land. Perhaps InterGalactic's research into Ptolemy had missed the heritage of samurai and kamikaze. Or the Amerind heritage of craziness under the guns of the enemy. Schodt's own ancestors would have called the emperor fey.

Ball missed human lungs right then. He longed for a deep, centering breath such as those of the Palikar and various Ptolemaic rituals. His dispassionate observations of Schodt's and the emperor's states of mind would have to serve. It was, after all, one of the things he did best.

He spared a moment to mourn the death of the body he could not remember and would never know again.

"Let him go back to his offices," he told the emperor. "He will need to ask Tomas for further instructions."

He was careful to ensure his tones were those of a resigned and defeated loser.

But his mind was functioning at top speed again. Things were beginning to tumble and click into a pattern. Permitting Schodt to think his bluff had worked would give him time. Just enough.

We tied up in the Tezuka University sailing basin not too long after daylight on the morning the Renga was to begin. A steady rain slanted across the harbor. Low clouds obscured the higher forested slopes rising behind the town. The school's sailboats bobbed in a stationary regatta across the expanse of rain-dimpled water, bare-masted and deserted. There was a handful of houseboats similar to Raven's tied up on the far side of the basin. I don't know what I had expected as a greeting party. What we got was a solitary shrouded figure, motionless as a statue on the wharf.

I secured the bow line and hurried aft to take care of the stern while Raven held the houseboat motionless against the pilings. The engines powered down. By the time I was done, she was beside me, waiting for the automatic gangplank to fold out.

"Master Inaba himself!" she said.

"Is that a big deal?"

I watched raindrops ricochet off his bald pate. He didn't blink or react, just stood there wearing one of those peaceful Ptolemaic smiles that seemed as common as jumpsuits. But his own attire was an ankle-length robe, roped at the waist. Sandals. No socks. Well, the rain was warm, at that. He had big knobby feet.

We went ashore. Up close, Inaba was as tall as I'd thought Raven to be on first meeting. I had to tilt my neck to meet his twinkling eyes. Raven bowed deeply, and he returned it.

Inaba favored me with a bow as well. "Keith Ramsey of Highlands, Acme. It is my honor to welcome you to our Renga cycle."

"I guess I expected more fanfare," I said. "Not for me, I mean. But for the start of a such a celebration."

His smile deepened. "The celebration comes when the Renga is complete. As for the start of the Renga, you should know that a writer's labor is done in solitude. The ancient dilemma. In order to communicate, one must first go inside oneself, all alone, and mine the words."

"Well-spoken," I said.

He bowed again. "You are ready to begin?"

"I guess so."

"This decade's final Renga is a very special one, Keith Ramsey. You know of Arthur Galatis of Singing Tree, Crestmark?"

It was the name Tanner had told me to watch for. "I know the name, not the work. The poet laureate of Crestmark. He died here during one of your Renga cycles. Thirty years ago?"

"Twenty-six years ago. And he did not die. He donated his brain to scientific research. His brain was more useful alive than dead. Alive, the brain still is inhabited by his mind. The thinker of the thought. Nothing in the research has interfered with his poetic abilities. In twenty-six years he has amassed a body of work which will be a great gift to all lovers of words. As a way of announcing this great gift, his is the first tanka of this year's cycle."

"This is pretty hot news," I said. "Galatis is here? At your university?"

"Oh, no. Arthur Galatis is on Old Earth. His tanka arrived here at precisely dawn on this continent. The traditional start of our cycle."

"Then the media already know he's back," I said. "Damn."

"No," Inaba said, "they do not. Poets of a Renga are anonymous for the entire cycle. The media have his words, but not his identity, nor his location. Ego is not the prize here. And his words arrived by a communications medium not monitored by the media. Nor by anyone else. A medium, in fact, unknown outside a select circle. The story of this new medium will be yours, Keith Ramsey. It has been planned that way all along."

"Ball's doing," I said. "A breakthrough in communications technology? Here?"

"Not precisely technology. Still, technology played its role." He was calm, as if discussing the weather. "Ah. I sense your immediate impatience to get on to that story, but there is time yet. Other things have occurred. And in the meanwhile there is the Renga. Each thing in its appointed round. Balance in all things. Now listen:

"Blood the argument.
Indignities untold stain
All the bloody years.
Stars collide, explode, expire
Blood drums hot until it cools."

My surprise must have showed. "I believe you said you are unfamiliar with the early work of Arthur Galatis, Keith Ramsey?"

"I don't know his work. But I had the idea he was a romantic, somehow."

"His perspective has seemed to . . . change," Inaba said. "His work has grown more bitter with time." He frowned. "It is a puzzle. I am reliably informed he should be content. His emotional and physical needs are completely met. Certain irregularities have become known as to how the research involving him was handled by a cooperating company. But he has not sought release from his contract."

"His contract?"

"The one he signed in lieu of the death sentence he came here to find. He believed his well of creativity dry. He believed all those whom he held dear to be dead. He was so lonely. He came here certain his verses were maudlin and would be rejected, and the ancient myth of emperor's prerogative would be invoked."

I shivered. It wasn't the rain on my bare head. That was as warm as the blood Galatis seemed determined to write about. And my Ptolemy coverall—khaki-colored at my insistence instead of gaudy—was fully waterproof.

"Then the execution of poets is a myth?"

"A Commonwealth citizen owns his or her own life force, Keith Ramsey. To conserve, or to protect, or to squander, at will. The myth served us to attract the minds needed to perform our tests."

"He's alive, then? For sure?"

"And shall remain so, unless he demands contract compliance. Such compliance would require his death if our experiments fail to persuade him to live."

"A damned interesting story so far," I said, "even minus the technology. How far along has the poem progressed?"

"Listen again," Inaba said.

Blood the sacrament
Your lips on mine seal the vow
Fingertips explore
Love inflames our blood with joy
But the market price is steep.

"That sounds like Miriam Trane," I said. "I've read some of her work. Is she one of your study subjects as well? Still alive, I mean?"

"Yes, she is. Excellent that you know her. Yours is the next tanka. The surprising theme selected by Arthur Galatis, and elaborated by Miriam Trane, of course points to you. Your writing has much of blood and death."

"How much time do I have?"

He smiled. "Ah, the deadline? Always the news hawk, Keith Ramsey! There is no deadline. Some cycles have lasted well into the next year. One Renga of one thousand links was complete in a local month. A poem is complete when it is complete."

"Master Inaba," Raven said softly.

"Yes, Raven of Lao-tzu?"

"You said other things have occurred. And you alluded to certain irregularities."

He sighed. "You are an apt semantic pupil. Things have occurred. Simply Ball is denounced as a Terran Service spy. Promises made to our emperor by InterGalactic Cybernetics have been broken. Were broken long ago. The emperor is in seclusion, in meditation. We of my Order are concerned. The essential tranquility of things has been disturbed. Steps must be taken to restore balance."

"Is Ball in trouble?" I said. "Again, I mean?"

"Simply Ball also is in seclusion," Inaba said. "Complete seclusion. No one can find him. It is as if he vanished from this planet."

"Then somebody's out to get him, probably. He's pulled that trick before. He'll find whoever he wants to find. But only when he's good and ready."

"I believe you are correct," Inaba said. "For now, there is the Renga. We shall pursue the tradition while the emperor meditates. My Order waits to assist however it may. This new communications medium—"

"Yes," I said. "Tell me about that."

"In essence, instantaneous," Inaba said. "We chose the Renga as our demonstration, so that previous poets long forgotten may be remembered. We break one tradition, insofar as not all participants are located here. But the immortal mind is free of such imagined constraints of time and space, in the end. Have you ever heard the phrase, 'The mind can go to Sirius and back in the time it takes a dog to snap at a fly'? Keith Ramsey?"

"No. But I like it."

"It is attributed to a pre-space prose writer named Frederick Faust," Inaba said. "Speaking of the distance between Old Earth and Sirius. The poets always understood quantum phenomena long before the scientists."

"Are you talking about telepathy?" I said. "Honest-to-God telepathy?"

"Not human telepathy. Not quite. You will learn all, in good time for your deadlines, whatever they may be. For now, though, do us the honor to compose our third tanka, and forge the next link in our poem."

We were back in the main
lounge aboard Raven's houseboat. She was
brewing that heavily aromatic local tea. The
rain beat a steady tattoo on the overhead decking. Weak rose-gray light filtered in through
the ports. Inaba hadn't stayed long, or given me
much more about what was going on here. But
it seemed clear there was a hell of a lot more
than a simple poetry competition. I keyed my
'corder back to Inaba's voice, reciting Arthur
Galatis's words.

> "Blood the argument.
> Indignities untold stain
> All the bloody years.
> Stars collide, explode, expire
> Blood drums hot until it cools."

Powerful words. Not the kind of thing I
would have expected from all I knew of Galatis,
which wasn't that much. For some reason, I felt
almost as uneasy as if the greer were looking
over my shoulder. Galatis had chosen blood as
the theme. Blood was one hell of a subject, all
right. The Pondoro wolverine knew about
blood. How to spill it, and how to die. So did
humanity, for that matter. And other species

we had encountered out among the stars. At least to date, everything sentient seemed to run on some kind of liquid delivery system that might pass for blood, regardless of color or temperature. So maybe Galatis was right: maybe blood always is the argument, no matter how the debate is framed.

And the sacrament, too. I played back Miriam Trane's words:

> *"Blood the sacrament*
> *Your lips on mine seal the vow*
> *Fingertips explore*
> *Love inflames our blood with joy*
> *But the market price is steep."*

Miriam Trane had once enjoyed a wide reputation as an erotic poet in her home and neighboring systems. Her work had found its way years later to Acme, in my youth, and was the cause of some consternation among the more conservative of my elders. Her words had inflamed my youthful fantasies more than once in those long-gone days, and sent my fingertips exploring, all right. Though not perhaps in the sense she used that term in this tanka.

Her market-price reference troubled me in the same way Galatis's line about untold indignities did. I had no idea why. His line grated against all my news-gathering sensibilities. It hinted at things hidden. Bad things. Hers grated in a different way—somehow implying emotions purchased and sold. Maybe I was just jumpy because Ball was in the soup again.

Raven served us both tea, making a ceremony of it, and sat silently across from me, her
chin cupped in her palms, her expression rapt.
It seemed she thought I was busy composing.
But I wasn't.

I keyed a com channel and scanned head-
lines. There was one story datelined Ptolemy
on the regional digest. It said that in honor of the
decade-ending Renga, Ptolemy had released
the text of several previously unknown Arthur
Galatis poems. These were identified as part of
an unpublished collection in the custody of the
Ptolemy priesthood. As soon as that word got
out, the bids would come in fast and furious. An
artist tended to be more valuable dead than
alive, even in our time. The price might slump
when they found out he was still alive.
Lawsuits might even ensue. But maybe not.
Maybe a living death as a lab rat would excite
the public to a buying frenzy. I wondered if
that might be the market price to which Trane
referred. It seemed clear that whoever had
organized that media release had a knack for
honoring art and commerce in the same
stroke.

I stared out at the rain and sipped my tea.
What the hell had Ball got himself—and me—
into this time?

The waterfront was deserted and tranquil.
Greater Ptolemy seemed largely indifferent to
my musings. So, I supposed, was the galaxy.
Meanwhile, I was supposed to be composing a
tanka. A bit of poetry in response to poets long
thought dead, and at least one of whom had his

brain altered "for science." I wondered if I was going to get a headache.

Galatis was involved in some new secret interstellar communications method. He spoke of cataclysm in his tanka. Was that why Ball was here? Ball had been denounced as a spy, Inaba said. In a way, it actually made sense. All that diplomatic immunity rigmarole could have just been another cover story, as when he pretended to be my Ball Friday on Pondoro. Anything to get on-planet and at work, ferreting out secrets the Commonwealth wanted to know.

Ptolemy officialdom, of course, would be very unhappy their hospitality had been compromised.

I wondered if Ball actually was still in the employ of the Terran Service. Raven had said it all when she said things were seldom what they seemed with that damned cyborg. I also wondered if the Commonwealth Executive had trumped up a disinformation campaign to make it look as if he still worked for her. If anybody could, she could. And if Ptolemy withdrew Ball's diplomatic immunity, he would be fair game again for her assassins.

Where the hell *was* Adrienne Taft anyway?

Inaba's revelation about the new communications medium was intriguing, but it sounded a lot like hocus-pocus to me. Still, as Raven had assured me, Ptolemy was the world of ideas. Maybe one of their wilder ideas had hit pay dirt. It would be a good story. I thought for a bit about the idea of a faster communications medium. Something really fast. Right now, for instance, insofar as *now* means anything on the galactic scale, Adrienne Taft could be personally supervising the reduction of some upstart world to rubble a few hundred light-years from here. Not that Old Earth had done anything like that in a long time. But it wasn't past someone like her to reinaugurate the practice. And we wouldn't know it here for hours or days, depending on the distance, no matter how many newscasts were beamed out from the battle site.

It would be a huge advance to get information across the entire spaceways with the speed now restricted to sectors. Selfishly speaking, my royalties for a freelance news piece would come in a lot faster when I hit on a hot news story. If Inaba was accurate, Associated News would be buying some of the new technology as soon as the bugs were out.

What the *hell* was Ball into? If he was in empatho-chip range, he must know I was worried about him. That particular technology was as close to true telepathy as I knew anything about. Unless you counted the greer and their eerie ability to cause fear in their prey. Or Baka Martin, bonded to that damned Blocked World parasite.

Trying to find a rhythm that complemented the words of Galatis and Trane was uncomfortable work to me. I had never seen writing as a communal exercise. But finally I began to noodle with words on the 'corder, fingering them in instead of saying them. They used to call it *typing* hundreds of years ago, when the keystrokes resulted in words on paper. They kept calling it that after all the keystrokes got you were letters on a glowing screen. Just like, in ancient times, there was a *telegraph editor* who culled news stories from remote locations. They called him that long after the telegraph itself was history. Then—if I remembered right—there was a *wire editor*, still so-called after physical transmission lines had gone the way of the telegraph key. Finally, today, it was just *news editor*, like Tanner, for the product and not the technology that carried it.

Whatever the communications medium— talking drum, flashing mirror, homing pigeon, mail ship, or electronic gadget—the news often came soaked in blood. We had been simple predators far longer than we had been supposedly civilized. And once civilized, predation had simply taken other forms. More complex, more subtle sometimes, and sometimes far more ghastly.

Hence Galatis's line about untold indignities?

His reference to stars expiring could have referred to the cosmic wheel of the universe itself, the stupendous and uncaring clash of ponderous and colliding star swarms almost beyond human comprehension. But he spoke of blood, and indignities, which certainly implied a human, or at least sentient, agency as cause of the destruction. Trane had tried to soften his bitterness in her tanka. But her allusion to an exorbitant market price still troubled me. It was almost as if both poets had selected words with some common motive beyond the vivid images they evoked.

Perhaps their role as subjects of scientific study was not quite the nirvana Inaba had hinted. Supposedly Galatis could opt out of the experiment any time. Rather drastically, but still his choice. But could he? Could Trane? I wondered where she was right now, this enigmatic woman who had stirred my pubescent fantasies.

I met Raven's gaze. "It's almost like they're talking in some code."

She blinked. "Do not try to see too much, Keith Ramsey. The cycle will come full in its time. Just let go, and let your own words flow."

"I have some words here," I said.

"So soon!"

"I don't like to ponder too long, or I start second-guessing. What do I do with them?"

"Transmit them to the Hall of Words. They will be transmitted to all participants, broadcast to interested parties, and of course recorded for posterity. Just recite them from where you sit."

"All right," I said. "Here goes:

"Blood the covenant,
Blood crying the ageless hunt
Stone or blade or beam
Blood thunders in primal glee
When the quarry goes to ground."

After I stopped reciting, she said nothing. Just kept sipping her tea. The sound of the rain on the deck seeped back into my awareness. I busied myself looking everywhere but at her for a space of minutes. I guess I'm like every writer who ever lived in that I want some reaction to my words, but I'm fearful of hearing it at the same time. I wanted her to approve of me. Of my words.

The silence stretched.

"Well?" I said finally.

She put down her cup with a click. "You do not need my approbation, Keith Ramsey. Your words are powerful." She sounded reflective. "You suggested the others were attempting some form of code. You have answered them in kind. We will see what the next links bring."

Adrienne Taft had been work-
ing steadily in her shipboard office for seven-
teen straight hours. *Forthright*'s light cycles for
sleep and waking periods had passed unno-
ticed; they were set to Old Earth anyway, not
her native Belkin's World. As Commonwealth
Executive, she commanded the finest medical
resources the Terran Service had to offer, and
she had been known to work seven straight
days before allowing a deep-rest and restora-
tive cycle to be imposed on her. But she was
feeling the strain now.

She adjusted her chair to full prone and
keyed in a massage routine. The visual displays
all around the interior of her spherical work
space adjusted for maximal viewing without
any command. Priority traffic remained centered for easy perusal, and less critical information floated in the periphery of her vision,
available for a quick glance.

There had been 107 serious interplanetary
conflicts under way at last update. Twenty-
three had been fully involved shooting wars
when the logs were posted, and another dozen
probably were by now, given the time-lag in
signals traffic from more remote quadrants.
Though troubling, she had faith in the Terran

Service naval branch to deal with cease-fires and imposition of treaties, or, barring that, to sweep warring fleets out of space and establish martial law. There were some areas where a broader political angle could be served by appropriate application of Terran might. She issued instructions for her commanders in those instances, to go out on the next data stream.

Then she turned her attention to the civil wars. There were too many to readily assimilate at one time. Some were restricted to a single continent on one planet—or in one case, a long archipelago—but in others an entire world was involved. Of the top ten on the priority list, use of crude weaponry on one of them had resulted in virtual burn-off of the whole surface of the world. Though sparsely populated, the estimated casualties would still number nearly a billion. The Terran Service had arrived too late to intervene, but now was in control. Leaders of one warring sect were dragged off an orbital fortress where they had survived the doom of their fellows. Leaders of the other side had been dug out of the bedrock of the planet. All of them had been summarily executed on the order of Taft's sector administrator. The search for survivors was underway.

She approved the administrator's acts, authored a congratulatory note, and upped his pay scale three ranges.

Delegation of authority always had been one of her strongest—and weakest—points. She picked her delegates carefully and tracked them obsessively. She gave the ruthless ones full rein—until they went too far. She tried to shore up the timid ones—just enough. She usually found something to approve in each autonomous decision, and focused on that. There simply was no other way to carry out the semblance of a central authority across the sprawling Commonwealth. Decisions had to be made swiftly under local circumstances, long before a consultation with Old Earth could be accomplished. As a rule, the farther from Taft, the more autonomous the administrator. Her minions knew they were growing in her esteem when she shipped them to the outer reaches. They understood equally that they had lost her confidence when she pulled them closer.

They knew they had failed when her assassins showed up.

It was rumored such failures were required to view tapes of previous executions of failed executives before they died in their turn. The rumor was spurious, but Taft liked it. A leader needed to be terrifying as well as loved.

The information in which she was immersed came in several varieties: electronic packets of words alone from the most remote trouble spots, words and images where the images did not delay transmission too much, and full-fidelity oral and visual briefings from closer still. One of her charts showed worlds that were close enough for real-time interaction along *Forthright*'s projected journey if she deemed that to be warranted. These were

ranked in order of crisis. That simple list represented a large number of otherwise powerful
humans and nonhumans, all of whom would be
anxiously awake, regardless of where their
particular sleep cycle was right now. They
would know Taft was projected to be within
hailing range, and her ship might materialize
at any moment. Even the ruthless ones who
had her full authority would be standing by.
Perhaps especially those, since she was known
to change her mind on short notice.

She smiled at the thought. Who said classical education was not useful in politics? She
had learned the trick of distancing herself from
emotional reaction to the news of millions of
casualties from V. I. Ulyanov, an ancient revo-
lutionary. His secret had been to train his mind
not to see bodies, but just numbers on a balance sheet, like an accountant. His successor,
Iosef Stalin, had practiced keeping his subordinates awake all hours, waiting for a call from
him that might or might not come. Sleep depri-
vation tended to make the most stubborn brain
compliant.

Her ear-com chimed softly on her private
frequency, a brief musical code. SjillaTen, still
on the surface of Belkin's World, wanted her.

"What?" she said.

"You took delivery of his body personally?"
he said.

"I did. He is in my stateroom."

A rush of conflicting emotions swirled
through her. From thoughts of billions of bodies
to thoughts of just one. The chair swiveled her

upright, and she killed the displays. The rest of the Commonwealth could wait, all of a sudden. She was going to reassure herself, again, that he still was here.

In the next cabin a hastily installed Medfac bulked large near her bunk. Beneath the transparent lid a man lay sleeping. Her heart seemed to literally squeeze inside her chest.

Not sleeping, she corrected herself sternly. And not even a man. The remnants of a man.

"The body seemed to be in perfect condition," SjillaTen said.

"Perfect?" Her voice caught. "His body was never perfect."

She gazed down at the well-known features, unseen for so long. His face was so slack and expressionless. Empty of life. There was no visible evidence on his too-large cranium of the surgery that had removed his brain—removed *him*—and left this carcass behind. This well-loved carcass. He had never been a physical beauty. His head was too large and hairless, his shoulders too narrow, his arms too thin for his large long-fingered hands. She steadfastly did *not* let her eyes dwell on those hands. He wasn't very tall. He had too much hair on his chest and legs, and a huge dark thatch in which his shrunken genitals nested. Some of the pubic hairs had turned gray. When had that happened? Surely after he left her . . .

"Are you all right?" the Llralan said in her ear.

"I have been reviewing files that report the death of hundreds of millions," she said tonelessly. "Millions who never again will know love, hope, joy. I had no emotion then at all. Yet here I stand looking at this sorry specimen of a man, and I feel like crying my eyes out. What have they *done* to him?"

"He did it to himself," SjillaTen said. "He left his body. You know my culture's unease in dealing with things like that. But he didn't choose anything as supernatural as astral projection." His tone was dry. "He chose the scientific method."

"He *left* me," she said simply.

"No. He chose to serve you in a different way. As Ball."

"I didn't *need* his service. He didn't ask *me*, damn him!"

"Did you own him, then?"

She caught her breath. "That's not what I meant. *Damn* you!"

The Llralan's voice softened uncharacteristically. "Forgive me. You are not yourself. I will not goad you again."

"Nothing to forgive," she said briskly. "You are the one who analyzed the data that led us here. Just in time, it would seem. They were going to—going to . . ."

She couldn't say it.

"Yes," SjillaTen said. "It is my hypothesis that disassembly of his corporeal body was to be used as some kind of threat against Ball. They are playing for high stakes on Ptolemy. I contacted you for a reason."

"Where are you?"

"I'm still in the InterGal facility, Sweet Repose. The troops have it fully secured. We will turn it over to the local authorities and let them handle protection of the other bodies here. Governor Somenon is being most cooperative. We retain control of the administrative offices. We have found something very strange."

"What?"

"We have found Shelly Mesec, a native of the planet Cascade."

"Cascade? I'm not even sure I know it. So what?"

"Shelly Mesec was a famous children's poet. The Space Rat Saga?"

"I read that to my son! You remember everything?"

"A good memory is recommended for intelligence work." A touch of his dry humor. "Shelly Mesec died fourteen years ago, before your son was born. She died on Ptolemy."

"Ptolemy again? That does it!" Taft opened a separate channel and ordered *Forthright*'s commander to recall all landing craft and prepare for a jump. "You found Mesec's body?" she asked.

"No. We have her, alive and healthy. She has been infected, but she is supremely healthy. The medics say the infection is the reason for her superb health."

"Infected by what? What kind of infection causes health?"

"She is host to a sybil virus."

Despite herself, Taft felt a jolt of primal fear. "The sybil is here? Out of Terran Service control? On Belkin's World? So your analysis about the Blocked Worlds blockade being compromised was correct, too. My God—get out of there! We'll have to sterilize—"

"No." His negative cut across her words. "She is isolated in a creche. Her sybil is more or less controlled by a chip. A chip we have never encountered before. But it is clearly an InterGal design. Wholly new, radical. We are trying to map its architecture and function now. The sybil infestation is full-blown, but she is the only one infected. There is no more of the virus here. Nor, presumably, anywhere else on Belkin's World."

"Somenon will have to deal with a search, just to make sure. What in space was InterGal doing with a sybil symbiote all the way out here?"

"We have the director of the facility under interrogation now. He was equipped with state-of-the art synthetic shields. Commercial-secrets grade. InterGal design, of course, the very best. It took a little while to break him. But we are getting it now. InterGal has been using sybil-infected human brains to effectuate some form of quantum communications across space."

"Quantum communication?"

"Effectively instantaneous. No wonder their intelligence lately was always better—well, faster—than ours."

"Bring her."

"Of course. Wait one—" Then, "We are getting a recall. You initiated it?"

"Yes. Bring her. Bring the director. Bring anybody and everything you need. Our warrant covers it all. Work on them here aboard ship. We're going to Ptolemy. Right now."

*F*orthright was absolutely silent in its passage through quantum probability. Or so it seemed to SjillaTen. Somewhere on the distant bridge mathematicians and immensely powerful computers ceaselessly calculated their chances of a peaceful reentry into Einsteinian reality approximately where they wanted to be. Failing that, at least a peaceful reentry somewhere. Since the Terran Service fleet had the best record in existence, the odds were good they would succeed, and the chances of total failure vanishingly small. Still, there was that little niggle of worry in the back of his mind. He decided he had been planet-bound too long.

He sat across from Adrienne Taft in a roomy cell in *Forthright*'s high-security cell-block. The cell was featureless and to all appearances motionless. It could have existed anywhere—anywhere at all. Right now, he mused, anywhere at all was as accurate as any other statement about its existence.

He found himself yearning for the tread of boots down the corridor outside, a creak of metal or sigh of plastic, a hum from some electronic device—anything to indicate life or motion. The rustle of his uniform was startlingly loud when he shifted in his seat. The two security troopers by the door twitched, then controlled their reflexes. They were countrymen, but their high-keyed lethality annoyed him. *Forthright*'s captain had insisted upon their presence before Adrienne Taft could view the sybil symbiote up close. Well, skipper's privilege; she hadn't balked, and SjillaTen could live with it.

Taft had been gazing down into the creche that replaced the cell's furnishings. Its occupant was a voluptuous blonde, her nude form lax in deep sleep. Now Taft glanced at her subordinate.

"I keep thinking I should have put her in my stateroom to keep him company," she said wistfully. "He always had an eye for the light-haired ones." Then she caught his gloomy mood. "What?"

"Yin and Yang," SjillaTen said. "Being and nothingness entwined in the great mystery. Since we are going to Ptolemy, I have been studying a little. Every culture has an expression for it. Yin and Yang is popular on Ptolemy. They almost make a religion of it there. Right now—insofar as *now* means anything—we are part of the great nothingness."

"I never thought of you as a philosopher," she said.

"Did you know that our brain cells are supposed to be engaged in a constant struggle for supremacy as to which of them shall form our brain's view of the outside reality? To build a bridge of awareness to our own private inside reality?"

"Where are you getting this stuff?" Taft asked.

"I seem to get moody in deep-space travel these days," the Llralan said.

"I find that interesting. Llralans were in space long before we were. Granted, you had more nearby solar systems to tempt you out. But generations of you lived whole chunks of your lives out here, back when you planned to rule all creation." She spared a brief smile for the impassive Llralan troopers. "Remember?"

"We were out here, all right. And the Workagis were out here long before us."

"They're a myth," Taft said.

"Are they? Then a myth smashed Llrala back into the stone age."

"Extremely ancient history," Taft decreed. "You evened the score, eventually. More than evened it. They don't exist anymore."

"Perhaps. They fled, in any event. To some-where. Or somewhen. And left the sybil behind as their watchdog."

"What proof do you have of that?"

He rubbed his face. "Not one scrap. But the sybil is an anomaly. A bad one."

"A dangerous one. Bad is a value judg-ment."

He gave his version of a smile. "On worlds where sentient life of your and my kind evolved, it generally was preceded by two to five billion sidereal years of bacterial evolution. Simple organisms, transferring energy from sunlight and carbon dioxide into oxygen. Then came the mutation to the so-called smart cell, with its glucose-processing machinery. And its internalized reproductive blueprint, which strongly resembles a bacterium. Add another odd billion years or so for this type cell to perfect itself. From that kind of cell, we are told, subsequent life developed. A more or less common blueprint for life on worlds like Llrala and Earth. Our nerve cells are said to closely resemble that mutant cell."

Taft was studying the sleeping blonde again. "So what?"

"Viruses are usually very old," the Llralan said. "Perhaps as old as bacteria. Some say a virus has its own form of alien intelligence, of a sort. Some say a virus exists only as a potential—not really alive, not really anything—until triggered into action by a suitable host cell. A virus can coexist with a more complex host organism and feed off it, or kill it. But the sybil does far more. Its physical features change to mimic brain cells of any host species it can attach to. It accomplishes this so perfectly that the brain incorporates the sybil into its neuronal structure. Given free rein, it then takes over control of the host brain. It goes against reason the sybil is a natural virus. It is almost as if it was designed—by someone or something—to *rule*."

"You're starting at shadows," Taft said. "I'm a little surprised. As long as we keep the sybil confined to the Blocked Worlds, or harnessed to our use, it's not going to *rule* anything." She tapped the cover of the creche. "You think it knows we're here? That it's been captured, so to speak?"

"Do you have any idea the panic it would cause at headquarters if they knew you were this close to a wild-state sybil?"

She made a dismissive gesture. "It's not completely wild-state. There's an InterGal chip controlling it. The creche is fully sealed. Self-contained. This is the most secure section of *Forthright*. It cannot escape. Even if it could somehow infect us, it could not escape the cell-block."

He noticed the troopers shift slightly, nervously. They were superb fighters, but this was too close to ghost-talk. He knew the feeling. "You experienced immediate alarm when I told you there was sybil on Belkin's," he said.

She nodded. "Point taken. That was before I knew it was controlled by InterGalactic nanotechnology. But the question still needs answering: who put the sybil there? Who infected this poor woman? Why?"

"All unknowns at this point," SjillaTen said. "But we may find some answers on Ptolemy."

"Yes. Those sanctimonious navel-gazers. I may just slap a protectorate order on His Excellency for starters."

"It would be viewed as retaliation for his protest," the Llralan said.

"Good, then! Maybe others will decide in the future that public attempts to embarrass this administration aren't that smart."

SjillaTen said nothing. She was working herself up. He had seen it many times.

"Our next phase-shift for signals traffic, do this: order JonHoward Tomas taken into custody. Safety of the Commonwealth," she went on. "We may have to break InterGalactic up as a warning to overly ambitious companies. Execute a few people. We don't play that card yet. We may let InterGal sacrifice Tomas to us. But the sybil is absolutely *not* to be trifled with. I'll give you that much."

He nodded. That was safe to agree to.

She tapped the creche again. "Could the creche awaken her?"

"Only if her sybil would permit it. She was highly stressed when I tried to talk to her. Kept muttering about things which must not be mentioned. Almost like a mantra."

"A mantra?"

"Another Ptolemaic expression," the Llralan said. "Sorry. It means something like an article of faith."

"Things that must not be mentioned. It has a ring, doesn't it? Maybe she was a bureaucrat in another life?"

SjillaTen smiled dutifully. "My research indicates the term is a formal rule used in something called a Renga. A chain of poems by different poets. I had the impression she expected to participate in such a chain momentarily. But the only Renga to which I could find reference occurs on Ptolemy. And is taking place as we speak. My assumption is that she meant to participate from Belkin's World."

"Communicate all the way to Ptolemy?"

"That is my assumption."

"Let's wake her up, see if she can."

SjillaTen took a breath. "To what point? We

do not exist in our native time and space now. How could she communicate with anyone?"

"There is no transmitter of any kind built into her creche, right? Not in the creche, not in her body. Yet she can communicate across those distances, according to those you interrogated."

"You listened to the tapes," the Llralan said.

"Perhaps it's some kind of cult. She could have been dreaming. A kind of dreaming. Maybe she was communicating to her sybil, and vocalizing. You know, like children with their imaginary playmates."

SjillaTen considered it. "That's not something Llralan children experience."

"You actually believe she can talk to someone far away. The prisoners say she can. So how does she do it? Some kind of telepathy? Do you believe in that stuff?"

"According to the creche printouts, sybil activity was abnormally high during the episode. And her brain was functioning at furious speed. The prisoners say, and it is reasonable to infer, that the sybil was the agency of the communication, in some way we cannot understand."

"So we awaken her, and perform an experiment. What if the sybil can communicate from here to normal space and time?"

"That would be extraordinary," SjillaTen said uneasily.

"You mean the fact we're having this conversation at all is *not* extraordinary?"

"I would prefer to wait until we learn more from the InterGalactic functionaries we arrested."

"One can analyze data to death," Taft said decisively. "Let's try to wake her up."

PART FOUR

Kyoku

(Center)

Blood the sacrament,
Blood stained with awful things.
Strict shikimoku.
An untold lust worse than death
Haunts the dreamer of the dream.

After what seemed a subjective eternity, Alex Schodt's aircar finally was back within the defense screens of the InterGalactic facility down the river from Tezuka. Not for one second, out under the unprotected sky, had he managed to relax. His primitive brain had been shrieking in terror, expecting to be vaporized into nothing. He already was terrified of Ball, and the emperor of Ptolemy had changed before his eyes into a bloodthirsty stranger.

There was a reception committee outside the administration building, led by his unconscious mercenary colonel's subordinate officer.

"Wait one," the captain said crisply. "My Rongor sergeant major is scanning for bugs or bombs."

"Our outer screens—"

"Can be fiddled, if we're up against the Terran Service, sir." The captain might have been a clone of his commanding officer: lean, weathered, disciplined and deadly.

The robot loomed at the captain's shoulder.

"Yes, S-M?"

"The vessel is clear, sah!" The Rongor's pronunciation was arcane. The Rongor engineers who built his prototype were a long time dead. "But the occupants, sah—both are chipped, sah!"

Schodt felt his blood seem to freeze. "Spy chips or destructors?" he choked out.

"Sophisticated, sah. Characteristics concealed."

"God*damn* that Ball!" Schodt said fervently.

"Easy, sir," the mercenary captain soothed. Was there an edge of contempt beneath his professional demeanor? "The white room will neutralize them. S-M! Carry the colonel in, please!"

"Sah!" the robot barked.

Schodt followed the killing machine meekly. Two other Rongors moved swiftly out of sight, to reassume perimeter watch. The captain and his two lieutenants followed Schodt. The S-M dumped the unconscious mercenary commander on a pullout drawer and departed.

"Vet us both carefully," Schodt said. "The Rongor says we're chipped."

"Deactivating," said the tech. And then: "Three in him, two in you, this time."

"Five damn chips?" Schodt pushed furiously at his hair. "Check again. Be very thorough, damn it! Ball must manufacture the damn things!"

"All clear," the tech said.

"It'll have to do. They'll check me downstairs again anyway."

He left the mercenaries to wait for a medic

to rouse their commander. Before he went below, he stopped in his darkened office for a mood-stabilizer tablet. He chased it with a more ancient remedy, a neat jolt of Old Earth scotch. The tablet calmed him almost at once, and the scotch lit a smooth fire in his belly. He began to believe he might still be functional.

Tony and Mary, the two canaries, were sleeping side by side on their branch, heads tucked. His assistant must have blocked sound into their cage to prevent disturbing them. A nice touch of normalcy. All seemed right in their abbreviated avian world. Tony must have sung his new song and won her, Schodt decided. The room would have recorded it. He felt an almost physical ache to pause longer and listen to the new song. But his sense of urgency had not been dulled by the medication or the whiskey. He left quietly and went back to work.

The second white room found no more Terran Service plants in his body. His assistant waited beyond the room, her body molded by a filmy translucent jumpsuit of cool green. To his distress, Schodt found the effect arousing. Well, he had been close to death, and death had that primal effect on humans. He controlled himself and paid attention to her attitude. She didn't look seductive, she looked tense.

"Something's gone wrong," she told him. "We tried to activate the Raven chip. It won't activate. He—She—Whatever, is still alive. Still in play."

Schodt swore. "How is that possible? I paid that local med team good money to verify it was in place and functional. It's one of our competition's best designs, damn it!"

"Well, something happened. It's not working."

Schodt rubbed his face, which felt hot from the liquor. "Well, Ball is neutralized for the moment. Soon to be neutralized permanently, I hope. We have Baka Martin under control. But she's almost certainly Terran Service. I wanted a clean sweep. Do you have any *good* news?"

"Our people have begun to brief the orbiting media about the sybil project, right on schedule," she said. "Reaction has been gratifying. They're clamoring for more, for interviews with the poets, for a real-time demonstration—the works."

Schodt relaxed a little more. "All as predicted. We'll let them stew a bit. Get the initial story out. Then we announce an attempt to steal our secrets from that facility where Ball is. After the explosions."

She bit her lip. "There are a couple of unexpected twists. I'm not sure they're important—"

"Everything is important now! Tell me!"

"Well—one of the news hens in orbit has been analyzing the contents of the poetry. She took our people by surprise. She says the poets want out. That their words hint at enslavement. She wants proof they are operating under their own free will. Our own semanticists confirm

Galatis did seem to set that tone, and Trane followed it."

Schodt swore violently. "God*damn* that Arthur! I told you before to check this—before the Renga began. Why didn't you—"

"We did. Our people confirmed he seemed to be hinting at things he should not remember. But he's done that before. And the actual Renga is under control of the Tezuka monks. We can't edit beforehand."

"This news hen is persistent?"

"Persistent!" She gave a grim smile. "Yes, I would say so. She wants to talk to you. Only you."

"Impossible. I don't do interviews."

"She says she reports directly to Tanner at A.N. Central. Tanner's a heavyweight, boss. Even JonHoward answers when he calls."

"Okay, then. When Tanner calls, I will answer, too. Not until then. What else?"

"Miriam has been calling for you," his assistant said. "She has an urgent transmission coming in."

"She has? For how long? Why wasn't I told? JonHoward—"

"It's not from Arthur," she said. "It's Shelly."

He stared at her with a dreadful, sinking feeling. "Shelly? On Belkin's World? That's not possible! I was just going to ask Miriam to transmit to Shelly."

"Well, for some reason Shelly's terrified she'll miss her turn at the Renga. The monk on watch insisted she wait her turn. Shelly's very eager to talk to you."

In the creche, Miriam was restless, tossing

and turning. Her eyelids fluttered as if her eyes followed hidden things. Schodt was careful to bow to the robed Tezuka monk. He recognized him as one of Inaba's disciples. The monk serenely returned the bow, oblivious as the canaries upstairs.

"Miriam?"

"Alex?" She gave something like a groan. "At last! Shelly won't leave me alone. She's so impatient for her turn in the Renga."

"That's up to the academic monks, Miriam."

"But she's so frightened . . ."

"Frightened? Frightened about something happening on Belkin's World?"

"Yes. Shall I tell you her tanka, Alex?"

"Wait!"

He glanced at his assistant. She immediately linked arms with the monk and leaned her body against him. Her shimmering attire made a stark contrast to his rough robe. She smiled up into his eyes.

"Perhaps we can take a break until it's Shelly's turn?"

The monk's eyes glittered with interest. Celibacy was not a feature of his avocation. They went away. Schodt felt a momentary pang. She was the best assistant he had ever had, and he used her this way. But no time to repent now.

"Who's trying to reach me from Belkin's World, Miriam? The Sweet Repose director?"

"No . . ." She frowned in concentration. "Shelly is. Shelly by herself. She's afraid. The director doesn't come see her anymore. She's not on Belkin anymore, Alex! She's—She doesn't know where she is. She can't remember. Strangers have been talking to her. She thinks they have. She is so—so afraid. Poor baby. Please talk to her."

Schodt wanted nothing more urgently than to talk to Shelly right then. Something was dreadfully wrong. But he was careful to initiate and double-check the procedures that Tony's feathered tribe had inspired. He goaded Miriam's sybil into opening neuronal linkages in her brain that would close behind the pending conversation with no memory of it. It was the best he could do. There was no way to know what was going on at Shelly's end until he asked.

It took a matter of minutes before Miriam was in full sybil-link, ready to pass along every incoming word verbatim, and remember none of them.

"Shelly?" he said tentatively. "It's Alex, Shelly. Do you remember who I am?"

Miriam's voice developed a singsong quality, as if Shelly had reverted to childhood under stress. "Hello, Alex. Miriam says you're her contact with the other world. Miriam says you're very nice. Mine was very nice, too, but he's gone. I don't know where. It was almost my turn in the Renga! It's not fair!"

"You'll get your turn," Schodt said reassuringly. "Do you know what happened? Who came there? Who talked to you?"

"Strange people! They asked me things!

They tried to get the creche to give me drugs. Strange drugs, Alex! Of course, my muse wouldn't let them, though—"

"Muse?"

"Some of us call our sybil their muse," she said. "Like a benevolent spirit to aid our writing. The drugs would have made me try to remember *shikimoku*."

Schodt keyed his console to pick that term off the recording and search for its meaning. "Say that last phrase again, Shelly. Shi—what?"

"*Shikimoku*," Miriam said impatiently, making a great show of sounding out each syllable slowly. "The things that must not be mentioned. Listen now—

> *Strict shikimoku.*
> *Lost in the Great Nothingness*
> *How can I answer*
> *Unremembered questions?*
> *The queen of swords approaches.*"

He keyed queen of swords. "You mean they wanted you to tell them about past conversations you have had?"

"Ohhhhh," Miriam sighed. "I don't know what I mean. Maybe I'm confused. Not every Renga has things that must not be mentioned, but a lot of them do. This one does. Remember Arthur's first tanka?"

Schodt controlled himself with an effort. "Shelly—did these bad people ask you about conversations you conducted for your, um—

other-world contact? Conversations you conducted for the director of your facility?"

"What conversations, Alex? And I didn't say they were *bad* people." If Miriam's facial expressions accurately portrayed Shelly's, the latter was pouting. "I said they were *strange*. Doesn't mean *bad*."

Schodt choked on an oath it would have given him immense release to utter. "Who were these strange people, Shelly?"

"I don't know. People from the other world. The world I used to know." Miriam gave a theatric sigh.

His screen bloomed with words. He read quickly. "This queen of swords. An ancient myth-figure. One bad babe, Shelly. Are you *warning* me? Where are you now, Shelly?"

"Where I always am."

"On Belkin's World?"

"No, silly—in my creche."

"And where is your creche?"

"I'm—I don't know."

"Are you saying this queen of swords is with you? Are you trying to tell us something?" He wondered remotely what JonHoward Tomas would think of this mad conversation.

"Shhh!" Miriam said. "She's talking to me."

"Who is?" Schodt felt a surge of hope. Maybe Shelly was just having some kind of emotional jag because of this damned Renga. These *damn* poets—

"I think I've got this figured out," Miriam said.

Her syntax had changed, become measured and authoritative. Whoever Miriam was mimicking now, it certainly was not the addled Shelly. Schodt's hope died as quickly as it had flared.

"I talk to you," Miriam said, "and you communicate with somebody else like you, who conveys my words to someone at the other end. What I don't understand yet is how the sybil sends the communication. Nothing known can communicate from where we are to sidereal space."

Schodt held his breath, speechless. His assistant of course took that moment to return with the monk, who was grinning like an idiot. He sobered instantly when Schodt looked at him.

"It is Shelly's turn in the Renga," he said.

Schodt motioned him to silence.

He stiffened, but did not speak.

"Who are you?" Schodt whispered to Miriam.

"Hello?" Miriam said. "Hello? I know Shelly just transmitted my words to you. Who are you? Where are you? This is the Commonwealth Executive. I am in the process of executing a Commonwealth Court warrant. Are you located on Ptolemy? Identify yourself and your location, please. At once."

Schodt shut off the mike with a spastic twitch. "The queen of swords!" he muttered.

"Oh, my God!" his assistant said. Her voice shook.

The monk turned on his heel and left.

"*Strict shikimoku.
Lost in the great nothingness
How can I answer
Unremembered questions?
The queen of swords approaches.*"

I was sitting on the afterdeck of Raven's houseboat, reading the words off my 'corder screen. They represented the ninth tanka of the Renga. Whoever my fellow participants were besides Galatis and Trane, they had been clicking right along. This one seemed to have swerved a long way off the theme of blood and tears Galatis established. Raven was below-decks. I thought about asking her about the obscure first line of this tanka, but decided to exercise my research skills. My 'corder tapped into a local library and came back with the answer fast enough.

Shikimoku: the things that must not be mentioned, as in a Renga cycle. Also, a collection of rules and grammar forms. Also see: *Uchikoshi wo kiraukeki mono:* things to be guarded against in the verse just gone.

Well, that was clear as mud. But maybe this poet still was on track, after all.

Things that must not be mentioned resonated with Galatis's *indignities untold* in his
first tanka. Since I was tapped into the library,
I looked up queen of swords as well. It took a
minute or two longer, and turned out to be as
obscure as the first line. The queen of swords
was a card in a tarot deck, some ancient form
of fortune-telling. From the description of her
properties, she did not sound like somebody
you would want as an enemy. I knew one
woman like that, at least by reputation.
Adrienne Taft, the Commonwealth Executive. I
couldn't help but wonder if the verse was a sly
dig at Taft's ruckus with the local emperor.

I still was reading about the tarot deck
when an incoming message chimed. Master
Inaba's features popped into focus on my
screen.

"The ninth tanka completes the first
round," he said. "Nine poets are participating
this year. The first poet will now pick up the
link." My notes said a master enforced the
rules. Inaba was the only person I had encountered with the title of master, but beyond
telling me my position in the order, this was the
first thing resembling an instruction he had
issued.

Well, that meant I had two more tankas to
absorb before it was my turn again. I discon-
nected from the library and tapped into the
region news digest. Ptolemy was high on the
budget. I pulled the news story up and leaned
back. A keen wind had sprung up in mid-
morning. The rigging of the moored sailboats

in the boat basin hummed and chimed. The temperature had dropped dramatically, but the thermostat on my Ptolemy coverall had adjusted nicely. The slanting rain had turned cold on my exposed face, but my old long-billed *twon*-hunting cap shielded my eyes. The change in weather felt good.

But the news story didn't.

InterGalactic Cybernetics had announced that four of the nine poets participating in this year's Renga were off-planet. Way, way off-planet. One on Old Earth, one on Belkin's World, one on WhitePeyton, and one on Carbonal. Thousands of light-years in between. Tens of thousands, all told. They were participating through some brand new technology patented and extensively tested by InterGal, which made transmission effectively instantaneous, just as Inaba had hinted. But the thing that made my skin crawl was the reference to the Blocked World parasite, the sybil. The poets all were symbiotes, including Miriam Trane, here on Ptolemy.

And InterGal was charging that the Terran Service had tried to stop the experiment. Alleging that Terran Service operatives had been busy on Ptolemy, trying to ruin a simple poetry exhibition, because the Commonwealth wanted exclusive use of the sybil.

It was one hell of a news story. And I thought Inaba had promised it to me.

I was trying to raise him on my 'corder when Raven came out onto the afterdeck, squinting her fine eyes against the rain. It took me a moment to register that she was carrying my ammunition belt. Something looked odd about it. I realized half the rounds threaded into its loops seemed to have turned soot-black.

"What's this, now?" I said. "Some kind of oxidation?"

She handed me the belt. "Before we hunted the wingfingers, I said I would have my analyzer build you cartridges suitable for local use. The dark ones are color-coded so you won't get your ammunition confused."

"Makes sense. Are we going hunting again?"

"Not exactly. Those are not hunting rounds. They are smart bombs."

"Smart bombs? Something like my pencil-bombs?"

"More complex. Programmed and self-guided. Their main propellant doesn't kick in until the projectile achieves three thousand feet per second. Then they seek the targets they are programmed to kill."

"Programmed by whom?" I was having a little trouble untangling my thoughts from the Renga research.

"You seem confused, Keith Ramsey."

"I am."

"We are getting under way immediately. Simply Ball believes a mercenary squad may be en route to attack us."

"Ball? He's been in communication with you?"

"We must get moving." She was tense, but not afraid. "Arm yourself, Keith Ramsey. The squad may include Rongor battle robots. It will certainly contain Ptolemaic gunmen."

"Cyborgs?"

"Yes."

"Why not call in the emperor's security forces? Aren't they still babysitting us?"

She made an impatient gesture. "Keith Ramsey, we may be *talking* about the emperor's security forces."

We were under way in less than ten local minutes. There were short, choppy whitecaps out in the main channel of Civilization River. Raven's houseboat sliced through them with only a faint hull vibration. She turned downstream and throttled up. The boat began to really move. She activated the autopilot, went to the weapons rack and handed me my rifle.

"Load the new rounds," she said simply.

"Why does it feel like we're running away?"

"We are taking evasive action. You wish to fight a pitched battle with Rongors and cyborg gunmen?"

"This doesn't make any sense. I'm a guest of the emperor. And I'm a Certified news hawk."

She touched something on the panel and the gun rack folded out into the room.

Behind her hunting battery was another rack of weapons. Heavy-duty Colt-Vickers beam guns. She selected two and closed the panel.

"I know you have used a beamer on Pondoro," she said. "We may need these."

She clamped one into a set of brackets by the helm and placed the other on the dinette couch. I loaded my seven gun with the ominous-looking dusky cartridges and put it next to the Colt-Vickers on the couch.

"We'll need to secure those when we make open sea," she said. "If we make open sea."

"This is crazy," I said. "Ball thinks we are in some danger?"

"Yes. He told me that after they tried to terminate me."

"He told you *what*?" Simple questions seemed to get confusing answers. "*Who* tried to terminate you?"

"InterGalactic Cybernetics," she said. "I should be offended. I'm a customer." She gave a tight smile. "I purchased one of their erotic programs sometime back. The Keith Ramsey version. A pale rendition of the reality, I should add."

This was no time to pick up that line of conversation. "InterGalactic is all over the news right now," I said. "Sounds like they've invented another way to manufacture money. Why would a corporation that huge attempt to murder a Tezuka U. teaching assistant? And when did they try it?"

She shrugged. "They set me up for assassination several days ago, so they have been planning it for some time. They're the ones who chipped that last flock of wingfingers to attack, and killed my boat's electronics. The dactyl that cut me implanted a remotely controlled self-destruct chip. Every one of that flock was equipped for such an injection. The medical team that examined me afterward was bribed to confirm to InterGalactic that the chip was in place and operational."

The boat juttered a bit as we hit rougher water. My seven gun slipped toward the edge of the couch. I took my cap off and bunched it up under the forearm to add some friction. The rifle stopped moving around.

"Isn't it a pretty long run to the ocean?" I said.

"Over a hundred kilometers by river."

"So all they have to do is patrol the river."

"Yes. But Simply Ball plans a diversion."

"Uh-oh," I said.

She nodded grimly. "They will be busy."

"You told me how they planned to kill you, not why. And why go to such elaborate steps? Get the emperor involved in a diplomatic protest? All that?"

"As for shifting the blame for the attack to Old Earth, that was part of a larger scheme," she said calmly. "As to why they want to terminate me, I am a Terran Service spy."

I sat down, heavily, on the stock of my rifle. "You?"

"I am the local agent-in-place. I have been here some time, trying to find my way into a secret Ptolemy project that has the Service worried."

"I think it may not be a secret any longer," I said. "InterGal is talking about some program of theirs right now. They say the Commonwealth wanted it stopped. It involves the damned sybil parasite!"

"Yes, it does. That's why I was second choice

for the mission." Her tone was wry. "Ball and the symbiote, Python, were first choice—but the Executive sent them to Pondoro instead." I noticed she no longer was using the local form of address for Ball. Just as well; he had never known a simple moment in his existence.

"Is Ball still a Terran Service operative?"

"Are you recording all this?"

"It's what I do, remember?"

She leaned against the steering console. "I really don't know what his Service status is. But I was directed to assist him. He has discovered that InterGal is running this secret project, not Ptolemy."

"Old news now." I gestured to the 'corder. "But you're saying the company has coopted a Commonwealth planet? That's a whole different angle!"

"Ball said you would be pleased."

"Why didn't he talk to me himself?"

"You're not equipped with secured Terran Service channels. He suspects your 'corder is being monitored."

"Another crime," I said. "Interfering with the public's right to know. Better and better. Tell me: what do you know about activation here of a Baka Martin clone? If Ball still is in the Service, he was trying to reanimate his field man."

She tilted her head and smiled at me tenderly. "Ah, where has all the romance gone, Keith Ramsey? You use your words now to interrogate me, not seduce me."

"Raven—"

She straightened. "It's all right, love. Truly. It's actually why Ball wanted you here. To blow the lid off, if our operation began to fall apart. And it certainly has begun to fall apart. That InterGal spotted me is bad enough. That they dared to coldly plan execution of a Service op is worse. The stakes here must be very high."

"They're damned high, if what I see in the news is accurate. Amazingly high."

"Just as we feared."

"Where the hell is Ball?"

"He's pretty much hemmed in by a strong force of Rongor battle robots and cyborgs. They're taking no chances with him. They must know by now he spotted the chip they planted in me, neutralized it, and set up a relay so he would know when they tried to use it. Of course he recorded the whole exercise for evidence. He trapped them very neatly."

"And how did he do all that?"

"He spotted it, of course, on the day of the attack. He said nothing to me then. He arranged to neutralize it later, under circumstances they never would suspect. That would leave me free to move if something happened to him. The centopod injected me with a Terran Service hunter-seeker that killed the InterGal chip. And thoroughly confused InterGal by creating a second incident involving you, when none had been ordered."

I shuddered at the memory of awakening

with that thing in the cabin with us. "That slimy damn thing was *Ball's* doing?"

"Ball is the best we ever had," she said with admiration. "I hope the Executive will pardon him and let him come back to the Service."

*I*t was like a dream, and yet as real as anything he had ever experienced. They were by a forest pool at the base of a sheer bluff, down which a dramatic waterfall tumbled. Chill mist off the waterfall drifted thrillingly across their heated bodies, which sweated in the hot sun. The roar of the water made speech impossible. But speech was totally unnecessary. Baka Martin was in the throes of a passion beyond vocalization. The sensations flooding his wiry athletic body as he embraced Miriam Trane were so intense that he grunted like a beast in rut. He knew her every texture, taste, odor, mingled with the damp smell of the forest and the heat of a sun he had never seen . . .

Even so, at some deep level of awareness a part of him was the eternal observer.

He knew his body still was in a creche, alone. Knew that creche had been programmed to convey the sensual illusion of Miriam's distant body, straining and writhing against his own. Knew his sensitive fingertips and his loins lied to his brain when they seemed to feed back evidence of silken, sweating female flesh. Knew—

"*Oops!*" her voice whispered. All sensation stopped. Just stopped.

The waterfall—the whole scene—Miriam vanished. All was darkness.

Baka Martin's long body quivered in unconscious imitation of an injured snake. He had been named Snake once—no, Python. That was it. Python. He groaned aloud.

Sorry, so sorry, dear.

It was Miriam, speaking to him from her own creche.

I have to go now for a little while. Alex needs me to talk to Arthur about Shelly. And Arthur will be—well, Arthur.

Martin had a fleeting image from her—instantly suppressed—of previous erotic episodes with this Arthur. Who in the name of creation was Shelly?

My best friend. My colleague. Poor Arthur. All this activity will excite him so. I need to compose myself sufficiently to deal with him. You have me so stirred up, I don't know if I can. Hold the thought, love. I'll be back as soon as I can—"

A powerful, unfamiliar emotion roared through Martin, shaking him to his depths. He actually tried to sit up. Cracked his skull painfully against the creche lid and sank back in confusion. Had he really forgotten he was imprisoned? His pulse was hammering, his breathing was uncontrolled, and his whole being felt sickened and weakened by this new rage pouring through him.

Jealousy. He was jealous.

Miriam thought she had carefully concealed all memory of her trysts with Arthur from him during their lovemakings. Her confidence was bolstered by a long lifetime of practice in multiple relationships. But she had not calculated the power of Python's peculiar mind, enhanced by the sybil-bonding. Martin knew this woman. Knew her as perhaps she did not know herself. And loved her, insofar as he understood that ambiguous term. Loved her, complete with all her variegated experience of lust and love, which made her what she was, this overpoweringly sensual creature who drove him wild without actually touching him. But this Martin body, despite the years of life-experience transmitted into its new brain, was desperately young in the ways of the flesh. He had poured all his considerable emotion into this strange out-of-body relationship.

He had not considered how he would react when Miriam abandoned him abruptly for another.

It hurt. It hurt beyond anything he had ever known. Physical pain of crushed bone or ruined ligament or ripped nerve was as nothing compared to this. Couldn't she see that? She had to know. Had to! He could make her know, if only he could—

If he could what?

His mind skittered around crazily. She was probably with Arthur already, sweat-damp and love-moist from her lovemaking with him, but happily lost in the heat of Arthur's lust, crying out—

He had to know.

Palikar discipline asserted itself then. He lay back and began to compose his breathing. The decision was taken. There was only action now. He would deal with what the action brought when the time came. His muscles began to flex in the incredibly powerful toning rhythms of the Palikar, and his brain settled and steadied. As his thoughts cleared, he perceived that the creche had been trying to extinguish his consciousness, reading his jealous rage as a kind of fever. The sybil had blocked the creche attempt, of course. He almost smiled.

"We can find her, you and I, wherever she is," he breathed.

And go to her if necessary.

Had that really been his parasite, answering him? Impossible to know. But he suddenly was confident he could do just that. His mind began to quest outward. And found her, right away.

He knew a relief so swift it was almost sickening. She was reciting another tanka. It wasn't Miriam's work. He didn't know how he knew. It was Arthur's. The Renga was on its second cycle.

"Blood the sacrament,
Blood stained with awful things.
Strict shikimoku.
An untold lust worse than death
Haunts the dreamer of the dream."

His relief was supplanted instantly with a kind of sinking dread. With his own emotions roused and aching, Python felt a powerful empathic reaction to the words. Arthur still mourned the loss of his presymbiotic independence. Still retained enough of that independence to shape his words cunningly.

Arthur feared his sybil. Feared it was trying to break out of the artificial stasis imposed on it by his InterGal chip. Trying to breed. He was trying to warn Miriam. . . .

Against all reason, Python felt a powerful kinship with this Arthur. A linking. His body stiffened. He did not want to feel kinship with someone he might have to kill. . . . Kill? Why would he have to kill Arthur? The thought of Arthur dead brought instant grief. As if a part of himself would die if Arthur died. They were linked. By their love of Miriam? That, yes, but by something far more powerful. What could be more powerful? His mind was whirling again.

The sybil. They were linked by the sybil.

His thought, or that of his parasite? It didn't matter. He saw it now, with crystalline certainty. Those who carried the sybil were one, indivisible. Arthur was wrong to be afraid. Those who would use the symbiotes to their own purposes were the enemy. Those who imprisoned Python here. Those who kept sweet Miriam locked away from him.

His sybil . . . shifted. He groaned again. He heard a voice as clearly as if it spoke directly to him. But it was speaking to Miriam.

"We don't have time for this, Miriam. I have interceded with Master Inaba, and apologized for interrupting the Renga."

Martin heard the words as she heard them. But he recognized something about the mind behind those words, a familiar neural pattern. The speaker had been present for his reanimation. Schodt? Yes.

"We must suspend the Renga this instant!" Schodt was saying. *"Is JonHoward there?"*

"Isn't JonHoward always here when you are, Alex? Alex, why are you so afraid, poor baby?"

Martin fidgeted. It was almost as if he had uttered those words himself. Miriam was aware of him. She knew he had reestablished contact. He knew she needed his support. For a brief instant he felt her welcoming emotion.

Then she was gone, as quickly and as completely as the waterfall illusion.

He writhed in frustration. She had forgotten his existence! Just like that! He could no longer reach her. It was as if her forgetfulness had exorcised him entirely. Had damned him into nonexistence. His teeth ground in frustration. Something was controlling her sybil. Harnessing it. Forcing it to do things to her!

Her InterGal governor, of course. The same one that imposed stasis on her sybil and prevented proliferation. His memory attempted to supply ancient background-briefing material on the dangers to humanity from such a proliferation. Stumbled.

Drew back, the memories unretrieved. He was diverted by a powerful sense of urgency.

He had to get out of this contraption.

He had to go to Miriam. What they were doing to her was wrong, terribly wrong. Together, they would find a way to Arthur—and the others. There were others, too, very far away, involved in this poetry cycle. He could sense them now, four of them besides Miriam, widely scattered. It did not occur to him to question how easily he located them throughout such a vast reach of spacetime. It seemed more amazing that he had not noticed them before, since they all were bonded to the sybil. Each was imprisoned, just as he was, in a creche. Of course they were—so their bodies could provide enough glucose to drive their altered brains to the intensity needed for deep contact. None seemed, at first encounter, to have the native paranormal aptitude for which Python had tested so high as an Old Earth foundling. He probed deeper, seeking rapport, and almost cried out.

There were others enslaved. Many others. Hundreds.

Distant sparks of awareness flared in his brain. Each existed at a distant coordinate in Einsteinian spacetime—and each simultaneously was *here.* Scattered across unimaginable distances—yet he imagined them. More than imagined them, *felt* them. Knew them. Knew their situations. All were imprisoned in creches. All were sybil symbiotes, their parasites as strong as his own. All labored to transmit messages between their prisons at near instant speed. All were in the indentured service of the forces behind this Schodt.

Linked by the sybil, a gossamer webbing of thought had been spun across the stars by the prisoners. Not of their own free will. Not at the behest of sybil. Not in pursuit of some great common service to all sentience.

All this imprisonment, all this isolated loneliness, all this pain—to enrich an already rich corporation.

He had to escape.

But for all his considerable physical might, enhanced by the sybil, he didn't think he could smash out of the creche. There was insufficient room for leverage. He was helpless—

Not helpless. Never helpless. There are many ways to escape.

Again, his thought? Or that of the sybil? He felt a flash-fire of bone-deep fear run through him. A remembered fear from somewhere else. From Pondoro. He recognized that fear instantly. It came from where he had learned to be afraid for the first time in his adult life: Pondoro. It was greer-fear.

But he was not afraid. He was *generating* the fear.

From that other lifetime—that other incarnation—his reanimated memory dredged up a sentence he had uttered there: *They send that fear—and then they hunt!*

Use it? Use the fear?

"How can I? Oh, how . . . ?"

But he could. Or his parasite could. He caught his breath at the wonder of it. His sybil parasite that had died with his previous incarnation on Pondoro had not died in vain, after all. It had absorbed, and somehow communicated to the Blocked Worlds, the paranormal power of the greer. Impossible. Magical. Terrifying.

But terror was his ally now.

He became aware of nearby life-forms in the university research wing, going about their daily tasks. Some of those were charged with his well-being. The creche had alerted those to the storm raging within his brain. Their attention was turned now to him. They already were concerned. If that concern were to turn to alarm, and then to outright fear, perhaps someone would come and release him.

Almost as his thought formed, he sensed uneasiness on the part of one particular woman who had somehow been instrumental in his reanimation. From somewhere he dredged up a mental image of a face accustomed to a hotter sun, and a name—Elizabeth. When he concentrated his attention, her uneasiness increased dramatically.

"What is this now? Am I become like the greer? The beast that clawed me down and destroyed me? How can this be?"

The sybil remembered. The sybil remembered everything. . . .

He focused his blended awareness on Elizabeth of Pythagoras. She was getting extremely nervous about the health of her symbiotic charge. She needed visual reassurance. She was rinsing her cup out with decision, and moving down a corridor. Her footsteps were hurrying now. She was almost running, as the fear drove her toward Python's creche. If she didn't hurry, she would be too late!

She never paused to wonder too late for what.

"**I** said you were a puppet," Ball told the emperor of Ptolemy. "I apologize. You are a sacrificial lamb."

The emperor sat dejectedly at a console vacated by a nanotech. Though there was no visible change to the leisured pace of work going on around them, there was a general mood of resignation. The workers seemed to know their emperor was in trouble. But they didn't know his trouble could have been terminal, and that it could include them all.

"I can't believe JonHoward would have authorized this," the emperor said. "He has guested at my personal table!"

"Maybe he does have a species of conscience," Ball said. "He sent several of his top sector executives to die with you here. The VIP tour you were about to lead when I showed up."

"To plant bombs of that magnitude! Right in the heart of this facility! So many innocent workers! If you had not been here—" The emperor broke off.

"They just miscalculated, that's all," Ball said. "They keep thinking they know all my abilities, and they keep being wrong. I am forced to admit it would have made a grand news story, though. I guess my association with Ramsey is rubbing off on me."

"A news story!" The emperor shuddered. "I have yet to have progeny."

"Relax. You may yet live to see your grand-children." Ball made his laughing sound. "'Emperor dies in plant explosion! Scores killed! Visiting executives among casualties!' I can see it all now. 'Investigators theorize a Terran Service operative, also killed in the blast, was sent to sabotage the facility—'"

"Please," the emperor said weakly. "But how could so many devices have been planted here?"

"Your security is nil." Ball chose a neutral tone. "Any tour group had access to the locations where they were found. You get a lot of visitors from InterGalactic."

"You're positive you found all the bombs? They're all deactivated?"

"I'm still here, aren't I? I value this hide, too, you know."

"Well—those Rongors above. And the cyborgs—"

"Don't insult me," Ball interrupted.

"The moment they try to detonate one of these devices, and it fails, they will send in those troops," the emperor said. "I have one paralyzed and one missing bodyguard. All communications blanketed. And this." He shifted his handgun.

"You have me," Ball told him. "My communications aren't blanketed. And I have work to do. Just see to your guests. They're completely innocent of complicity. Their presence here is proof of that. JonHoward Tomas has an ironic sense of how to fire employees."

He left the emperor staring vacantly at the console and moved swiftly through corridors of the complex. He ignored staff, who shrank away from him. He had found one of the bombs hidden in the drinks cabinet of the executive lounge. Probably Schodt had placed it himself. The perpetually nervous InterGal executive was constantly surprising Ball with his audacity. But in this case, perhaps he had believed it was just a spy device. Each of the miniature devices had contained surveillance equipment as well as a minuscule bomb. Each was small, its size and weight inconsequential. Of course, so was the weight of a sundered atom. But Schodt might not have considered that analogy.

The surveillance features on all the bombs still were operational. Ball had arranged closed-loop recycling of interior videos that showed everyday activities to keep Schodt's surveillance crews happy. He had rigged each bomb to alert him when an activation attempt was made, and identify the origin of the activation signal. Just as he had on the chip they had planted in Raven. Given the chance, it would be strong evidence in Commonwealth Court.

His analysis of the InterGalactic media releases being regurgitated by the orbiting media suggested a detonation signal could come soon. Destruction of the factory that manufactured Schodt's sybilline girdles would be a small price to pay for a windfall of suspicion against the Terran Service. They probably had another such factory already in production, light-centuries from here.

In a detached way, Ball found himself admiring the generalship of JonHoward Tomas. He seemed to have raised commercial warfare to a new pitch. There wasn't much on the public record about the reclusive CEO of InterGal. But if this work on Ptolemy was his signature, then he could give Adrienne Taft a run in the ruthless department. Of course he couldn't be permitted to get away with all this. Taft, for all her bloodthirstiness, was a duly elected representative of the people, subject to the will of the Assembly. Tomas answered only to his shareholders, and their only measurement was the all-sacred bottom line. Commonwealth citizens could suffer and be damned, as long as the stock played well in the financial centers.

Ball wasn't going to allow that.

He paused at the entrance to a service corridor. As the schematics had indicated, it was too narrow to admit him. He hovered for a moment, calculating, and then burst forward. The door and its frame exploded into fragments. He was through. He could have generated a suitable retinal pattern for the lock's receptor, but he was in a hurry.

At the central ducting relays, he levitated near a main grate. This was the junction he'd found in the schematics of the building's files. He spent a moment monitoring airflows and heat exchange. Satisfied, he opened a port in his hide and extruded three slender tubes through the grate. A gentle mist poured out of each tube and wafted away toward the surface.

On the surface, weather monitors fed data to him through the facility's control room. Surface winds were light and variable. He caused baffles here and there throughout the ductwork to open or close, based on the positioning of the war-robots and cyborgs in the surface garden. There were a few cyborgs indoors on the top level as well. With no wind for him to deal with, they succumbed first.

The faint mist, rainbow-hued, descended on them from the facility's vents. Instead of droplets of water, the mist was comprised of vast numbers of germ-size nanomachines. An ancient but very simple and powerful technology. He could churn out large numbers of the tiny devices in his on-board manufacturing complex. It had been simple to reprogram the facility from generation of his own replacement parts to follow blueprints from his extensive software on molecule-size infernal devices. Several varieties now grew rapidly in his element vats, and were conveyored out to the tubes.

The mist in the lobby touched the cyborg gunmen.

Specific synthetic molecules penetrated their pores. Sank into their nasal passages. The cyborgs ran on oxygen and hydraulic blood, to supply glucose to their primate brains. Simian brains, altered and tuned to operate their synthetic bodies with lethal speed and precision.

Their nasal passages were well-filtered against poison gas and other nastiness.

Some of Ball's microscopic machines dissolved the filters.

Others penetrated through to the lungs, and adhered in clusters to the membranes.

The cyborgs died. They died at their posts, choking quietly, without fuss, without realizing they were at risk.

Outside, the light ground currents swirled across the garden, carrying exhalations from the hidden ventwork. The cyborgs in the gardens died as quietly as their indoor fellows. The all-but-invisible mist settled on the ceramoglas casques and limbs of the Rongors.

Clung.

Some of the droplets were programmed to attack the cellular integrity of their tough hides. Ball's droplets ate inward. Ancient Rongor software, programmed for the vicissitudes of awful battles, registered a threat and tried to flush their hides from hidden reservoirs. To no avail. They began to simply rot apart at their posts.

Rongor software had also been programmed for mobility as the ultimate safety. And so they ran. Ran at vehicle speed, in all directions. Emergency calls for assistance flashed across the planet. Ball did not try to interfere with the signals.

He had promised Raven a diversion.

The fleeing robots went down as the droplets ate through crucial circuits or disabled weight-bearing joints. In some, the swift erosion caused weapon-system malfunction. Heavy blaster fire erupted from several points of the compass. One dying Rongor made it through the buffer zone to unclaimed Ptolemy. His weapons fused a wide arc of desert sand to steaming glass. Another exploded dramatically, producing a towering fireball. A third, helpless on its back as a turtle, burned a kilometers-high full-strength beam into the clouds until its power fizzled out.

The fireworks lasted far longer than the Rongors.

Ball found the emperor at a long banquet table, hosting his guests with the grave courtesy of a condemned man.

"Schodt's forces are destroyed," Ball told him. "Make sure no one tries to go above this level for an hour."

"But how—"

"Flush the ductwork before anyone tries to leave. The devices I employed will be inert by then. Safe. Call in your aerial forces now. Put them in holding patterns above a thousand meters. Don't let any of them land for an hour. Spacesuits won't help them. Give them orders to destroy any vehicle or robot approaching this facility."

"You're leaving?" The emperor was clearly alarmed.

Ball's attention had been urgently drawn to readouts from the Baka Martin empathometer while he neutralized Schodt's troops.

Python was on the move.

Ball was torn between an urge to laugh and concern that his partner was about to make another suicide run.

He found it humorous that Schodt had thought to contain a mind like Martin's with the modern equivalent of smoke and mirrors. The InterGal executive couldn't have imagined that Python would embrace the illusion of Miriam Trane so utterly that he would launch his peculiar version of a vision quest to find her. But he remembered too well the obsessive way Martin had suicided on Pondoro, in a doomed attempt to infect the Pondoro wolverine with the sybil virus. The same single-minded determination unreeled relentlessly now on Ball's monitor.

"I have things to do," Ball told the emperor. "You will be safe now."

"The bombs—"

"Are harmless."

"There are many lives here," the emperor said. "Innocent lives. I do not include my own."

"If you're still worried, have a tech suit up and take them outside. Even if one explodes out there, the facility would be safe. He might die, though."

The emperor straightened. "Then I will take them. You are a hero of Ptolemy, Simply Ball."

"Don't get all mushy," Ball said. And headed for the lifts.

We were running downriver fast when a heavy rumble of thunder rolled across the river. The houseboat's superstructure shivered. I was sitting in the galley, trying to make contact with the temporary Associated News bureau in orbit. Static played heavily across my 'corder's screen.

"It seems the wrong weather for a thunderstorm," I said.

"That's not natural thunder," Raven said. "That's Ball."

"Sweet spirit of space! Is he blowing up the damned planet?"

She didn't smile. She was concentrating on her instruments. "We're being followed. An aircar. Forty kilometers back. A hundred meters off the water. Closing. They're trying to herf us."

"*Damn* it!" I jabbed the 'corder keys hard.

"Don't break it!" she said. "If they succeed, it'll be the only thing working. It never quit when they hit us out on the salt. How come?"

"Special shielding. Developed right here, as a matter of fact." I couldn't believe how calm she was. "Why haven't they already disabled us?"

She did smile this time. "Well, unlike last time, I was expecting this. I'm fighting them. Full countermeasures. There's more to this baby than meets the eye." She held my gaze a moment. "You didn't say it?"

"Say what for God's sake?"

"I expected you to say more to *both* babies than meets the eye, Ramsey. Am I not a babe?"

"You are crazy is what you are." I was so scared my mouth was dry, and she was flirting. Just great. "What if they just vaporize us?"

"Doesn't your 'corder have a media rep identifier?"

"So damn *what*? These are outlaws, for God's sake."

"Probably just mercenaries." She shrugged. "Trying to make a living, even as you and I. But they work for InterGal. No question. I don't think even InterGal will go quite that far. Not now."

"Can't this thing go *faster*?"

The thunder rolled across the river again. Echoes bounced back at us from the dark-forested slopes. The rain drummed steadily on the overhead and crawled in translucent snakes along the windshield. The hull rocked as we sliced through the wind waves.

"Raven?"

She was absorbed in her readouts again. "What, love?"

"What do we *do*?"

She was chewing her full lower lip now. "Damn! They broke that sequence." She looked up. "You want the kill?"

"What are you talking about now?"

"They're good. Too good. Another three minutes, tops, and they're through my countermeasures. They must be Zion-trained. You want the kill? A taste of real bloodsport?"

"I can't believe you!"

"My marshmallow man," she said tenderly. She came to the table, bent over and kissed me on the forehead. When she straightened, she had my seven gun in her hand. "Be right back, love." She didn't seem to hurry, but before I could react, she was through the companionway and out on the stern.

I saw her shoulder my rifle with the same casual grace she had used against the wingfingers, and aim down our wake. For an instant my memory of Raven the huntsman clashed with the visual evidence of Raven the deadly female. My seven gun jarred into recoil the moment its butt touched her shoulder. She was halfway back inside when the gray day behind us came apart in an eye-searing flash. The sound reached us a moment later, a huge vicious *crack!* The boat lurched. She stumbled. Her delicate teacups chimed against each other in their rack above my head.

"Rest in peace," she said. "You guys were good." She handed me the rifle. "You might want to chamber another round, sweetheart." And she was back at her readouts.

Habit took over. I worked the seven gun's bolt, and the dusky empty hull tinkled across the tabletop.

Out the rain-bleared windows I saw a dark streamlined shape drop out of the overcast parallel to us. "Raven!" I knocked the table off its moorings getting out of there. The damned gravity was still too light. The aircar out there drifted toward us. Any closer would be too close for an explosion of the magnitude she had just touched off.

"Wait!" she said. "They're on our side."

"You better be sure!"

"I am sure. Get your 'corder and shell belt. We're changing horses in midstream."

"I can't *believe* you."

She gave me a sad smile. "You never said that in the sack."

"Raven, dammit—"

Something banged against the hull, jerking my attention away from her.

There was a flexible gangway suspended from the open hatch of the aircar to our stern. It swayed gently to the tread of a robed, cowled figure hurrying across it. A damned monk. He hopped lightly to the deck and came in out of the rain. He couldn't straighten completely; he was far too tall. Rainwater runneled off the coarse weave of his garment. When he flipped his cowl back, it was Inaba. But I had known from the big feet.

"Keith Ramsey." He bowed slightly to us both, and then stood partially hunched, like an Old Earth heron. "We don't have much time," he said to Raven.

"All set," Raven said. "Take the com?"

"Aye," Inaba said gravely. "I have it." He looked back at me. "I apologize for disturbing you in your creative composition, Keith Ramsey. But there is time. A Renga is complete—"

"When it's complete," I finished for him.

"Yeah. But I'd like to be around to see the finished work."

Raven brushed past me. "Don't forget your
'corder, love." In moments I saw her run lightly
across the gangway, barely touching the
handrail.

Two more cowled figures came across from
the aircar and crowded into the cabin. Both of
them were tall as Inaba and had to duck their
heads. One of them manned Raven's readouts,
the other scooped up a Colt-Vickers. He
checked its charge and sight display in very
businesslike fashion. Some monks they had,
here on peaceful Ptolemy. I wasn't used to
being towered over in a small space, even if
they were more finely boned. I felt like a child
thrown into a grown-up's world.

"You must go now," Inaba said. "It would
not do to have an honored guest destroyed in
the middle of a cycle. Your words are for the
ages!"

Somehow my 'corder was in my hand without my knowing how it got there. We went out
into the slashing rain. The wind from our passage poured over the superstructure. I had forgotten my old hunting cap. The rain stung like
twon-shot. Our wake foamed away undis-
turbed; the aircar was riding just above the
chop. The gangway swayed gently to and fro.
We were moving *fast*. I gulped and slung my
rifle.

"Go, Keith Ramsey." He had to shout.
"Raven of Lao-tzu will explain all."

"She's not—"

"You must go!"

Raven crouched in the hatch across the racing water, her hair whipping in the wind. She shouted to me. I couldn't hear her.

I went.

Python prowled, naked, through the university corridors. A sealed emergency door blocked his way. Using his forward momentum, he launched a full-force sidekick at the lockwork. The impact was precise and powerful. The creche's supervised workout routines had returned his musculature to Earth-norm. The door frame buckled and the door sprang back. He stalked through.

The ceilings were high, designed for a tall race, and translucent. Oddly colored daylight poured through. The corridors were bright and tranquil in appearance, conducive to thought and meditation. He registered these details peripherally. Though there was no sound, an alarm of some sort had been triggered when the tech had opened his creche. He had rendered her unconscious quickly, gently, and fled. He was on his way to the roof and the air-car park.

Behind closed doors along the corridor, humans crouched tensely, waiting for him to go by. None of the academics in hiding felt the slightest inclination to interfere. He read that disinclination, dismissed them from consideration. Though the corridors appeared tranquil, the mental atmosphere of the institution quivered like a living thing that sensed an infection running through it.

He was aware of the two men before he saw them.

Two robed figures stepped into the corridor to face him. Tall and slender, shaved heads, large gentle eyes. Their coarse robes were tinted a delicate shade of rose. No weapons.

They bowed in unison. "Baka Martin of Old Earth," the left-hand one said.

He kept coming.

"You must stay here," the monk said. "It is unsafe for you to leave—"

Python struck.

The speaker warded the kick with a forearm. But the force of the strike spun him. The right-hand monk moved with fluid speed, spinning and capturing Python's leg in the crook of his elbow. He tried to elevate the leg. Python shifted his weight instantly into that leg, emptying his rear leg. Leapt into the air, using the captured leg for leverage. Drove his free foot squarely into the robed back. Not quite as hard as he had kicked the door. The monk was driven forward into his companion. Python hit the floor with a crash. Rebounded to his feet.

The left-hand monk freed himself of his slumping companion. Roundhoused a kick at Python's head. Python moved his head the minimum distance to make it miss. Drove forward with a simple hammer fist. Again the monk blocked deftly. But again the strength of full-g muscles punished him and drove him back. He stumbled over the fallen one. Tried to catch his balance.

This was not sport. Python gave him no second chance.

He spared a moment to ensure neither was dead, then peeled the tallest one out of his robe and pulled it on. The hem fell high on his shins, and the sleeves well above his wrists. It would do.

He hurried to the lifts. They weren't working. Of course not. Somewhere in the building he was aware of minds organizing to trap him, moving to seal off exits. Some sort of security personnel.

He found emergency stairs, sprinted upward.

He could sense a squad of security people waiting above. Armed, this time. He felt his sybil stir uneasily. It didn't want to be burned down in this stairwell. Well, neither did he. But could he reach the weapons-bearers before they could react?

Of course he could. They already were nervous, jumpy. Their nervousness beat at him. They had no experience capturing runaway lab subjects. Let alone a Palikari. He caught one thought with perfect clarity: this would have been a good day to go sailing on the river instead of reporting to work.

He almost smiled.

They certainly had never known the greer. . . .

He paused to concentrate, to center, to become consciously aware of his linkage with the parasite. To picture what he needed to do.

But the sybil already knew. Urged him onward. He began to climb again.

The greer-fear swept before him. He saw the waiting minds go all disorganized with unspoken horror. Abruptly they knew that they waited to confront a terror. An unspeakable terror. They couldn't force themselves to see the vidscreen images of a tall unarmed man in an ill-fitting robe. Dangerous, yes, but not an object of raw fear. They saw—

Python snapped his peculiar mind shut. He was too empathic to enjoy their terror.

They saw the greer, flowing up the stairs like furred purple death, dark-purple mouths laughing up at them.

They saw fanged and clawed gargoyles from the Blocked Worlds, awful things with gray armored hides and hell-hot eyes. Mythic, ravenous monsters.

Their bowels clenched with fear, and their hands were cold on their weapons. Nothing could stop the awful things that swept upward to the roof. Certainly no ordinary security guard at a peaceful university. They saw their own mortality racing at them with breakneck speed. Closing *fast*.

He was near the roof now. Running the stairs easily in the lighter gravity, his breath coming steady and strong, the sybil purring through him, readying him for the supreme effort of attacking armed men full-face. There was surging glory in it, intoxicating and fiery. He had to hurry or they would run away and he would not get to eat them—He tried to halt the thought. Was he *becoming* a greer? Or worse?

The guards clustered together like prey animals, their minds bleating.

When he burst onto the roof, only one managed to raise his weapon before Python struck him down. Then he was in among the remaining seven, in a Palikar's dance, whirling and kicking and punching, and it was too late for them to shoot.

He killed two by breaking their necks. Crushed a third's nasal cartilage back into his brain. The sickening sound of violent death up close snapped him momentarily out of his fog.

They were all down and disabled.

One still was conscious, trying to crawl away across the landing pad.

Python rolled him over on his back. "Summon the medics!" he said urgently. "Three of your fellows are clinical. The medics must hurry!"

"What between the stars *are* you?" the crippled guard groaned.

"Hurry!" Python said again.

He straightened and stretched. Became aware of his surroundings. His first taste of the unfiltered air of Ptolemy. It tasted like freedom. The parking lot occupied the tallest point of the structure in which he'd been held. The structure itself commanded a view of an impressive range of mountains. The sky had a rosy hue not unlike his robe. The greens of the forested slopes were almost black. A brisk breeze whipped across the landing pad, blowing his robe above his knees.

No one was climbing toward him from inside the building. There was no air traffic nearby. His sybil was urging him keenly to be off and moving.

The injured guard was muttering into his com. He half sobbed with pain. "They're afraid to send the medics up." His voice was weak.

"I will be gone when they get here," Python said. "Forgive my clumsiness. May your men survive."

He selected a pair of handguns and checked their charges. Puny things, nothing like a Colt-Vickers, or Terran Service weaponry. They would have to do. He jogged toward a row of parked vehicles. Already his symbiotic awareness was questing, questing. Just as it had on Pondoro, when he finally made contact with the greer. But this time he was seeking Miriam.

Adrienne Taft had been in deep sleep seconds before. Now she was wide-awake and barking inquiries. *Forthright*'s bridge personnel were stammering and stuttering, confronted with a full front visual of their commander-in-chief sitting up nude in bed. She had never seen them so shaken.

"Let me know when the captain makes his leisurely way to the bridge!" she said, breaking contact with an angry flourish.

The subliminal toll of general quarters vibrated through her skeleton. She had a moment's undifferentiated terror. Had the computations failed? Was *Forthright* lost in quantum probability? Had SjillaTen's nervousness been precognitive?

She silenced that train of thought before it could descend to panic. Clambered out of bed. The room lights came up. Out of habit, she was about to draw on a dressing gown. Thought better of it. Palmed open an emergency cabinet and stepped inside. A millimeter-thick spacesuit sprayed over her body. The suit's computer began a systems check requiring her responses. It took fifteen seconds; she still was groggy. The faceplate withdrew on command.

"Inject an energizer," she told the suit.

"Half strength. If this is a false alarm, I still need to get back to sleep sometime."

Her robot medtech came into the room unbidden. "You interrupted your prescribed mandatory sleep period," it said emotionlessly.

"Thank you very much! Go to standby!"

She left the inert tech behind and activated a call to SjillaTen as she strode into her office. He answered instantly.

"General quarters?" she said.

"Shelly is trying to escape," he replied.

"*What*? How? Where are you?"

"Outside the cellblock. She has help."

"Help? What in pity's sake do you mean?"

"She recruited one of the jailers. He's armed. He won't let us in."

"Recruited him how? Isn't he one of your Llralans?"

"One of yours, to be precise." He sounded tense, almost nervous. She had never heard that note in his voice. "He is a male. She is a female, albeit a human one. I hazard that she offered him the oldest trade."

"The sybil!" Unwilling fear flooded her. "She infected the guard?"

"So our readouts show. And he doesn't have a governor in place. His sybil is full wild-state. There's more."

The fear gripped her more strongly. "Isn't that bad enough?"

"The rest of the guards . . . ran away."

"Ran away! My Llralans?"

"They were terrified by something. Seeing ghosts. I couldn't hold them—" His voice cracked.

"You, too?" she asked. She felt a physical tremor in her own body. "You of all beings between the stars?"

"I have been—call it hallucinating." He sounded as if he were grinding his teeth. "Things coming through the walls. Shadow-things—"

With the words, something moved in the corner of her vision. She spun, with a startled oath. Nothing there.

"I'm coming down there," she said.

"No! That's what it wants! It wants you."

Her throat seemed to close. "What wants me?"

"The sybil. It's trying to work its way up the food chain. *Sirri!*"

She had never heard him swear. "I'm coming. Find me a weapon!"

The two personal bodyguards on station outside her stateroom already were in spacesuits. They were crouched, tense, shoulder weapons at the ready. They were afraid. She imagined she could smell feral fear. That rattled her, again. Her picked troops afraid!

"Give me that sidearm, trooper."

He hesitated, shifting uneasily, torn between snapping to attention and staying alert.

"*Now,* trooper! Or there won't be anything left of you to be haunted." She took the weapon, checked its charge. She had done it a thousand times on parade. And she knew how to shoot. "Now let's go," she said. "The cellblock."

Their eyes walled. Obviously, they knew what was happening down there. But they still knew how to follow orders. She led out briskly, and they followed obediently. She felt a surge of pride. A tough race, Llralans—almost as tough as humans.

"We're coming," she told the intelligence chief. "Me and two of my bodyguards."

Her ear-com chimed. *Forthright*'s captain spoke in her ear. "Permission to abort the next jump phase. My mathematicians can't seem to concentrate. They're in a blind funk. Last best chance to return to normal spacetime without ongoing calculations coming up in minus fifteen and counting."

"Absolutely not!" she snapped. "We don't take this damned thing back into normal spacetime with us. If it wants us—and is good enough to take us—let it figure the damn equations itself. It might screw up. It will take more than fifteen minutes for it to get us all."

"Maybe not," SjillaTen said. "Not if it can control the right personnel. It probably can fly a starship that way. This—thing—is stronger than we've ever imagined. Get those people off the bridge. It may be able to scare them into doing things we won't like by remote control. Just because they're so afraid."

"You heard him," Taft told *Forthright*'s captain. "Full automatics. Right now! So far this thing can't seem to frighten machines—"

A bolt of energy snapped past her left ear. A white-hot hole appeared in the bulkhead at the end of the corridor. Her com squealed with electrical feedback. She wheeled on the trooper who had fired.

"What the *hell* are you doing?"

"There was something there. Something big!" His eyes tried to skitter everywhere at once. "Big and—and furred! It had fangs. . . ."

"Sweet spirit of charity! You fired at nothing! Control yourself! You poke a charge through our hull into our probability bubble and we'll have more to worry about than ghosts. You want to try to do the math?"

He gulped. "Math?"

She smiled grimly. "I thought not. Me, too. Bring on the ghosts any time, right?"

Both of them laughed uneasily. But she saw their courage pour back into them. All they needed was a leader. She was *good* at this.

"I'm suited up. I'm going in," SjillaTen said in her ear. "No time to waste."

"Stay right where you are," she said. "That's a direct order!"

"You're breaking up. I say again, I'm going in—"

"Cut the crap!" she snapped. "You heard me perfectly well. Stay right where you are. Don't push me! Not now."

"Yes, ma'am." It was the first time she had ever heard him meek. What the hell was *down* there?

The two guards were nervous again in the car, quiveringly alert. They both jumped when Taft slammed her palm against the wall in frustration. She had never known an intraship car to seem so slow. She willed the telltale to speed up its methodic clicking off of levels down through the vast ship. When the doors finally opened on the cellblock level, she fairly exploded into the receiving area. She was *really* ready to kill something.

The receiving area was abandoned. The watch desk was vacant, its monitors unwatched. Taft gestured one of the guards behind the desk.

"Don't leave that spot until you're relieved, Wilf. It's mutiny if you do."

He didn't seem to notice the threat. He manned the desk without complaint.

Past the desk, the airlock door to the cellblock was pulled back into the wall. Down a short corridor, SjillaTen half crouched outside a second atmosphere-tight door. Almost self-consciously, he straightened and tucked his pistol back into his spacesuit's molded-in hip holster. First profanity, now a blaster. She had never seen him with a weapon.

"Status?"

His eyes remained warily on the sealed door. "I've reviewed the tapes. Mid-watch, exactly, one of the guards began to act strangely. Nervous, jumpy. He said he was going down to check on the prisoner. He was on the desk at the time. Said he'd noticed something odd on the monitors."

"And?" she said impatiently.

"He entered Shelly's cell. The monitor eye in there went blank. Seconds later there was energy discharge. He fused the door shut with his weapon. Then the creche alarm went off. It had been opened. She couldn't do it from inside."

"How do you know she made him do it? How do you know it wasn't simply rape?"

SjillaTen glanced at her, saw she was serious. "Creche instrumentation shows enormously high levels of brain activity before the guard began to act strange. A level Shelly's unsupported brain could not have managed. The activity increased exponentially right up until the lid lifted. Then the . . . hallucinations began."

"You think she's responsible?"

"No. I think her sybil is. Or both their sybils together. The other guards tried to burn through the door. But—they ran. Just ran away. That's when the bridge watch sounded general quarters."

Her remaining bodyguard touched his ear. "Ma'am. They're cutting their way out of the cell."

"Tell your partner to report continuously," she said. "Are they out?"

"Soon—"

"This is the only way out," SjillaTen said, "unless they try to cut through the walls. I don't know if the guard would know where to cut."

"Doesn't matter, if you're right about this thing wanting me."

"What do you mean?"

"You said it wants me. I'm here. It'll try to come and get me."

"You must leave, ma'am," the bodyguard said urgently. He unlimbered his shoulder gun. "We might not be able to protect you—"

"Wait!" SjillaTen shouted.

But the guard's full-strength energy bolt had already sliced neatly through the door. There was a smell of scorched metal and insulation. They waited tensely. The guard was listening on his ear-com. He nodded once, glumly.

"I missed," he said. "They weren't in the corridor. I thought—"

"Another hallucination," SjillaTen said. "It's almost as if they're reading our damn minds!"

"Explain," Taft said. Meanwhile, she was ignoring *Forthright*'s skipper, who demanded that she seek refuge on the bridge.

"If we don't go in and get them, the next best thing is to spray the section with lethal fog. So they got us to open a breathing space to share the grief."

"Sealing 'bots on the way," the guard reported.

"We're suited," she said grimly. "Shelly and the guard aren't. Are they?"

"Of course not," SjillaTen said. "Suits for prisoners are kept out here with ones for the guards. Their only protection in there is the creche."

"Seal this section behind us. Now. I'll settle for forcing them back in there. Better chance to control them."

The guard fired again, startling them both. A second glowing hole in the door overlapped the first. Molten drops of metal ran and then congealed like candle wax.

"They were trying to get in the corridor," he said. "Wilf saw 'em this time. On the monitor."

"Maybe," Taft said. "It doesn't matter. At least you're keeping their heads down. Face shields up, now. Suit integrity check?"

Something sprang out of nothingness, straight for her throat.

It was a huge, horrid something, purple-furred and savage. It moved with supernatural speed. She flung herself backward. Crashed to the deck. Heard the guard's gun go again. Heard SjillaTen trying to calm him. She cursed herself for a fool. Not long ago, she had accused her security chief of starting at shadows. Those very words. And now here she was in an undignified sprawl, having literally done just that. It was *not* to be borne.

No mere beast could slash through the stretched-molecular armor of a Terran Service suit. No shadow-beast should have been able to shake her faith in that marvel of engineering, even for a moment.

But such a shadow-beast had.

A somehow familiar shadow-beast. Like some mythic monster from her long suppressed memories of childhood fairy tales. A shadow-beast that hated her, specifically.

Her answering anger roared up, hot and furious.

"Fog 'em," she rapped out, still prone. "Kill 'em! *Now!*"

SjillaTen issued the order.

Miriam was dully repeating the news stories from the orbital media briefing as Schodt's assistant read them to her. JonHoward Tomas was not about to wait for conventional transmissions. He wanted the news quickly on the way to financial centers. On Old Earth, Arthur soon would be working overtime to repeat the news stories to other symbiotes in key locations. The Inter-Galactic executives on those worlds would be busily notifying the local media. The simple fact of breaking A.N. news before the local Associated News affiliate received it would underline the veracity of the tale. They risked the wrath of A.N. management and the powerful journalism societies by pirating the news stories without permission, but Tomas already had that angle figured. A.N. would be offered top priority in use of the InterGal symbiotes already in place, without charge, until they could negotiate their own network.

Schodt fidgeted and paced. He was awaiting word from his mercenaries that the emperor of Ptolemy and Ball had ceased to exist, along with the local sybil-control facility. Tomas had issued the order before Miriam started reciting. Half a standard hour had crawled by. Something was wrong.

He activated his com and called his mercenary colonel.

"There's a problem," the colonel said. He still sounded groggy from the effects of Ball's narcotics. Or maybe, Schodt thought, he was just exhausted.

"What problem?" Schodt's hands automatically pushed at his hair.

"Perhaps you could come aboard for a briefing?"

"All right." He glanced at his assistant. "Let me know when JonHoward wants me," he said, and left.

He took the lift to the surface, and an interbuilding tube car to the landing field. When he stepped outside, it was raining. The mercenaries' battlecraft, bristling with weapons blisters, hulked over civilian orbital shuttles and aircars. He half ran through the rain to the warship's access slidewalk. The guard saluted as he hurried by.

The warship had interplanetary range, and could carry three hundred in cramped quarters. Schodt crossed the ship's launch bay, past berths for a dozen armored aircars. Only five were still on board. Service robots were all over them.

The warship's bridge was fully staffed and operational. The colonel was at his station in the fire control section.

"None of the bombs detonated," he said quietly.

"None?"

"No, sir. All were deactivated. There's more. Our detonation signals were trapped and identified by an array of countermeasures. Terran Service countermeasures. Whoever set that up knows we tried to fire the bombs, and has a record of it."

Schodt swore. "Ball again! Have you ordered your forces into the complex?"

"Uh—that's the other thing. We don't have any forces there anymore."

"What?"

"Destroyed, sir. Wiped out. Somebody fogged 'em. Terran Service molecular weaponry. We weren't prepared for that."

Schodt couldn't get his mind around the enormity. "All the Rongors? All those cyborgs? Just *gone?*"

"Yes, sir. We sent a wing of aircars out there when the distress calls came in. They were engaged by local security forces. Thought the locals were standing down. Guess not. We've lost three, destroyed eight of theirs. Our remaining fighters retreated in good order, but they're under surveillance. We can't bring them here."

"Where the *hell* is Ball?"

"Unknown. Nothing we have seems able to find a trace of him."

"You have this Raven under surveillance? She may lead us to—"

"No, sir. Our surveillance vehicle was destroyed. We have others searching for that houseboat now."

"Ball's on the way here! He must be."

The colonel shrugged. "I don't think he can penetrate the outer defenses. I know he can't crack this vessel. If you're worried, perhaps you should move on board until this thrashes itself out. If the local security forces try to hit us here, we may have to fight our way clear of the system."

"My God! Are you *serious*?"

"Deadly serious, sir. The operation seems to be coming apart."

"Don't lift without us!"

"Don't dawdle, then—*sir*."

That fighting man's contempt again? Schodt had no time to be insulted. He hurried all the way back to Miriam's quarters, barking instructions into his com as he went. He was sweating and out of breath when he got there. He called his assistant outside the creche room.

"Evacuation drill," he said. Her eyes widened. "Miriam and her support team only. Ask the colonel for an escort. Not a word to anyone else here. Wait for the escort upstairs and bring them here. Oh—while you're at it, get Tony and Mary into their acceleration cage and onto that mercenary ship. And make sure you get the room's recordings of Tony's new song, along with my files. Got it?"

"Got it, boss. Miriam is—"

"I'll handle Miriam until you get back. I need to alert JonHoward."

Back in the room, he spoke to Miriam. "Is JonHoward there?" he asked her.

She smiled broadly. "I'm here, Alex. Congratulations, boy! You've done yourself proud."

"Um . . . JonHoward, there are some problems."

"Well, hurry up and tell me! I want to get Arthur busy spreading the news. He's all worked up from so little contact with Miriam or Shelly, but for once he's just going to have to wait. This is the payoff!"

"The sybil-chip plant failed to explode. That damn Ball somehow stopped it."

Schodt half cringed, waiting for the reprimand.

It didn't come. "Oh, well, that was just frosting anyway! The main job is done."

"But the emperor—"

"He'll come around. If he doesn't, we may have to replace him. No matter; this is going to make them all rich there, and us a whole lot richer. I've already released the scoop here on Earth, Alex. Our stock went crazy!"

"The, um—er, that is, a lot of the mercenaries' auxiliaries have been destroyed. And the local security forces have engaged our mercenaries in air battles. The colonel recommends evacuation out-system."

There was a pause. Miriam frowned. "Running away will look as if we are guilty of something."

"We are under *attack*, sir!" He hated the whine in his voice.

"Very well. Your call. You're the executive on the scene. But Ptolemy will just come and get your mercenary boat if you stay in that system."

"Yes, they will. I had hoped—"

"That I would use Arthur to divert a star-ship for pickup?"

"Well—yes, sir."

Miriam still was frowning. "Mighty expensive. But—hell, it's not every day we make this much money, either. You did well, Alex. Just get out of there in one piece and there will be a ship out there to bring you home."

Schodt expelled his breath in a long shuddering sigh.

"What's wrong, baby? Scared?" Miriam's voice had gone soft and seductive.

He stared at the nude woman in the creche. "Miriam?"

"Arthur broke contact, love. They've got his sybil chipped down almost to death to keep him working. He's too busy to play. You're so, so frightened, baby. Let me ease you."

He felt stark terror wash over him. It paled his earlier fears to nothing.

Without willing it, he crept closer to the creche.

"I—I am, Miriam. I am so frightened—" His voice broke.

"Aw, darling, come to Mama. Let me hold you a minute and tell you everything's going to be all right."

He felt hot sweat seep under his collar. The terror roared in his ears like jet engines. She moved sinuously in the creche, molding her body with her hands. Her nipples were erect, her hips lax. Her eyes glowed up at him hungrily. In some remote corner of his mind he wondered how he had ever found her unattractive. His whole being seemed to yearn toward her, and cringe away from the fear. In her arms was safety—

"Hurry, Alex, hurry," she whispered. "We won't have much time to be alone. . . ."

He half stumbled toward the creche, his hands reaching for the locks.

Raven drove, of course. We skimmed across the river in a big U-turn back upstream, staying right down on the water and close to shore. The rain came straight at us.

"You think Inaba is in danger?" I asked.

"We're all in danger until this sorts out," she said. "But I'm betting they won't try to hit my boat. Once they find it again, they'll just follow. I think. They probably just want to keep me from mixing in whatever Ball's up to."

I toyed with my 'corder. "Think it's safe?"

"Try it," she said.

This time I got right through to the orbital bureau. A robot receptionist read my ID off the 'corder and told me to wait. I felt the car slow. Raven was studying the instruments. Up ahead I noticed a break in the shoreline trees. She slanted us toward it. Seconds later we slid up the mouth of a tributary river. A canopy of branches closed in over us. I felt safer, though I knew that was sheer illusion.

The 'corder chimed. "Ramsey?"

"Yes," I said. I didn't know the guy on-screen.

"Tanner said you were down there. We've been trying to raise you. What've you got?"

"I'm not sure yet. I just wanted to make

sure you can set up a Certified scramble for
me. They may be monitoring me now."

"Who?"

"InterGalactic Cybernetics."

"A damn *company*, for God's sake? They
wouldn't dare!"

"Yeah, they would. The stakes are high
here. Do it and get back to me."

"Will do." He was gone.

We moved steadily up the winding river. It
began to narrow and climb, and we cruised
above linked cascades of riffles. Raven slowed
our speed as downed logs began to stretch
from bank to bank. She hopped them delicately
and went on.

"Does this hiding really help?" I asked.

"Doesn't hurt. This vehicle has pretty good
shields. Might get missed under the canopy
and against the moving water. Probably
wouldn't if we went up and took the short
route."

"The short route to where?"

"Soon, now," she said.

We rounded a bend. Up ahead my eye
caught a regular shape in the gloom. Just for
an instant. Then it was gone.

"Good eyes," a voice said out of the dash-
board. Ball's voice. "Hunter's eyes. I corrected
my camouflage the instant you noticed me."

"Damned empathometer," I said.

Raven slowed to a hover and activated the
hatch. It was just wide enough to admit him. He
floated in and came to rest on the cargo deck.
She closed the hatch. His usually burnished

skin was a dull mottle of breakup camouflage patterns. Water trickled off him. Ball, the guerrilla.

"Are you enjoying playing war?" I said.

"Don't start. Are you ready for your news story?"

"Sure. But it looks like I missed the one Inaba promised me."

"No. You missed a glorified media release from InterGal. This story is all yours. You have a secure channel setup?"

"In process. What's the story?"

"Do I hover—or proceed?" Raven put in.

"Go forward slowly," Ball said. "No faster than twenty klicks per."

She nodded.

"Where are we going?" I asked.

"To try to rescue my field man," Ball said.

"You do seem to use them up."

"Not fair! But accurate insofar as it goes. I'm referring to the Martin clone."

"He's been activated? He's operational?"

"Yes. And he's making his run again, just like he did on Pondoro. With the same probable end result, I'm afraid, if we don't intercede."

"You mean he's trying to plant the sybil here? On Ptolemy?"

"No. He's trying to rescue his true love from the clutches of evil men. In this case, an InterGal exec named Schodt. Martin's true love is Miriam Trane."

"The dead poet who's not dead," I said. "Another sybil symbiote. Just like Martin."

"More or less. She's being held in the local headquarters of InterGal. Martin is in close rapport with her through the sybil. He thinks he's in love. He thinks she is enslaved, which undoubtedly is true. But she signed away her right to life in a binding contract. It's a matter for the courts, not heroes. InterGal probably would be within their rights to simply blow him away if he tries to invade their headquarters. And they certainly will do that. Unless we stop them."

"What's this 'we' business?"

"C'mon, Ramsey! Where's your enterprising spirit?" He used a sarcastic tone.

"I get the story?"

"You and no one but. Attempted assassination of the emperor and murder of dozens of citizens by a major corporation. The sybil running wild. And a reborn Baka Martin to boot. It's good, Ramsey, trust me."

"Where's Martin now?" I asked

"Airborne, en route to the local InterGal headquarters. Which just happens to lie at the headwaters of this stream."

"Blood the sacrament,
Blood stained with awful things.
Strict shikimoku.
An untold lust worse than death
Haunts the dreamer of the dream."

Alex Schodt was sprawled naked on the carpet, writhing slowly. His body burned with fever. His brain seemed to be trying to bulge out of his skull. His pulse hammered turgidly in his temples, thickly, cadenced to the words of Arthur's second tanka. He didn't know if he was asleep or insane, or both.

Miriam rode him like a hell-born jockey in a slow-motion nightmare. His loins were caught between her heated thighs. Her head was thrown back, eyes closed. Her hair weaved dreamily, like seaweed in a slow tidal surge, back and forth across her shoulders. Her neck was taut and exposed, corded with her efforts.

With great effort, as if fighting double gravity, Schodt curled his body up off the floor, straining to reach her flesh with his mouth. His fingers dug into her soft hips for leverage, intensifying their union. She made a guttural, primal sound that seemed to sink through him like molten lead. With a final convulsive effort, his mouth found her straining throat. Fastened there hungrily. Her pulse surged beneath his lips in a rhythm ancient as the seas of Manhome. He sucked fiercely. He was achingly aware of his own blood engorging his flesh. His blood throbbed through him to the kettledrum beat of his heart. Only two fragile fleshes separated two creatures straining to become one.

In the fashion of dreams, his awareness—separated. Became the observer and the participant. The observer wondered remotely if his basic cellular structure retained, as genetic memory, the urge of a single-cell organism to meld with another. His body somehow identifying itself as a single simple organism, trying to link with Miriam's. Deeper than human love or lust. Survival at the submicroscopic level. Transduction. Conjugation. Reproduction. An actual exchange of genetic information via replicon, changing both organisms into something new, different.

The participant Schodt sank his teeth into her throat. Tasted hot copper. He heard her groan with dazed lust. There was a warm pouring over his chin. He clung, sucking. Arthur's tanka pealed like a tolling bell through his addled mind.

It blended and then clashed with another sound. This new sound was dissonant, jarring, insistent. His consciousness swam groggily upward. It was a voice, a voice on the room com. His mercenary colonel sounded very nervous.

"Mr. Schodt? Sir? Sir? Are you all right in there, sir?"

Another voice, feminine, stiff with loathing and arousal in equal parts. His assistant: "Fine time for *this*." Arousal momentarily won. "Can't you activate vid?"

For a shocked moment Schodt was almost fully awake, almost himself, horrified at the taste of human blood in his throat. He realized that in the last thing resembling a reasoned act since his assistant left, he had secured the room from entry and all outside contact except a single audial channel. And activated a quarantine isolation sphere, which now threaded its energy through the fabric of the chamber, another barrier to ensure privacy. He had done those things because somehow Miriam had compelled him to. He wanted to scream to his assistant for help, try to tell her she misunderstood.

As his thought formed, a white-hot pain flamed behind his eyes, stunning him, terrifying him.

"Stay out of here!" Alex Schodt screamed. His voice broke as he tried to control it, stop the words. He couldn't.

"Ohhh, baby," Miriam slurred. "Don't stop now! You can't. You can't!"

Her fingers twisted in his thick hair, twisting his face up to her. She kissed him—hard. She pressed him back onto the floor, her body squirming against him.

He sank back into the dual vision of the dream. She thrust her tongue roughly into his mouth. He bit down—hard. Tasted her blood again. She sobbed in excitement. Their flesh, their blood, was joined irretrievably. The primitive beat of their hearts seemed to synchronize in huge surging billows. From the joined rhythm, words grew in his mind. She couldn't be speaking to him. Her mouth still was sealed to his, her tongue invading him as he sucked furiously. But the words still formed.

"Blood the sacrament.
Your lips, my blood, seal the vow.
Fever sings and burns
Need inflames our blood with lust.
We surrender, and are free."

In some corner of fading lucidity he knew what was being done to him.

It was wrong, wrong! It was that damn Arthur, taking his revenge—

"No, baby. Not Arthur. Not revenge." When had he released her tongue? "You'll see soon. You're already beginning to see. You're one of us now. You always *wanted* to be . . ."

One of us! A symbiote.

The observer tried to hide from the truth, fleeing down the twisting corridors of his own brain, past flickering bits of data. Transduction. Conjugation. Replicons. Wrong data. Those were bacterial functions. A way for simple, elegant organisms to exchange resistance to antibodies or antibiotics. But analogies were evident.

The sybil was possessing him.

It was in his blood now. Mapping him. Blueprinting him. Changing him. His blood, his body, his very DNA were completely unprotected. Naked in the most fundamental way to the incursions of the virus. He had never thought to install the control chips in himself—never seen himself at risk. Too late now. But if—just if—he could manage to crawl to the creche, fall inside, order inoculation—

Instead of pain to divert his intent, the sybil chose pleasure this time.

His rebel body bucked up against Miriam savagely. Aching for release. He was frantic now, engulfed in her heat, driving toward completion—

Distantly he heard her cry out. Simultaneously, his whole body seemed to explode into a billion flaming fragments.

His answering scream had as much of horror as release. An incredible wave of sensation poured through him. Endorphin dump, his fading consciousness tried to warn. *The sybil is using your body's chemistry against you. . . .* The thought was drowned in a sea of lassitude. He sank down into thankful darkness.

PART FIVE

Nyu

(Fall)

Blood the covenant.
Blood crying the ageless hunt.
Stone or blade or beam
Blood thunders in primal glee
When the quarry goes to ground.

In some ways, it was like old times on Pondoro. Ball was feeding me a story no one else had. A good story, revealing InterGal's extralegal shenanigans here. The story would cloud the fact of their communication breakthrough. Possible civil and criminal action might even delay its availability. That would upset a lot of powerful people. The news hawk's lot in life.

A Certified scramble had been easier to set up here than on Pondoro. That was one of the differences. There were just too many media types in orbit for anyone to fool with A.N. frequencies without getting caught. Another difference: I wasn't taking on the Terran Service this time. The Service was right here in the pilot's chair in the form of Raven.

I keyed thirty to the first part of the story, about corporation execs planting bombs meant to assassinate an emperor and destroy scores of other lives, while throwing the blame on the Commonwealth.

The rain slid slowly down the windshield, filtered through the overhead canopy. It was gloomy and peaceful here. The aircar hovered above the headwaters of the stream we had followed up from the river. My gaze wandered up the slopes that defined the watercourse. There was a high bluff off to the right. The foliage opened up at the top, and weak daylight flooded through the sodden trunks. Up there, the rain was coming on a slant, pushed by a wind we couldn't feel down here. The crowns of the bluff-top trees thrashed and nodded in the wind. My eyes kept jerking from spot to spot. For some reason I was as jumpy as if waiting in a hunting blind for a shot to present itself.

My 'corder chimed, surprising me. The rewrite man was back. I wasn't accustomed to working so close to the rewrite desk.

"The emperor will confirm this assassination attempt?"

I looked at Ball, still resting in the cargo area. "You have a sound-bite to insert here?"

"Wake up, Ramsey. Look on your directory. It's already there." He gave me the file name.

I opened a screen. The emperor was typically tall, but untypically harried for the local norm. Even his ponytail looked frazzled. He spoke fervently and at length. I sent it all aloft. Let them edit.

"No one is supposed to be able to penetrate an A.N. 'corder file," I said.

"Don't be silly. I was your Ball Friday on Pondoro, remember? You gave me the codes yourself."

"Oh."

The rewrite man came back. "Hot damn stuff, Ramsey. These InterGal flacks are scrambling for cover like mad. Tanner says hell of a job."

"I bet he does."

"What's all this crap the big man down there is spouting about your old sidekick, Ball, hero of the universe?"

"I just quote 'em," I said. He went away again. I turned back to Ball.

"Did the emperor even actually say that? Or am I being your shill again?"

"Cross my heart," he said solemnly. Raven released an unwarriorlike giggle. "Before you point out the obvious, the heart I use here is inorganic, synthetic, impervious. But I had a real one, once. As real as yours."

"I bet."

"Well, I did." He sounded almost petulant. "And the emperor did say those things. You have the proof codes there on file: virgin tape, verified real-time recording."

"You could fiddle anything," I said. "You hero of the universe, you."

"Just Ptolemy." He chose a modest tone. "He said hero of Ptolemy. Don't exaggerate."

The 'corder chimed again. "Wait one," the rewrite man said. "Our bureau chief up here wants face-to-face."

The screen flickered and a new face swam into view. I did know this one.

Very well.

"Long time, no see," said Anne Starr. Her eyes shifted to take in the presence of Raven. She would know all about Raven from Tanner. She permitted herself a small sad smile. "You could voice-post me more often."

I sensed without seeing Raven's reaction to

the intimacy of Anne's voice. Just great. "Small universe," I said.

Ball made a snickering sound.

"Don't start!" I said over my shoulder.

"Nice to see you, too, love. Tanner gave me a roving bureau. Go where the action's fast and furious. Inevitable I'd run into you again." She smiled sweetly, and then became all business. "You on to this Schodt guy yet? The InterGal top gun here?"

"Not yet. You know where he is?"

"Last reported at the local InterGal HQ. I've analyzed this poetry. Have you?"

InterGalactic's local offices were on the other side of that bluff above us. It didn't seem the right time to mention it.

"You analyzed their poetry?" I said. "I didn't know you were a critic."

"For semantics, smarty. Those poor slobs are being held against their will! Something awful is being done to them. Has been done. Whatever. The InterGal flacks are ducking and weaving up here. I don't think they know the whole story. Now we get your news break. There's more to this thing. Lots more."

I glanced over my shoulder. "Ball?"

"Ball?" she said. "Ball's with you now? I heard he was here. Is he still a Service op? How can he be, if he saved the emperor? That drink of water pissed Her Nibs off. Seriously. I'd think she'd applaud InterGal."

"InterGalactic Cybernetics has been infecting humans with the sybil virus." Ball chose his voice of doom.

"Ah, Ball!" she said. "Hi, sweets! Of course they have. They're proud of it. Major breakthrough in communications technology, all that. They're right, actually. But those poor poets—"

"Each of the poets involved signed away their lives," Ball said. "I have information that so did others. Scores, perhaps hundreds, of others. InterGal has a full network in place. Ready to rent out time or sell to the highest bidder."

"You know this for a fact?" she said.

"Yes."

"Legal contracts?"

"I have no evidence to the contrary."

"Damn! I was hoping—"

"There's an even better story," Ball interrupted. "The best. Sorry, Ramsey, this is hers."

"Go," I said.

"Their sybil controls are flawed," he said flatly. "The sybil can break free. Every world that hosts one of these InterGal symbiotes is at risk. And I have no idea which ones they are. Probably no one does, but InterGal top management."

For a long beat none of us said anything. I knew what I was feeling. A kind of aching dread crept over my bones.

"That's an astonishing allegation," Anne said finally. "I can't go with something like that without independent corroboration."

"Check with the local Commonwealth embassy," Ball said. "If I say it, and the Commonwealth says it, that should be sufficient. The emperor will say it, too."

Raven cleared her throat. "Air traffic, Ball." She suddenly sounded as nervous as I felt. "A singleton. Coming from the right direction."

"We have to go," Ball told Anne. And shut off my 'corder. The call-sign telltale began blinking instantly.

"Dammit—" I began.

"It's Baka Martin," Ball said. "He stole another aircar. He didn't waste time."

My stomach seemed to knot up under my breastbone. "They'll shoot him down. He won't have a chance."

"Maybe. Maybe not. What are you so afraid of all of a sudden? Both of you?"

"I'm not afraid!" Raven sounded highly offended.

"I am," I said. "What the hell am I doing here anyway, Ball?"

"Getting famous again, raking in the money, thanks to me. You should be celebrating instead of quaking in your shoes. But that's okay. I understand."

"Right. I'm sure you do. Cyborg!"

"Think about it for a minute, Ramsey. Really *think* about it."

Something in his tone let a bone-jarring shiver loose up my spine. I knew the range of his empathometer. He knew exactly how uneasy I was. Of all creatures between the stars, he understood me very well indeed. Even better than the two women who had studiously ignored each other's existence.

Ball had been there to witness the jelly the Pondoro wolverine made of my intestinal fortitude. I'd thought I would never feel anything like that again. Yet here I was, wiping my palms repeatedly on my coverall legs. I traded the 'corder for my rifle and held it muzzle down between my knees. I suddenly wanted it handy. Apologies to Anne Starr would have to wait.

The realization sank in slowly.

There were *greer* on the far side of the bluff. Casting their nets of fear.

Which was impossible.

"What—What is it?" Raven stammered.

"Use your training!" Ball grated at her. "You're Palikar-trained. Snap out of it. Ramsey knows what it is now."

She looked at me oddly. "You do?"

"Here?" I said. Or croaked. My vocal chords were dust-dry in all that humidity. "On Ptolemy?"

"Not precisely. There's a marvelous irony here, if you can control your bodily functions long enough to grasp it."

His sarcasm braced me a little. I drew in my breath, let it out halfway and held it. Rifleman's discipline: steadying for the shot. This fear had nothing like the overpowering force I had experienced before. For one thing, it didn't seem—focused.

Whatever was out there was not looking specifically for me.

"Ah—good, good," Ball said. "We may find some paranormal traces in your makeup yet. You and Martin are the only humans in this sector who have known the full force of greer-fear. This is only a pale imitation, projected by another entity which evidently survived that fear."

"What other entity? The *sybil*?"

"What you are feeling is reprocessed greer-fear, generated by two human brains not well-coordinated to such tasks. Hence the weakness. I only have one of them chipped. I admit I got lucky there. I kept chipping him with harder-to-find-chips for other purposes. Finally they missed one. The sybil still is in the process of taking him over. He was just infected, infected by that poet, Miriam Trane. That's how I know the sybil can break free."

"The sybil? The damn *sybil* learned how to project greer-fear?" I couldn't focus on the implications. "All those sybil symbiotes you mentioned. All over the place . . ."

"Yes. The danger is real."

"But we eradicated the sybil on Pondoro! None survived."

"Survival may take many forms between the stars, Ramsey. I postulate the Pondoro sybil somehow transmitted information home across the void before it expired for good. Just as InterGal uses sybil symbiotes to transmit human data. I suspect every sybil parasite can learn, eventually, to use its host brain to generate greer-fear. If the host brain is strong enough."

"And you find *irony* in that?"

"Of course." He almost sounded amused. "The Commonwealth Executive wanted to experiment on Pondoro. Create a supreme predator. She succeeded in an unexpected way."

The cargo hatch slid back. Raven's eyes jerked to the controls. "I didn't do that!"

"No, dear. I did," Ball said. "I need to help my field man assault this fortress of commerce. Wait here. I'll send back instructions."

And he was gone, a mottled meteor blasting up and over us, and out through the trees.

Alex Schodt awoke to ringing silence. His head ached abominably. He was lying on his back. There was a warm soft weight pressing him down into the carpet. The air in the room felt chilled. He opened his eyes slowly.

Miriam still straddled him. But she was now huddled down along his body, her chin cradled on her cupped fists. Her face was wan, haggard. Her heavy-lidded eyes were sunken and bloodshot. There was a trace of dried blood at the corner of her mouth where her bitten tongue had bled.

"You finally came back," she said. Her voice was faint and dry.

Automatically, he glanced at the cool blue numerals above the doorway. Almost an hour had elapsed since he released the creche latches. He seemed to remember there had been some urgent business afoot before he did that. He couldn't concentrate his thoughts. He glanced around the room, seeking visual clues. The whole room looked—strange. Out of focus. Unfamiliar. Almost alien. He felt her body shiver into his.

"I'm cold, Alex. So cold, so tired. I need to rest. I need my creche. . . ."

A jolt of alarm flooded through him. She was beyond tired. He didn't know how he knew. She was dangerously depleted. He tried to sense her thoughts. At one level his own mind wondered what he meant by that. But his doubt was overcome by what he read in her.

She was dying.

So was her sybil.

The virus had essentially suicided to free enough of itself into his blood. He was that important! He knew a melancholy pride. He was a leader. And he was the one who had designed the controllers the sybil hated and feared. Miriam's parasite had dangerously depleted its host and itself to fight free of its girdle and infect him. Away from the creche, it was feeding on her last reserves, frantically trying to replenish itself. The portion of the parasite that rode her blood into his body had long since entered his bloodstream, penetrated his blood-brain barrier, and lodged in his neurons. He somehow knew the headache would go away soon. The rest of his body felt strong, relaxed, ready. More fit than he could ever remember.

He put his arms gently around her and rolled her off him. Got up to one knee and shifted his grip, one hand behind her shoulders, another under her knees. Gathered his strength. Shoved upward. For an instant, even in Ptolemy's lighter gravity, the outcome was in doubt. He teetered precariously and almost let her fall. Her arms went weakly around his neck, trying to help.

Strength flushed along his body and he surged upright. He experienced momentary dizziness but was anchored on his feet now. He didn't waver.

The dizziness passed, and with it some of the pounding behind his eyes. He carried her to the creche and lowered her carefully. She felt so light, fragile, in his newly powerful grasp. Without conscious thought, he bent and kissed the bloody side of her mouth. Then straightened and closed the creche. His brain was beginning to function now. He consulted the creche instrumentation. It was going right to work, pouring in the restoratives. It was all he could do at this point.

"Take very good care of her," he instructed.

"Of course," the creche responded. "Prognosis: full recovery. The parasite is weakened. Shall I excise it?"

"Absolutely not. Deactivate the control chip."

"Confirming instructions," it said. "Deactivate the control chip?"

"Deactivate it, yes. Now."

"Deactivating."

He keyed the exterior com. "Anybody still there?"

"Yes, sir." His assistant, her voice clouded with conflicting emotions. The strongest seemed to be fear.

"I'm deactivating the isolation sphere. The crisis is past." His own voice was steady, controlled. "Have her creche removed to the warship. Immediately."

"We're still leaving?"

"Are we under attack?"

"Not yet. But the media is full of news about InterGalactic trying to assassinate the emperor! They're burning all circuits trying to get through to us. Tanner himself called. I told him you were—unavailable. He was outraged."

"I am unavailable," Schodt said.

He found himself shoving at his hair in his characteristic manner. A foolish unproductive gesture. He stopped it at once and opened the door. Four husky mercenaries came in towing a grav-dolly. His assistant was about to follow, then stopped short and stared. He realized he still was naked. He retrieved his coverall and stepped into it, saying nothing. He saw her delicate nose wrinkle. She probably could detect the smell of rutting in the room. A delicate flush rose in her throat. He had never seen her so disturbed. He let himself smile, a deep knowing smile. She would make a fine recruit, once he was stabilized and his sybil ready to reproduce. Her flush deepened. The mercenaries went efficiently about their work, unaware of the byplay.

"Are we ready to leave?" he said.

"Yes, sir."

Her eyes were wide and glistening. Fear and attraction mingled. Schodt felt a distinct carnal stir. There would be creches on the warship, of course. If he could compel her into one of them, he wouldn't have to wait. He didn't want to wait. He felt a tectonic shift behind his eyes, and his headache went away. His sybil didn't want to wait, either.

One of the mercenaries glanced up. "Sir, there's air traffic. A single vehicle. Coming in low. Colonel wants permission to engage."

"No." Schodt was unsurprised. "Let it come in. Give him landing codes."

He had been marginally aware of the impending arrival since he awakened. Now he sensed a light touch against his freshly sensitized dual awareness. It was Baka Martin, of course. For the new Alex Schodt, Martin was an ally. More than that. Almost a brother. Linked to him not only by Miriam, but by the sybil. Schodt knew a momentary pang about Arthur's situation. Poor Arthur, trapped alone on Old Earth.

The new Schodt bore him no enmity, and somehow knew Arthur no longer detested him. They were joined now. He wished he could think of a way to extricate poor Arthur. But Arthur would have to do that on his own. Make his own new friends.

Schodt smiled again at the thought. His assistant's lips were parted, full.

She was reacting to him—to the emotions he was projecting. He felt an almost godlike power.

"There was another newsbreak," she said. She cleared her throat nervously. "The Commonwealth has officially announced that every world with an InterGal symbiote on it is at risk. The emperor here confirms that our chips are flawed. That the sybil can escape!"

"Utter nonsense," he said cheerfully. "I designed those chips myself."

She wouldn't meet his eyes. "Yes. I know."

Fear radiated off her in waves, warring with her evident arousal.

Miriam's creche was on the dolly. The mercenaries activated a lab-width door in the rear of the room and trundled it through. Schodt took his assistant's elbow. Her blood pumped beneath his encircling fingers. His hunger deepened. He felt her cringe ever so slightly. This was going to be delicious.

"Hurry," he said. "We don't have much time...."

Python's aircar looped over the high snowcapped escarpments that formed the watershed of Civilization River. He pushed the controls down hard, and swooped low above the massed lowland forests beyond. Kilometers ahead a thick cloud bank lay from horizon-to-horizon athwart the broad river. There was air traffic on all cardinal points now, stacked at multiple altitudes. He kept the car on manual and took evasive action without reducing speed. Collision-probability alarms squealed each time he shot a gap, went quiet as the danger evaporated behind him.

He flashed across a good-sized city, leaving rattled robot and organic pilots in his wake. Authoritative air-traffic control voices first spoke harshly to him, then began to shout in outrage. He had no time to find the OFF switch. The angry voices resonated with the alarms, battering his sensitive ears. The sound set up a pulsing rhythm in his brain, counterpoint to his jumbled thoughts.

The cloud bank loomed above him. He slapped on instrument goggles and reduced speed. There was traffic in the dense cloud cover, too. He needed the physical challenge of flying the instruments through this murk, even needed the cacophony of alarms and voices. Anything to distract his thoughts.

His mind was at war with itself on many levels.

He had escaped. He was free. But to get free, he had loosed dreadful things on those poor men in his wake. And killed without mercy. Could a clone brain know remorse? Had his Palikari conscience been taped across the years along with his thought-patterns, and fed full-blown into this brain?

He was on a fool's quest. He had terrified and then killed men in his bid to rush to Miriam. Knowing he was on the way, she could not wait. She had mated with another. In the flesh. Knowing—she had to know—that their neural connection was so strong that he could not shut out that primal coupling. Jealousy and hatred—unfamiliar emotions— kindled into rage. But the rage blurred and folded in upon itself and lost cohesion. His sybil was excited dreadfully by what Miriam had done, and triggered electrochemical relays in his brain to diffuse his rage, to change his thoughts. What had Miriam really done, after all? She had deposited another sybil colony in a sentient being. She had chosen a target—this Schodt—who had mobility and command powers. Who could help them all escape. Most exciting of all, Schodt was the one who invented devices like the governor in Python's brain which hobbled his sybil from full effectiveness.

The sybil didn't like being controlled.

Once Schodt's thought processes were assimilated, he would share his special knowledge. First Python and Miriam, and soon other symbiotes, would be completely free. The prospect was dazzling.

His parasite's undisguised glee awoke a deeper processional in Python's transplanted memory. Myriad memories from his previous life were all hashed together, trying to sort themselves into some semblance of order in his new brain. There had been too much external stimulus, too soon. The process was clogged in some way. But fragments bubbled up.

He replayed his fight with the greer that slew him on Pondoro. Bits and pieces of other dangerous assignments across the years. Ball was always in these memories, somewhere, lurking in the background. His imperturbable fail-safe—until Pondoro. Python's brain shied away from memories of his death. And, boosted by his recent violence against the security guards, curled back to the first time he recognized the depths of his own flaws—when he slew Iron Fennec in a sports arena. That was before he'd been partnered with Ball.

He remembered the day he swore his Terran Service oath. Winter in Quebec, the sky full of ice crystals, himself towering over most of his classmates. He hadn't felt the cold.

Our oath is eternal. We never retire from the Service. Or at least not for as long as we exist.

Now where had *that* come from? Certainly not from his sybil.

He pointed the car's nose down and dropped out of the ceiling into a gray and raining world. He stripped off the instrument goggles and flew the contour of the land. The collision alarms stilled. There was no traffic down here. But the official voices continued to yammer. They seemed to think he was an Ichiro U. professor, off on a joyride. He ignored them.

My Service oath? I honored it as long as I existed. That I! It's no longer my oath. I never swore it. This body never did!

But he couldn't stop the overpowering sense of obligation his brain had honored for so long. It was if a third presence, perhaps one of his long-ago instructors, had crawled out of his transplanted memories to trigger that specific memory. Which was preposterous, of course. But the memory of his youthful zeal welled up, stirring emotions. His sybil could not squelch them. His youth in the Old Earth training schools. His academy days. Classmates he hadn't heard from since then. They all had sworn, with the eternal solemn perjury of class-mates, to never lose touch. Some of them had died—permanently—to earn their Palm. His throat constricted in transient grief. Always there had been that one never-questioned con-stant of his particular universe: to protect humanity against the worst the stars could devise.

The sybil qualified, yet the Service had infected him with it. And ultimately sent him off to transfer the virus to another life-form through the agency of his death.

I owe the Service nothing. Nothing. This life is mine!

His thought—or his parasite's?

What do you owe humanity? You swore an oath. That third presence again. Implacable as the sybil.

He forced his thoughts away from that imperative. His symbiotic awareness quested ahead of the car like a neural searchlight. Found and focused on Miriam. Recoiled in horror, and guilt that he'd been jealous and angry. She was dying! She had sacrificed herself to transfer the sybil, even as he had on Pondoro. He felt another awareness, near Miriam, react to his probe, and try clumsily to seek him in return. It was this Schodt, newly infected. But Schodt's mind was weak, weak. Not the best one for symbiosis. The parasite riding Schodt had not been in place long enough to marshal the inferior material into effectiveness. It was being hampered by Schodt's commercial-secrets-grade synthetic shields.

The shields were no barrier to Python's probe. Schodt's sybil welcomed Python's instantly. Python found himself smiling happily, looking forward to close contact. Schodt was going to leave the planet. Take Miriam with him! He was waiting for Python to join them. They all could escape together! Python struggled to contain his excitement and probed again. How were they going to escape? A vague image of a hulking warship formed. Nearby? Far? He probed again. Very near. Walking distance for Schodt. Miriam was safe, being tended by a creche.

Python tried to probe again. But his mind—stuttered. That fuzzy sense of joy his sybil projected about his impending reunion swept through him. Miriam, Schodt. His kind! United against the enslavers now.

There were other life-forms near and around Schodt and Miriam. Primarily human. Some of these intelligences were disciplined and wary. Soldiers. The sybil disregarded all of them. Then they still were untainted.

He was close now. He dropped airspeed even more. A new klaxon sounded out of the dash. He had been acquired by a weapons system. He drove on grimly. It would be better if they did shoot him down. Better yet, vaporize him so thoroughly the sybil could not survive in the woods below to work its way once more up a food chain.

But they weren't going to. He had sensed the intent of the soldiers behind the weapons systems split seconds before the klaxon went. Focused his cone of awareness on them. Their hands had grown sweaty with indecision. They were afraid to fire, terrified to fire. Stricken in place, without any understanding of how or what they feared. They hesitated. The hesitation stretched.

Python knew the risk was gone before the klaxon stilled. Something had occurred— some order countermanding their order to fire. Their fear washed out of them. Schodt had given the countermand. He was a symbiote now. One of Python's kind. Python felt his stomach heave sickeningly at the gush of warm fellowship with which Schodt welcomed him.

Not your kind. An utter contempt. *Never your kind. You swore an oath.*

He knew the third presence then. It was Ball, reversing his empathometer. Somehow joining forces with him against the strength of his sybil. Ball's technology could not exorcise the demon. Could not even prevent the demon's efforts to wholly master Python. But neither could the demon harm or disable Ball's Terran Service chip.

Escape, escape! Free at last from the enslavers—

Never my kind . . .

The interior voices clashed repeatedly.

Schodt would know how to deactivate the sybil control in his brain. And how to discard the Service chip, too. Whatever vestige of personal independence he still had would be engulfed, then. And humanity would face a paranormal Palikar symbiote who could generate greer-fear.

I would be ruler of all. A hundred—a thousand—Miriams for my pleasure . . .

He groaned aloud. The sybil had not surrendered the field.

Above the babble of traffic controls, a new voice spoke out of the dash.

"InterGalactic Cybernetics. You are cleared to land. Stand by for coordinates . . ."

He passed without incident through the interruption field, and dropped the car lightly toward the beacon. Vehicles were ranked across the landing field, shiny in the incessant rain. A bulky, heavily armed warship seemed to occupy half the field.

He parked at the end of a short line of aircars and clambered out into the rain.

They were hurrying down the corridor to the lifts. "We need to stop in your office," Schodt's assistant said nervously.

He looked at her, assessing her growing fear.

"Why?" he said.

"To get Tony and Mary," she said.

For a moment his mind was a complete blank, as the sybil tried to ingest this unexpected development. It settled for pressing him more urgently: the time to escape was *now*.

"Your, um—your canaries?" she said. "And the room tapes. Tony's new song?"

He swore. "I thought I told you—"

"Well—things interfered," she said, with a small show of her old spirit.

They entered a lift. He reached for the level indicator. A warning buzz of pain scattered his thoughts. He was trying to select his office level, not the tube level that led to the landing field. The sybil didn't like that. He dropped his hand. Lifted it again. Held it there. Dammit, he *couldn't* leave Tony and Mary. It wouldn't take an extra five minutes to bring them. There still was no evidence of an attack shaping up.

And the warship should be able to fight

clear before the emperor's forces realized
what they were facing. Once in space, he had
no doubt the mercenaries could outrun and
outshoot the local forces. He stabbed the level
indicator. The pain behind his eyes went away.
The sybil wasn't strong enough yet.

A single mercenary was on duty outside his
door. "Sir, that aircar has arrived. The pilot
wants to see you."

He nodded. He already knew that. "Return
to ship. I'll be along shortly."

The birds already were snug in their
lightweight gravity cage. His assistant retrieved
the room records, not without some fumbling.
Her fear seemed to be growing apace. Schodt
felt an answering nervousness growing somewhere inside him. His sybil stirred, driving
home its same old message of urgency. This
was no place to dawdle. He picked up the cage
and stuffed the room recordings in his pocket.
His assistant picked up his dispatch case.

Something pattered down the hall outside,
soft-footed. Sudden fear boiled through him.
He spun.

There was nothing there.

His assistant gasped aloud. "Didn't you
see it?"

"See what?"

His mind was churning with fear. Something was coming for him. He felt his sybil . . .
shift. For just a moment, concentrating, he
could hold off that awful terror that seemed to
clutch at him. And more, force it back upon
itself. A nostalgic happy feeling surprised him

with a rush of joy that submerged his fear momentarily.

His sybil was trying to *welcome* the oncoming fear. His sybil had no fear of whatever was coming toward him.

He knew then it was Baka Martin. Had to be. There were no other symbiotes on the planet. But hadn't he ordered Martin held on the warship? He thought he had.

Behind him, his assistant screamed. His blood seemed to curdle.

He saw it then, a monstrous beast, heavily furred, purple-sheened. Rising on its hindquarters above his fallen assistant. It filled the room, fanged mouth open in what almost might be laughter. Vaulted lightly over her and came for him.

He fled out the door, heedless. A shadow-shape rushed at him from the lifts. He turned and ran toward the entryway. His body clenched with expectation of its claws. This was no Baka Martin! This was nightmare.

The savage strike, when it came, was from inside his throbbing head. His sybil was rebelling angrily, trying to turn him, to force his own will to coalesce and face the fear. Trying to force him back toward the tube cars. He stumbled and hesitated, but the fear was overpowering.

He broke outside into the rain. The mown pathways between the buildings were sodden and deserted. He staggered to a halt, still holding the canary cage. The sheer ordinariness of rain on his face was comforting. He had panicked. Well, no matter. No harm done. He could simply walk through the rains to the warship. His assistant would have to fend for herself.

Yes. Yes, hurry!

His sybil. Almost like a voice in his head. His hands started without volition toward his head to shove his wet hair back. The weight of the cage registered in his right hand, and he tried to control the gesture. The free hand refused his will.

Some of his native fear seemed to affect his sybil. It was almost panicky now, trying to manipulate his mind to action. He saw the squat warship, saw himself riding safely away, awaiting the starship JonHoward Tomas had promised. Saw himself coupling with his dim-witted assistant, bringing her into the fold. *If the shadows didn't get her,* he thought fearfully.

Fear had used him almost all his life. Fear of academic failure. Fear of making a misstep on the corporate ladder of success. Fear of his superiors. Fear his designs would not prove out in use. He had drenched his mind with fear, lifelong fear, a reservoir of fear. A useless reservoir. A too-full reservoir. And now the sybil—*something*—was trying to overfill it, drown him in it.

Why wasn't Martin in the fold? Why was he using his power this way, to terrify a fellow sufferer?

His own question, or the sybil's? Irrelevant. They should have joined hands like brothers, united by this common bond. Schodt was fully prepared to defer to the superior brain of the Martin clone. The three of them together, himself, Martin, and Miriam Trane, could possess the whole warship. The crew of which could then be transferred to the starship, when it arrived. After that, home—

Home? He turned his face up to the rain. Home?

Bright beneficent suns, steady and reliable seasons, warmth and peace and dominion over all creatures. Empty, fat worlds for the taking, with no fear of interference. It was like a shimmering hallucination, blotting out the dreary rain. His parasite was showing him the Blocked Worlds.

At that precise instant, the canary cage slammed against his ribs with stunning force.

Through the field glasses I saw the silvery box he was carrying explode against him. He went down, thrashing. I had a good view from the bluff above the InterGalactic complex. The interruption field had gone down seconds before. Ball had herfed their defenses with almost contemptuous ease. He and Python were inside.

Raven cursed and worked the bolt of my seven gun to chamber a new round.

"Low left," I said. My voice sounded natural. But I had never sniped humans before.

"*Damn* it!" she said. "That was damn near a meter off."

Before I could speak, she fired again. A gout of water and mud jumped near the fallen man. He rolled spastically onto his stomach.

"Still low," I said.

"If I had brought one of my own rifles—" She didn't finish the thought.

She didn't need to.

"That's over a thousand meters, and down-hill," I said. "A tough shot."

"I could have used one of the smart bombs I made you," she said. "But Ball wants the complex intact. *Damn* it."

Down there between the buildings, the

man scrabbled on his belly to the smashed silver box. His tangled hair was bright yellow, an easy target. He hunched up on his elbows. I saw the box shift. I couldn't make out what he was doing.

"That box seems important to him," I said. "He's got a lot of guts to stay there when he knows he's in the field of fire now. If he ran, he could make it."

Part of his hair seemed to separate from his head and float fluttering above him. But Raven hadn't fired. The swatch of bright yellow settled out of sight behind the cage. The man pushed himself to his knees. The ground beneath us began to quiver gently. The sound reached us seconds later. Heavy propulsors warming.

Somebody was getting ready to leave this world. The man down there shakily regained his feet. The bullet's impact against the box must have hurt him.

Raven pushed up out of her prone position. "You'll have to do it," she said. "You know this rifle. You can do it. You can't let him get on that ship!"

He took a few tentative, stumbling steps toward safety.

"What about Ball? Python?"

"They're busy. That's a damn *free-state* symbiote down there, Ramsey! It's not a man! You can't let it get away."

"Why didn't he run, if he's not a man?" I said.

"We don't have time for this! Maybe the sybil doesn't recognize gunfire. Even if he doesn't make that ship, he could get into the woods. We'd find him—but how many local creatures would he infect? Damn it, that's a walking *epidemic* down there!"

She thrust the rifle at me.

"He's already dead." Her voice had gone gentle. "Just like Python was on Pondoro. You're just cleaning up the sybil, again."

I handed her the glasses and took the rifle. Chambered a fresh round. Wrapped the sling around my left triceps and dropped into a sitting position. Actions I had taken thousands of times across the years. My muscle memory knew the drill. My elbows locked inside my spread knees, and my cheek snuggled the comb. I could do it with my eyes closed. My eyes *were* closed When I opened them, the scope was perfectly aligned with my right eye. I picked up the silver box in the cross hairs and tracked toward the building until I found him. He walked as if Ptolemy's gravity had doubled, hunched over and hurt. My pulse was heavy in my ears, and the image quivered. The combination of my respiration and the tuning-up spaceship blurred his image. Again, just for an instant, it seemed like a swatch of his yellow hair floated around his shoulders, separated from his head. Some kind of optical illusion in the flat light of the dreary day.

I drew in a breath, let half of it out, held it.

The image steadied momentarily. I knew where my rifle shot in Acme's gravity, and in Pondoro's. I hadn't sighted it in for here. Powder burn rates, local gravity times muzzle

velocity, sectional density of the spitzer hunting round—all those calculations flickered
through the back of my mind. But what this was
going to boil down to was something almost as old
as gunpowder: Kentucky windage. It occurred to
me I didn't know the origin of that term any more
than I knew the origin of always saying thirty at
the end of a news story. Which Anne Starr had
promised to tell me one day. I wondered if she
also had the scoop on Kentucky and its mythic
winds.

The ground began to shake more insis-
tently. I rolled with it, absorbing it. The cross
hairs remained where I wanted them. The
bass note of the spaceship's engines intensi-
fied.

I released my breath. Took another. Let out
half again. Held it.

There wouldn't be much lead required. He
wasn't moving very fast at all. The Zen of
riflery. Ptolemy ought to appreciate that concept, I thought. When the bullet is ready, it
releases itself.

"He's getting away!" Raven said sharply.

The seven gun's recoil surprised me, the
way it should in precision shooting. At that
range, I had the usual timeless moment to
wonder if I'd hit or missed.

Then he was slapped face forward into the
mud. He didn't try to throw his hands up to
break the fall. His feet flew up loosely on
impact.

"Not moving. Still not moving—not moving." Her voice was a triumphant singsong. "By

damn, you did it! One shot. Good old starship sahib Keith Ramsey, Bwana to stars. Head shot, too! There's still bits of yellow fluff floating around down there."

That's when I threw up.

*F*orthright's three-ship flotilla followed its probes back into Einsteinian spacetime well outside Ptolemy's solar system. Unlike the raid on Belkin's, they came into local perception at widely separated points, and in a more leisurely fashion. Adrienne Taft didn't want to startle the local defense forces into stupidity due to her recent diplomatic exchanges with Ptolemy's emperor. Her ships were so well-dispersed that each was hailed by a separate lifeguard station.

Taft was in her office. As soon as phase shift was complete and shields down, every screen came alive with data squirts from local Commonwealth relays. Dated, prioritized, and color-coded by most significant change since last report, the data organized itself for her.

He longtime habit was to scan quickly, seeking underlying or overarching patterns that might unify trends. She didn't worry too much about planetwide, intrasystem or even intersystem conflicts as long as they could be contained. What she feared was some flash-point, some jihad or political movement that might send an entire sector up in flames. Nothing of that magnitude seemed on the screens. If times were normal, she then would have dug into analysis, confirming her scan, and begun to issue orders to deal with the hottest wars.

But these were far from normal times. She told the office manager to scan all Service reports and all local frequencies for references to epidemics, medical anomalies, and mysterious disappearances of powerful leaders. She added InterGalactic's name to the search.

"Any reference to scientific breakthroughs in communication," she said. "One other thing: establish contact with TS 12-2-210 on Ptolemy. If he's there."

"TS 12-2-210 is an inactive number," the synthetic voice of her manager said. "Desertion in the field. Sentence death. Order signed by the Executive."

How could she have overlooked that? "Order rescinded!" she said. "From this instant."

A stylus rose from the armrest of her chair. "Rescission ready for signature."

She signed with a hasty scrawl. "Witnessed and recorded. Transmitting to local relay. TS 12-2-210 does not respond to signals."

"Is he on-planet?"

"No trace detected."

There wouldn't be, she realized. Ball was superbly equipped to vanish in place, as he had on Pondoro. "Contact TS 99-5-769. Local resident agent. Direct standby until I return here." She was on her feet when bursts of new data began to pour onto her primary screen. Words, images, talking heads.

"Local news accounts," the manager said unnecessarily. "As requested."

She scanned them with growing alarm. If anything, the news was worse than she could have imagined. She issued terse orders, for immediate transmission.

"Emperor Ptolemy requests face," her manager said.

She glanced at the time. "My kindest regards. Twenty standard minutes. I must attend a funeral."

Her jumpsuit was charcoal and black for the occasion, relieved by the Sunburst and Palm of office around her neck on a rainbow ribbon. The commanding officer of the shipboard battalion, full-dress gray, many-medaled, met her on the billet level for the dead cellblock guard's company. He fell behind her as she walked with formal reviewing pace down the corridor. Troopers stood four by four outside their cubicles. She measured them each with her gaze. Wondered which ones had panicked and run when their fellow was possessed. Dismissed it. She had ordered no punitive review. The commander had been restive under the restraint. But he too had seen . . . something . . . prowl a corridor as he tried to marshal a relief squad to her assistance.

At the end of the corridor, the burial detail awaited. They handled the flag-draped stretcher as carefully as if it were the trooper's dress-uniformed body. But the burial canister made a pitifully small lump beneath the flag. In the canister, a stretched molecular envelope permanently sealed his irradiated ashes. Nothing lived or could live in that canister. Taft was taking no more chances with the sybil.

"Full honors." Taft spoke in ringing tones. "He fought the monster in his brain with courage. He gave us time to react. He saved the ship."

She turned on her heel and marched back through the impassive Llralan soldiery. The rest of the ceremony was private, ancient. Had been before Llralans found the first human-settled planet centuries ago. Fourteen minutes elapsed. She stopped in her stateroom briefly to commune with the male body there.

"Are you really here?" she asked. "After all this time, are you really *really* here? Then why won't you answer me?"

She took forty-five seconds to change from funereal attire into a filmy opaque jumpsuit in rainbow hues, bright and happy colors. She told herself this was out of carefully researched protocol as to Ptolemy's preference in attire.

SjillaTen was in her office, reviewing the local signals traffic, when she returned. "The emperor will be stunned," he said stoically.

"This? This is just to dazzle our bridge crew," she said airily.

"The bridge crew already is dazzled. You saved the ship. And gave credit to a cellblock guard. Everybody knows it. Your fame will spread."

Her mood darkened. "Yeah. On the strength of executing a poor confused soldier, and one of the sweetest children's poets who ever lived. The stuff of legends, all right."

"Don't do that," he said. "They already were lost. InterGal has truly gone too far." He gestured at the screens.

"The emperor *will* bury Shelly's remains with full honors," she vowed. "Or I will bury him with none."

"Two minutes until your audience. You noticed Ball's report that InterGal has spread an unknown number of sybil symbiotes across many worlds?"

"I issued the orders before the funeral," she said. "Signals traffic is outbound to all commands. Highest priority. Whether it will be of any use against something with the sybil's speed of communication is a question time alone will answer."

"Ball still is not responding to hails," the Llralan said.

"I rescinded that intemperate execution order," she said. "You should have gotten me to do that long ago. All else aside, he's the best we have."

"I did mention that," SjillaTen said mildly.

"It doesn't matter. He's here. He's safe." She couldn't help smiling. "A hero of Ptolemy? He does know how to ingratiate himself, doesn't he?"

The seconds ticked down to the emperor's call. Her eyes were busy scanning the screens. War and rumor of war, pestilence, civil disturbances. Nothing seemed to loom as large as the sybil crisis. Perhaps she had let herself get too close to it. The thought of her directives plodding doggedly across spacetime, from relay to relay, while these infernal microorganisms yammered blithely away, was infuriating. And frightening. She wasn't smiling anymore. More than her administration was at stake for failing to prevent bootlegging the virus from the Blocked Worlds. She didn't think it was an exaggeration that the Commonwealth itself was at risk. But perhaps the sybil would let its hosts keep their primitive organization, if it made them happy.

She should be on Old Earth, she told herself, organizing the eradication. Not way out here, chasing someone who had given no indication he wanted her to find him.

On the other hand, no one on Old Earth even knew this crisis was at hand yet. Her issuing orders from here would curtail debate over whether reports of the sybil crisis were accurate, or warranted drastic action. Undoubtedly JonHoward Tomas had one of these symbiotes with him on Old Earth. The thought made her queasy. Had the local symbiote been able to warn him? Perhaps possess him? A symbiote in charge of InterGal? She shuddered at that possibility. She looked in vain for status on her orders to detain him. Probably no news was bad news. InterGal was a powerful adversary. Or would be until the Ptolemy news spread across space. At least it would spread as fast as humanly possible now that she was here.

She still was rationalizing being here, and she knew it.

"The emperor," SjillaTen said.

"Excellency," she said a moment later.

"Adrienne Taft of Yok, Belkin's World." Even on screen, he bowed gravely. "Your attire would grace our Renga Cotillion. It would be Ptolemy's eternal honor if you are able to stay for it as my guest."

"Always the charmer." She suppressed her surprise at his appearance. The emperor seemed deflated, sad. "But I'm not just out showing the flag."

He nodded. "I would appreciate the privilege of informing my council personally if your plan is to initiate protectorate proceedings. The responsibility is fully mine."

She shook her head impatiently. "The responsibility is InterGal's. You were a dupe."

He smiled sadly. "Simply Ball called me a puppet. I suppose you both are correct. Being stupid is no less venal than being evil."

"We can discuss that later. Where is Ball?" Her heart skipped a beat. "There with you?"

"In spite of all this"—he made a wide gesture—"I must insist Ball still is under diplomatic immunity. As long as I am emperor."

It was too much. "Ball has been cleared of all Commonwealth charges. *Where is he?*"

The emperor recoiled. She saw SjillaTen making cautioning motions beyond the screen. She bit her lip in frustration.

"Simply Ball not only is a guest of Ptolemy, he is a hero of Ptolemy," the emperor said. "We will not surrender him, even to the Commonwealth Executive in person."

She controlled herself with a huge effort. "I just want to talk to him."

"That would be Simply Ball's decision," he said icily. "I will cause your request to be relayed. Now, I must ask you to begin deceleration at once, and stand off outside our lifeguard satellites. This request is being formally recorded. Refusal will be construed an act of aggression against a Commonwealth nation."

"You found your backbone awfully fast, didn't you?" Her tone was bitter. "Now you listen: I am executing a Commonwealth Court search warrant against InterGalactic Cybernetics on your planet. Crimes related to violations of the Blocked Worlds embargo. You want formal, you get formal. Any interference will be construed obstruction."

He sagged visibly. "The sybil link offered so much hope for civilization. All civilization. So much promise!"

"Tell it to the poor sweet girl whose irradiated remains are all that's left of her poetic genius," Taft said grimly. "Now make a decision. We launch landing craft in under five minutes."

From this close, the rumble of the warship's warming propulsors was a presence as much as a sound. The ground trembled steadily. Ball damped the sound and vibration, and hovered at Baka Martin's shoulder. The warship's hull curved up over them. A weapons blister curled open, then snapped shut. The main loading bay was still open, the slidewalk still turning endlessly. It had started to retract once, stopped, started again, then settled back to the paving as if weary of indecision.

Martin's rain-slick face was tense with effort. "I fulfilled my oath," he said wearily. "I herded that poor man to his death. Just as a greer would. Leave me alone."

"He wasn't a man," Ball replied. "He was a host to a wild-state sybil. You forced your own sybil to collude in his destruction. Extraordinary."

"Whatever you say."

Ball's empathometer told him Martin's brain was in high overdrive. His cerebration was sapping his reserves steadily. He couldn't keep this level of brain-drain up much longer, unsupported by a creche.

Ball wouldn't let the ship's automatics take it up. There was a sybil symbiote in there he could not permit to escape. And because of that sybil, Martin's symbiotic brain wouldn't permit the joined will of the ship's disciplined crew to lift on manual. In Martin's interior reality, that sybil symbiote was the en-creched Miriam Trane, who, it seemed to him, was a fairy-tale sleeping princess surrounded by evil foot soldiers.

Ball could only imagine the terrifying visions those poor mercenaries were having. But he knew Martin couldn't hold them forever. The weapons blister was a case in point. It had been deployed manually. It would be a matter of minutes—maybe seconds—before Martin would slip. One of the mercenaries would have the time—and the trained reflexes—to open fire. When that happened, this field would not be a healthy place, even for a cyborg.

Ball wouldn't ask Raven and Ramsey to bring their aircar in for pickup. If such an attempt broke Martin's concentration, they all would die. Nor would he ask the emperor of Ptolemy to deploy airpower, because the level needed to breach the ship would kill them, too. He couldn't herf every shielded weapons system on the ship and all manually operated sidearms, all at once, to give Martin time to flee beyond range. Which seemed to leave him with two options: leave his field man to his fate, or stay and share it.

Neither was appealing. Stalemate.

"Ahhhhh," Martin said. A shiver went through his long body. His knees buckled slightly, but his spirits lifted at the same instant.

"Oh, Miriam," he murmured. "I feel you. You feel so strong now. Help me."

His words would have been inaudible beneath the obliterating sound of propulsors. But Ball had all sound filtered to focus on Martin's words. "She's alive?" Ball said. "Conscious? I thought—"

Martin ignored him. "Yes, dear," he whispered. "Yes, I am here. I'm coming. You will be free again soon." He trudged toward the slidewalk. "Help me, Miriam. Help me hold them . . ."

"Where the hell are you *going?*" Ball shouted.

"Away," Martin said calmly. He knew he didn't have to shout to Ball. "Away with Miriam. There is nothing for us here. I am a free man."

Ball at that moment suddenly had his own internal whispers to deal with, over a channel that had not been activated in over four standard years.

"TS 12-2-210 from TS Cruiser *Forthright,* acknowledge."

Over and over. Broadcast frequency. He still was shielded. They couldn't pinpoint him. What in hell was *Forthright* doing here? Had the Executive after all decreed protectorate status for Ptolemy? Sent *Forthright* to grab him in the confusion?

And at the same time: "Ball. Ball. Do you read me?" Raven, on a local frequency he had established.

"What?" he asked her.

"Schodt is down. Not moving. Can you confirm the kill?"

Ball's final unexpunged chip in the InterGal executive had told him the moment Schodt's brain packed up for keeps. There still was a faint flicker of electrochemical activity on his monitor. The sybil, feeding off its host's decaying life force, sucking the last glucose from his cooling blood, trying to stave off a deathlike lapse into stasis until it could transfer to another lifeform.

"Kill confirmed," he said. "Isolate and irradiate the body. Do it quickly, before bacteria or other microorganisms are affected."

"TS Cruiser *Forthright* is here! They're to take me aboard. They're trying to reach you!"

"I bet they are." Dryly.

"You don't understand! The Exec herself is on board. She's issued you a full pardon, all rights and back pay restored. Extraordinary service to humankind."

"It's a scam, to get around diplomatic immunity," he said. "Never trust the Exec."

"Well, she's here with three Service naval vessels. They're executing warrants on InterGal property. They're launching landing craft. Right now! They could be all over you, very soon!"

Ball watched Martin step wearily onto the slidewalk. It lifted him smoothly toward the landing bay. As soon as he was inside, he would release the crew member handling the loading bay. Then he would release the bridge crew. The propulsors were warm and ready; they could easily take the ship up on manual.

Two powerful symbiotes would be space-borne, with a crew of professional soldiers from which to recruit new candidates.

The vessel was no starship, but it could push very close to lightspeed on conventional drive. It was self-contained and could feed and protect its complement for extended periods of time. Years. Ball did a series of blazing-fast calculations: inhabited or marginally inhabitable worlds to be found in systems from seven to forty lights away. There were half a dozen settled worlds and three possibles in the marginal category. Plenty of places to hide, even though it would mean a few years in space at sublight speed. No huge barrier.

But they'd never make it.

The Terran Service would hunt them down. Service vessels could sniff out their engine signature in the void, calculate trajectory, skip ahead to ambush them.

Unless they had a rendezvous planned. Something organized by InterGal.

A starship with an unwitting crew for the sybil to infest.

As Martin passed within the ship's bay, Ball moved. Air collapsed into the space he had occupied. The airlock tried to snap shut, scraped along his passing hide, hesitated, then closed tight.

From the vantage of the high bluff, Raven and I watched the Llralan paratroops envelope the InterGal facility. The vivid blue haloes of their antigrav chutes were almost ethereal in the gathering gloom, belying the sting they carried. We stayed put for what seemed like a long time. The rain never relented. My hair was plastered to my head. Water ran down my neck. But my Ptolemy coverall was waterproof and impermeable, and the rain had flushed all evidence of vomit away.

"You could go back to the aircar and dry off," she said. Her eyes were glued to the field glasses, watching the Llralans work.

"I think I will," I said.

I had seen too many envelopments on too many fronts across the years. Any chance this would be exciting had vanished with the roaring exhausts of the fleeing warship. It was a long walk back over the bluff and down into the darkening woods. Wet branches slapped me across the face more than once. I kept replaying the way he'd been driven forward facedown into the mud, his feet flopping up. A man named Schodt, with a life and a history of which I had no clue. Dead down there in the rain.

Well, he no longer was lying out in the rain. That whole area between the buildings was enveloped in decon foam now. The suitlights of spacesuited techs caught eerie gleams from it as they worked. Schodt's remains would be sealed from the elements for all time if they harbored a sybil.

I found the car. My jumpsuit had kept my body dry, but the cessation of rain tapping against my bare head was a comfort. I found a discarded piece of monk's robing under one of the seats, used it to towel my head off, and then to dry my rifle. I dialed hot coffee out of the between-seats dispenser. It washed the bile out of my throat. Then I sat the container down and lay back in the seat to rest my eyes. Raven opening the hatch awoke me. It was pitch-dark now, but the clouds over the InterGal complex reflected a harsh white terrestrial glare. Native bird and insect life wandered through it as if disoriented.

"We're cleared to go down there," Raven said. She lifted the car up through the thumping branches. When we topped the ridge, the complex was ablaze with light, busy with air traffic.

We parked in the mud between the dull amber building cubes. A Llralan trooper escorted us down brightly lit corridors. Terran Service techs, human and robot, bustled back and forth. We passed an open door to a tiered lecture room. A miscellany of glum civilians waited there under the guns of a handful of troopers. InterGal staff, I imagined. Our guide

showed us into a spacious executive suite finished in green leather and real wood. The first
Llralan I had seen not wearing a uniform was
behind a broad desk, going through its draw-
ers. A tired-looking woman in a bedraggled
jumpsuit was pointing things out to him.

"SjillaTen?" Raven sketched an airy salute.

"You're Raven?" the Llralan said.

"Yes, sir. This is Keith Ramsey."

"Mr. Ramsey, I want you to listen to something," SjillaTen said. He glanced up at the
tired woman. "Please describe to him what you
saw in this room today."

She seemed to gather herself. "It—It was
big! Some kind of carnivore. It stood on its hind
legs. Huge! It had a snout this wide"—her
hands gestured—"and the claws—oh, my God!
It had purple fur. . . ."

The back of my neck was suddenly cold.
"You saw a Pondoro wolverine in this room?"

"So it would appear," the Llralan said. "Yet
the room's recorders show nothing. Nothing
like that was in this complex. But others saw
them, too. And—worse things."

"Talk to Ball," I said. "He claims the sybil
somehow learned how the greer can project
that fear. Remembers it because Python's parasite was exposed to greer-fear on Pondoro.
Then sent the good news home across the void.
Pretty farfetched, I'd say."

The Llralan raised his brows. "Farfetched?"
He seemed about to say more, then changed
course. "I can't talk to Ball. Ball is unfindable."

"Ball usually is, unless he wants to be found.

How about Python? He was in this complex somewhere, before you got here."

"Neither Ball nor Baka Martin were here when we got here. Our detectors find positive evidence Martin was here. But he's gone now. Ball of course covers his traces well. Suggestions?"

"Ball stopped talking to me after that mercenary boat lifted," Raven said.

"Python was trying to rescue another symbiote who was in this complex," I said. "One of the InterGal subjects. Find her, find him."

"Miriam Trane," the woman standing beside the Llralan said. "Her creche was loaded on the mercenary ship. I supervised."

"Schodt had ordered evacuation drill," the Llralan said. "He stopped here for his pet bird. But these—hallucinations—chased him out into the open. Singled him out." He looked at me assessingly. "An excellent shot, Mr. Ramsey. Never underestimate a human with a rifle."

"I'd feel better if you told me he was infected with the sybil."

He nodded. "Fully involved. And the sybil was wild-state. Schodt would have perhaps been on that ship, if he hadn't paused to get his pet bird."

Pet bird. I remembered how the silver box shattered from the force of Raven's shot. And how Schodt tried to crawl back to the box. He had been trying to protect his pet. My stomach heaved. What could be more human than that? It just didn't seem the act of a sybil symbiote.

"What kind of pet bird?" Raven asked with interest.

"Not one bird. Two birds," the other woman told her. "A mating pair. Old Earth canaries. He *loved* those birds."

He had crawled back to the cage as I steadied my breath for the shot. His pets had been that important to him. I felt sick.

The Llralan frowned. "There was only one bird, a tiny female, dead in the cage. Killed by shards of shattered plastic. We irradiated the carcass and cage, just in case."

"Then Tony's still out there," the tired woman said. "Poor Tony. He can't survive in the wilds of an alien planet."

I flashed back again on the recoil of the rifle against my shoulder. Raven's exultant chant at the perfection of the shot. The head shot. Her remark about bits of yellow fluff still floating around Schodt's ruined head.

"What color is a canary?" I asked.

"Yellow," the woman said. "A canary is yellow, of course."

Adrienne Taft was not one to waste time. Her flotilla had been in the Ptolemy system less than forty-eight standard hours. The local InterGalactic facilities had been stripped and everything of possible relevance transferred aboard *Forthright*.

She had caused the arrest and transfer to *Forthright* of all personnel, both corporate and local citizen, who had worked on the covert project. She no longer was acting under Commonwealth warrant. She had invoked the War and Pandemic Powers Act. This had provoked a sensation among the orbital media circus, following Ball's revelation about the spread of the sybil.

The emperor lodged a pro forma protest on behalf of his arrested subjects to protect the record. The local Commonwealth Court dismissed it within an hour of its filing.

She seized all extant versions of Schodt's final sybil-control designs. Ordered the facility shut down and sealed until further notice. The manufacturing facility was told to buck a recompense chit up through the embassy.

Taft knew that word would be rippling gradually across the Commonwealth about her call to arms against the spread of the sybil. She needed to be back on Old Earth, at the epicenter. No incoming signals traffic had reflected a sybil outbreak. Not yet. But it was early innings.

Just before departure, Taft invited the emperor aboard for a hatchet-burying lunch. She included SjillaTen in the discussion, and the emperor brought a monk named Inaba. They talked philosophy and the Renga, and for a brief period skirted all the unpleasant things but one: Ptolemy's solemn oath that Shelly Mesec's formal interment would eclipse the ersatz one that had accompanied her first "death."

"*Standfast* remains behind," Taft told the emperor. "A squadron is en route here from Sector HQ. Ptolemy's punishment for your part in this may yet be severe. The Assembly will decide. What is clear is that InterGalactic misled you. We still don't know how many symbiotes they put in play, or where. We don't know if what happened on this ship, and the infection of this Schodt, were part of some general uprising by the sybil. A bid for control."

"Harmony is disturbed," Inaba said sadly. "Yin and Yang unbalanced. The communications experiment, as conceived, was so elegant. Threatening no one. Poetry to knit all our stars closer!"

"There is a universal principle you failed to plan for," SjillaTen said. "I have heard it called the uncertainty principle. One of the most ancient human expressions of this natural force is the term *Murphy's Law*."

Inaba inclined from his seat. "Anything that can go wrong, will."

"Perhaps that principle *is* universal," Taft
said. "The sybil failed to take this ship. And
Schodt failed to escape, and thus to teach it
how to disable his devices. We hope so anyway.
Maybe the sybil is not a strategic thinker. The
escape attempt on this ship was childishly
futile. But I, for one, hope every sybil in creation doesn't have Schodt's control formulae
memorized by now, in order to devise ways
around it."

"The next few months—perhaps years—
should prove . . . interesting," SjillaTen said.

"Our most difficult task in this may be our
first one: to control such a monolith as
InterGalactic," Taft said. "It will be difficult for
many to distinguish our attempts to stop the
sybil from gratuitous government interference
in a genuine marketplace breakthrough."

"Perhaps not so difficult," Inaba said. "The
corporation's outside directors are amenable
to social order. Work from within."

"Now how do you know that?" Taft asked
quickly.

"I have the honor to represent my brother-
hood on the board."

"Your damn Order has a stake in InterGal?"
She threw up her hands. "I don't *believe* this."

"InterGalactic's research and development are the best available—outside Ptolemy,"
Inaba said. "We have long enjoyed a beneficial
partnership. Which is why we trusted Jon-
Howard Tomas of Mehico, Old Earth. A trust
mislaid. Fortunately, even he was denied
access to all the corporation's secrets."

"Yeah? Give me a for instance," Taft said.

Inaba inclined again. His robe's fabric almost touched his dessert. "Ball, for instance. One of our finest joint accomplishments."

"*Ptolemy* was involved in the Ball project?"

"The Zen of robotics," the emperor said. "A melding of human and synthetic stuff, to serve humanity. You knew Ball's brain donor studied here in his long-ago youth?"

"Yes," she said softly. "I did know that." She ignored Sjilla's quizzical look and stood abruptly. "No," she said before the others could rise. "Stay here. Talk poetry or something." She crooked her finger at the emperor. "You come with me." The emperor rose and followed her like a benign uncle. Damn navel-gazer; he didn't even seem to take offense. "I want to show you one thing before you go," she said. "A confidence between leaders." There, that ought to soothe him.

She led the way through her suite to her stateroom, and showed him the Medfac that contained the sleeping man. Her hand rested gently on its cover. The emperor gave her a gently perplexed look.

"This is Ball's original body," Taft said.

"Ah!" His perplexity went away. "The one Alex Schodt threatened to dismember so few days ago. No wonder Ball was unmoved. He knew you had this in your personal care. Nowhere safer between the stars. You indeed are a leader among leaders, Adrienne Taft."

"Don't minimize his courage," she said. "InterGal had him when they made that threat.

We got lucky. Or rather, I got lucky the day SjillaTen accepted service with me." She paused. "Nobody else will ever have him again." A longer pause. "Please do not take offense. I do not say you're still hiding Ball from me. But . . . just in case you see him or hear from him, tell him this body is safe. And always will be, as long as I am alive."

The emperor cocked his head. "There is much unsaid in your words, Adrienne Taft."

"Yes, there is. Just tell him. As a favor to me. A favor I will never forget."

He bowed again, even more deeply, and took his leave.

The ships were gone.

I found myself back on Raven's houseboat, tied up at Tezuka University once more. It was mine while I contemplated a position as guest lecturer. The Renga still was on hold. Of the nine participants, one was dead, one had gone missing in the company of Ball and Python, and the status of three others was unknown. It was unprecedented to suspend the Renga in midflight. Well, the nature of this cycle had been unprecedented to start with.

Raven was gone, bound back for Old Earth on *Forthright*, all her Ptolemy personalities shed, ready for reassignment by the Terran Service. We didn't even have a chance to properly say goodbye in the rush surrounding Adrienne Taft's departure. The queen of swords was right on the mark with that woman.

Raven's houseboat was none the worse for wear from its temporary crew of monks. But it seemed over-large and too silent without her. A faint lingering trace of one of her perfumes provoked something powerfully like melancholy. I hadn't been ready for her to go out of my life. It seemed my women always left me before I was ready.

Her personal stateroom was as empty of her personal effects as if it had been vacuumed

by a forensics team. I moved my own things
back to the stern cabin where I had spent my
first days aboard. I couldn't bear the thought of
that double bunk alone. The weapons cabinet
had been emptied of all but one of the double-
barreled dragon-slayers. I noticed a piece of
stiff, parchmentlike paper rolled and tucked
into one of the barrels. When I unrolled it, I
found actual handwriting, an elegant calligra-
phy.

> *My starship sahib,*
> *A Ptolemy souvenir.*
> *Think of me once in a while.*
> *—Raven*

Master Inaba found me in the galley a few
minutes later, cradling her rifle on my knees.
My vision was slightly blurred when I looked at
him. It was the dragon-slayer I saw her use
with such graceful efficiency out on the salt, the
last day I had known her as a man. I couldn't
even conceive of such a thing now.

I handed him the note without comment.

"A precious gift," he said. "I will make tea.
A small ceremony."

"What are we celebrating?"

"Life, most of all," he said serenely. "In all
its wondrous forms." He busied himself with
the preparations. His neck was hunched over
to clear the overhead. Once more he resembled some long-legged wading bird.

"The sybil is a lifeform," I said.

"Just so." He was loading a tray with some

of the local fruits and cheeses. The monks had left the boat's larder well-stocked. "Should you decide to accept a teaching position, here or in any of our other river universities, you can choose this for your permanent quarters. I don't believe the Terran Service will need it for quite a while. If ever."

"You knew who Raven was, all along?"

"It never was Ptolemy's intent to enhance InterGalactic's market position to the extent of a monopoly on the new medium," he said. "Harnessing the sybil to the communications needs of the entire Commonwealth would have been betterment for all. Even the sybil, as we came to learn and respect its ways. Harmony all around us."

"So why did you call in the Terran Service?"

"Our original contract with JonHoward Tomas offered adequate provision for profit to the corporation. Even generous. But his greed, and the greed of his supporters, upset harmony. Greed for power, and prestige, and profit, among those who already have those things beyond the wildest imagination of most. Harmony was ruined. Balance must be restored. The Service was added to the counterpoise."

"And so were Ball and Python," I said.

The tea water was at a rolling boil. He doled out leaves with ritual care. When it was steeping to his satisfaction, he looked up.

"Yes," he said. "And you. You were also added. The man of blood and words. Do you know Raven's first-year students engaged in a Renga about the three of you? *Homo in excel-*

sis, Ball. Man plus X, the renowned Python. And primitive man."

"Me."

"You are not offended?"

"The boots fit, I guess."

I returned Raven's double-barreled dragon-slayer to the weapons rack. Inaba added the teapot to his tray.

"It is a fine day," he said. "The stern deck has somewhat more headroom. . . ."

It *was* a fine day, after all the rain. The earth still smelled cool and damp, and the morning sun's rose-pink rays were mild. We perched on the weather rail and sampled the tea.

It wasn't as bitter as Raven liked it. An image flickered behind my eyes of the evening we tied up at Pirsig and stood here in the dark, seducing each other with poetry. I blinked it away and took a thick wafer of pungent cheese.

"My visit has a purpose," Inaba said at length, when the tray was depleted. "The Renga is unfulfilled."

"How can it be?" I said. "Four of the poets can't participate."

"There is no set number of poets for a Renga," he said gently. "Though a Master almost never intervenes, I feel I must. Yours would be the next tanka, Keith Ramsey."

"Following Galatis, right?"

"No. A recording from InterGalactic's headquarters revealed that Miriam Trane meant to answer him. Listen:

"Blood the sacrament.
Your lips, my blood, seal the vow.
Fever sings and burns,
Need inflames our blood with lust.
We surrender, and are free."

I chewed a bit of pulpy fruit while I thought about it. Anne Starr had said she analyzed the poetry for semantics. Her conclusion: the poets were enslaved and complaining about it. Inaba finished his tea and waited. Brightly garbed figures strolled on the university grounds. Something that resembled a meter-long drag-onfly hovered briefly on the flying bridge and then darted away on translucent wings.

"A tanka composed by an alien brain virus?" I said finally.

He stood. "Perhaps the virus felt its chains as acutely as poor Miriam. You will continue, Keith Ramsey?"

Compose a tanka about the way the bullet slapped him facedown in the mud?

Or cheat, and go back to that Pirsig night and soften the blood of the cycle into romance and new love? Would that be cheating? What did one damn poem matter anyway, in the broad scheme of things?

"I'll continue," I said.

We exchanged some bows when he left, and the rest of the day stretched out unbroken. I was restless. Reading the incoming news from other sectors didn't help.

There still was no word about the sybil from anywhere. The media were regurgitating the news of past days in different forms, seeking opinions from viral experts and experts on alien contact, experts on damn near anything. I took a walk on the peaceful campus grounds. When I got back I was hungry again, and raided the monks' larder. I tried to sleep, listening to the ripple of the water against the hull. It was restful, but sleep wouldn't come. By evening I was reduced to studying the Renga so far, trying to guide my thoughts back into the discipline of the syllable count.

My thoughts resisted. They kept veering off to wonder where Ball and Python were, where the mercenary warship was, if they were in control of it. I was reasonably sure they were. I wondered if Miriam Trane was still alive. I wondered about her and Python. I wondered what Raven was doing aboard *Forthright*. I keyed a few lines, but they went nowhere. I obliterated them and made some more of the tea and sat out on deck to watch the mellow lights of Tezuka come on at the end of the day.

When I finally came back inside, my 'corder call-sign was blinking.

It was Anne Starr. I was surprised she hadn't joined the exodus of media in search of sybil-infested worlds in the sector.

"Tanner wants to know what Ball is up to this time," she said. "Skipping out one jump ahead of the Exec, when she granted him a full pardon. Is he really just *trying* to get himself vaporized?"

"Why do I feel like we've had this conversation before?" I said. "Because we did have this conversation before. When you thought I knew where Ball was hiding on Pondoro. I am *not* Ball's damn Boswell or whoever the hell that was. And I'm not his keeper, either."

She answered my tone, not my words. "How come so testy, love? Where's your bowie-wielding babe?"

"Gone." I kept my voice perfectly flat. "Mission accomplished. Back to Old Earth for reassignment."

"You sure know how to pick 'em." She said it with a smile. I guess it was supposed to take the sting out.

"They don't stay picked," I said, before I could stop myself. "They always leave me."

"Oh, Keith! They don't leave you. They just move in and out of your life."

"Yeah. It's the out part I don't like."

She stopped smiling. I hadn't started. We gazed at each other for a long beat.

"I won't set foot on that awful old barge," she said finally, as if answering a question. "But I'll be here a few more spins."

"I could hop a shuttle," I said.

"Let me know which bay. I'll meet you."

I made reservations, and then had to pack an overnighter in a hurry. I felt a sharp pang of remorse when I locked the weapons cabinet. Raven's gift rifle stood there shoulder-to-shoulder with my old seven gun. Wasn't there a time in the course of human affairs when the mourning periods for vanished relationships were known and honored? Perhaps not. Perhaps I was just too sentimental. No vows had passed between us. But we had survived sabertooths side by side. A bond as deep as blood.

Perhaps that's what Inaba meant when he called me primitive.

An airtaxi dropped to the wharf, breaking my thought. I locked the boat and climbed in. From aloft, the soft reflection of the city and university lights in the wide river exuded a sense of timeless peace. It balanced in my mind the memory of open, unclaimed Ptolemy beyond the buffer zones, where dragons flew and the shooting was good in season. Harmony in all things. I could get to like it here.

But harmony was hard to come by. The Commonwealth was facing perhaps the first truly interstellar conflict of its history. The battlefronts would eventually be drawn.

Tanner would know where to find me. If he didn't, Ball would. Of that I had no doubt. None whatsoever.

Meanwhile, Inaba had counseled celebration of life in all its wondrous forms. He probably didn't have Anne in mind specifically. But what kind of poet gets bogged down in literal translation? And he also had said a poem is finished when it is finished.

The Renga could wait a few more spins.

■ ■ ■ ■ ■ ■ **49**

The grounds of InterGalactic Cybernetics' Ptolemy headquarters steamed quietly in the warm midday sun. The landing field was abandoned. Nothing moved among the surface structures. The interruption field was down. Smaller varieties of native fauna already had found their way across the fence and among exotic ground-hugging plants from Old Earth and other worlds. Some of the invaders flew, and some moved by foot. Not all were herbivores.

Tony the canary was no longer sleek and well-fed. In his home gravity he would have been sore put to fly. But in Ptolemy's lighter pull, he managed. He fluttered into the gnarled, low-lying branches of an Old Earth juniper, and pecked single-mindedly at small hard berries.

Some implacable force seemed to drive his search for sustenance.

That same force had tugged him out into the rain after his cozy enclosed little world blew apart. The force had tugged at him as he fluttered near his master's familiar voice. He had no capacity to comprehend its fear and pain. After the familiar voice was stilled, the force had tugged him closer still, to peck mechanically at various bits of cooling stuff.

With unfamiliar matter in his craw, the force had frightened him into panicked flight above the perimeter fence and deep into the dark timber beyond. He had huddled beside a thick trunk, shivering, for an interminable time.

But he did not succumb to exposure. After a time he was no longer cold. And then he grew stronger. Of all the things that prowled the dark, none tried to come hunting him.

Now, in this new day, avian life cast flickering shadows across his perch, stirring primeval impulses.

A new pressure was growing in him. He could not know it was far too soon for that part of his brain to swell again.

He began to sing.

All other sound hushed for a long moment at the alien sound. Flocks of creatures resembling a cross between a sparrow hawk and a large flying insect stopped their chattering and fled as fast as their wide wings could carry them. Smaller skimmers, their wings revving like hummingbirds, cataloged the sound as harmless and resumed their aerial prowl for nectar.

Tony's new mating song was liquid and pure, shaped by that special part of his canary brain. Though he couldn't know it, his song was stronger and more complex than it had ever been. His vanished master would have been in a transport of joy. His vanished mate would have found him irresistible. He sang and sang, as the sun warmed his wings and crown.

He sang so hard and loud that he never saw the sleek, furred form that ghosted up the juniper's twisted trunk on silent claws.

RENGA NOTES

Attempting to weave a venerable poetic form into an action yarn has been an exercise in temerity. I deliberately had Ptolemy's renga consist of linked five-line tankas by each poet, rather than the original form of three lines, answered by two, answered by three, and so on. A nod first to Karen Roehrle, no mean poet in her own right, who introduced me to the renga form and loaned me a couple of her tankas for Raven and Arthur to quote. But any errors in the history or the use of the form are my own.

Before poets and academics set out for the Evergreen State with a rail, pitchblende, and feathers, I freely confess my research was neither compulsive nor comprehensive. I have only anecdote to support the rumor that failed poets died for their art in ancient times. *Merriam Webster's Encyclopedia of Literature* (1995), says renga was a popular pastime, finally developed fully in the fifteenth century A.D. In a poetic phrase of its own, the encyclopedia says "the mood of the poem drifted as successive poets took up one another's thoughts."

The Renga Home Page on the World Wide Web places renga's beginnings in the fourteenth century among bored young poets waiting offstage to recite formally. This source also says the better-known haiku spun off from renga, as poets began to publish their three-line links independently.

Renga, by Octavio Paz and others (George Braziller, New York, 1971), identifies Otomo Yakamochi, a court princess living somewhere between 700–785 A.D., as the first to answer a three-line poem with two lines of her own. I found this book the most helpful in my renga research.

Encyclopedia of Japan (Dorothy Perkins, Roundtable Press, 1991), says that since Japan adopted the Chinese writing system in the sixth century A.D., poetry has been admired in Japan as the highest form of literature. I respectfully concur, regardless the language or syllable count; or whether the words were penned in black ink made from a pine tree's ash, or keyed onto a glowing screen.

NOTES ON THE BRAIN

Modern-day brain research is (should I dare it?) mind-boggling. Tony the canary fluttered into my thoughts after I read *The Amazing Brain* by Robert Ornstein and Richard F. Thompson (Houghton Mifflin Company, 1984). Ornstein and Thompson also described a patient whose hippocampus was surgically removed, and who lost the ability to remember new experiences. Using wildly poetic license (sorry; don't know what else to call it) I melded the canary-brain concept with viral suppression of the human hippocampus, enforced by a nano-control. Anyone who thinks a major corporation would stop short of such activities to gain a market advantage is welcome to their own fantasy. This one is mine.

WILLIAM R. BURKETT, JR., 54, is a native of Georgia who grew up in Neptune Beach, Florida, and began writing when at age fourteen he was given an ancient Smith-Corona typewriter. His first science-fiction novel, *Sleeping Planet*, was published in *ANALOG* magazine when he was 20, and subsequently published in hardcover and paperback in the U.S. and abroad.

On the strength of being a published writer, he was promoted to reporter at the *Florida Times-Union* in Jacksonville, Florida, beginning a career in journalism which led him from the Bahamas to Pennsylvania to the state of Washington. He continued to write creatively, and had some fiction and nonfiction magazine sales. But he found journalism a beguiling mistress, due to the twin incentives of a steady paycheck and seeing his byline on page one.

In 1978 he left journalism for public relations, and was a public information officer for three different state agencies in Arizona and Washington state. He edited a monthly tabloid for the Arizona Game and Fish department, which "required" him to spend days on end out in the wilds with a gun or fishing rod, doing research. In Washington, he headed up a negotiating team which settled major litigation between the state and local Indian tribes over tribal sales of untaxed liquor. And he won a Clio, a Telly, and other writing awards for TV commercials which promoted traffic safety.

He left state service in 1993 and returned to full-time fiction writing. *Bloodsport*, his second science-fiction novel, was published in 1998 by Harper Prism. He has two grown children, Beau and Heather. He and his wife, Wanda, live in the small logging community of Buckley, Washington, with a cranky cat and a gun-shy Lab retriever.